VAMPIRE HUNTER D

VAMPIRE HUNTER D

Written by

HIDEYUKI KIKUCHI

Illustrations by

YOSHITAKA AMANO

English translation by

KEVIN LEAHY

Milwaukie   Carson

VAMPIRE HUNTER D

Cover Illustration by Yoshitaka Amano

English Translation by Kevin Leahy

Book Design by Heidi Fainza

Published by
DH Press
a division of Dark Horse Comics
10956 SE Main Street
Milwaukie, OR 97222
dhpressbooks.com

Digital Manga Publishing
1123 Dominguez Street, unit K
Carson, CA 90746
dmpbooks.com

Library of Congress Cataloging-in-Publication Data

Kikuchi, Hideyuki, 1949-
 [Kyūketsuki hantā "D." English]
 Vampire hunter D / Hideyuki Kikuchi ; illustrated by Yoshitaka Amano ;
 translation by Kevin Leahy.
     v. cm.
 Translated from Japanese.
 ISBN 1-59582-012-4 (v.1)
 I. Amano, Yoshitaka. II. Leahy, Kevin. III. Title.
 PL832.I37K9813 2005
 895.6'36--dc22
                                    2005004035

ISBN: 1-59582-012-4

First DH Press Edition: May 2005

10 9 8 7 6 5 4 3 2 1

Printed in the United States of America
Distributed by Publishers Group West

VAMPIRE HUNTER D

Accursed Bride

The setting sun was staining the far reaches of the plain, its hue closer to blood than vermilion. The wind snarled like a beast across the barren sky. On the narrow road that cut through a sea of grass, high enough to hide all below the man's ankles, the lone horse and rider ceased their advance as if forestalled by the wall of wind gusting straight at them.

The road rose a bit some sixty feet ahead. Once they'd surmounted the rise they would be able to survey the rows of houses and greenbelts of farmland that comprised Ransylva, just another hamlet in this Frontier sector.

At the foot of that gentle slope stood a girl.

The horse had likely been startled by her appearance and stopped. She was a beautiful young woman, with large eyes that seemed alight. Somewhat tanned, she had her black tresses tied back. An untamed aura, unique to all things living in the wild, emanated from every inch of her. Any man who laid eyes on her, with those gorgeous features like sunlight in summer, would undoubtedly draw his attention to the curves of her physique. Yet below the threadbare blue scarf swathing her neck she was concealed to the ankles by the ash-gray material of a waterproof cape. Except perhaps for her snug leather sandals and what seemed to be a coiled black whip in her right hand, she wore no necklaces or torques, or any other accouterments that would have lent her a feminine feel.

An old-fashioned cyborg horse lingered at the girl's side. Until a few minutes earlier, the girl had been lying at its feet. Woman of the wild or not, the fact that she noticed a horse and rider, not running but approaching silently amidst the kind of howling wind that would leave others covering their ears, and that she stood her ground meant the girl probably wasn't some farmer's wife or the daughter of a pioneer.

Having stopped briefly, the horse soon began walking forward. Perhaps realizing the girl wasn't going to get out of the road, it stopped once again about three feet shy of her.

For a while there was nothing but the sound of the wind racing along the ground. In due time the girl opened her mouth to speak. "I take it you're a drifter. You a Hunter?" Her tone was defiant and full of daring, and yet also a touch worn.

The rider sat on his horse but made no answer. She couldn't see his face very well because he had a wide-brimmed traveler's hat low over his eyes and was covered from the nose down by a scarf. Judging from his powerful frame and the combat utility belt, half revealed from his faded black long coat, it was safe to say he was no seasonal laborer or merchant dealing with scattered villages. A blue pendant hanging just below his scarf reflected the girl's pensive expression. Her large eyes fixed on the longsword strapped to his back. Limning an elegant arc quite different from the straight blades cherished by so many other Hunters, it spoke of the vast expanses of time and space its owner had traveled. Disconcerted, perhaps, by the lack of response, the girl shouted, "That sword purely for show? If so, I'll take it off you to sell down at the next open market. Set 'er down!"

As if to say that if that didn't get an answer out of him then the time for talking is done, the girl took one step back with her right leg and crouched in preparation. The hand with the whip slowly rose to her side.

The rider responded for the first time. "What do you want?"

The girl's expression was one of amazement. Though the voice of her opponent was low, and she could barely pick it out over the snarling of the wind, it sounded like the voice of a seventeen- or eighteen-year-old youth.

"What the hell—you're just a kid! Well, I'm still not gonna show you any mercy. Show me what you've got."

"So, you're a bandit then? You're awfully forthcoming for one."

"You dolt! If I was looking for money, you think I'd go after a lousy drifter like you? I wanna see how good you are!" The wind shot with a sharp snap. The girl cracked her whip. It didn't look like she was doing any more than playing it out lightly with her wrist, but the whip twisted time and again like an ominous black serpent in the light of the setting sun. "Here I come! If you fancy some good eatin' in the village of Ransylva, you'll have to go through me first."

The youth remained motionless atop his mount. He didn't reach for his sword or for his combat belt. What's more, when the girl saw how nonchalant he remained when challenged to battle by a good-looking young lady who gave no reasons but showered him with a murderous gaze, a tinge of consternation rushed into her expression. Letting out a rasp of breath, the girl struck with her whip. The weapon was made from intertwined werewolf bristles painstakingly tanned over three long months with applications of animal fat. A direct hit from it would sunder flesh.

"What the?…"

The girl leapt back, her expression changed. Her whip was supposed to strike the youth's left shoulder but for some reason, just at the instant she saw it hit him, the whip changed direction and shot instead for her own left shoulder. The youth had reversed the vectors of the whip without the slightest injury to himself and turned the attack back upon its source. To grasp the speed and angle of that black snake striking so fast it escaped the naked eye,

and have the reflexes to do something about it, was something
that defied description.

"Damn it! You're good!"

Worked by her right hand, the whip did not strike her
shoulder but danced back through thin air, yet the girl stood
rooted to the spot and made no attempt at a second attack. She
realized his fighting skills were as high above hers as the heavens
were over the earth.

"Out of my way, please," the youth said, as if nothing
whatsoever had transpired.

The girl complied.

The youth and his horse passed by her side, but when they'd
gone a few steps more, the girl once again stepped into the road
and shouted, "Hey, look at me!"

The instant the youth turned around, the girl grabbed her
cape with her left hand and whipped it off in a single motion.

For a moment, the venomous glow of twilight seemed to lose
its blood-red hue.

Clad in not a single stitch, a naked form so celestial none
save the goddess Venus herself could have fashioned it glittered
in the breeze. At the same time, the girl extended her other hand
and undid her ponytail. Her luxurious raven mane splayed in the
wind. Her nakedness alone had been beautiful, but this was truly
enchanting. The wind twisted around, bearing nothing but the
scent of a woman in the full of her bloom.

"Let's try that again!"

Once more her whip cracked.

Through some masterful handling, the single tip whistling
toward the youth split into eight parts just as it was about to
strike. Each tip had a separate target, coiling around his neck,
shoulders, arms, and chest with slightly different timing, making
a hit much more difficult to avoid than if all struck simultaneously.

"You sure fell for that one," the girl laughed. "That's what
you get for letting a little nudity distract you." She hollered the

words, conceding nothing to the snarling wind. And then, almost disappointed, she suddenly added, "You're the ninth. Looks like I'm out of luck after all. How do you wanna play this? You drop the weapon you've got on your back and the ones around your waist and I'll have you undone in no time."

The reply she received was totally unexpected. "And if I said I wouldn't?"

The girl became indignant. "Then you get your choice of how I knock you out. Either I strangle you or I drag you to the ground. So, which of those suits your fancy?"

"Neither appeals to me."

With his words as her signal to start, the girl concentrated all her might into her right hand. Her power coursed down the whip to the tips, trying to send the youth sailing through the air. But it didn't! In fact, all eight loops passed right through the youth's body without losing their circular form!

"What the—?"

Not merely surprised but dumbfounded, the girl stood rooted and dazed. After all, here was an opponent who had beaten an attack that incorporated every bit of skill she possessed without so much as lifting a hand...

The youth's mount started to walk away calmly.

Though she remained in her absentminded stupor for a bit, the girl wrapped her fallen cape around herself and scrambled after the youth with a speed that was hard to believe from such slender legs. "Hold up. I apologize for that craziness just now. I'd like you to hear me out. I just knew you were a Hunter. Better yet, you're a Vampire Hunter, aren't you?"

The youth finally turned his eyes to the girl.

"I'm right, aren't I? I wanna hire you!"

The horse stopped.

"That's nothing to joke about," the youth said softly.

"I know. I know Vampire Hunters are the most skilled of all Hunters. And I'm well aware what fearsome opponents vampires are. Even though only one Hunter in a thousand is good enough to make the grade, your chances of fighting a vampire and winning are still only fifty-fifty, right? I know all that. My father was a Hunter, too."

A tinge of emotion stirred in the youth's eyes. With one hand he pushed back the brim of his hat. Long and thin and cold, his dark eyes were quite clear.

"What kind?"

"A Werewolf Hunter."

"I see, so that's where you get that trick with the whip," the youth murmured. "I'd heard all the vampires in these parts were wiped out during the Third Cleansing War. Of course, the war was a good thirty years back, so I suppose we can't put much stock in that. So, you want to hire me? I take it someone in your family or one of your friends has been attacked. How many times have they been preyed upon?"

"Just the once, so far."

"Are there marks from two fangs, or just one?"

The girl hesitated for an instant, then laid her hand to the scarf around her neck. "See for yourself."

The wind-borne cries of wild beasts streamed like banners across the darkening sky.

On the left side of her neck in the vicinity of the main artery, a pair of festering wounds the color of fresh meat swelled from the sun-bronzed flesh.

"It's the Kiss of the Nobility," the girl said in a low voice, feeling all the while the eyes of the youth bearing down on her from horseback.

The youth tugged down the scarf shielding his face. "Judging by that wound, it was a vampire of some rank. It's surprising you can even move." His last remark was a compliment to the girl. The reactions of people who had been preyed on by vampires varied with the level of their attacker, but in most cases the victims became doll-like imbeciles, with the very soul sucked out of them. Their skin lost its tone and became like paraffin, and the victim would lie in the shade day after day with a vacant gaze, waiting for a visit from the vampire and a fresh kiss. To escape that fate, one needed extraordinary strength of body and spirit. And this girl was clearly one such exception.

However, at the moment the girl wore the dreamlike expression of the average victim.

She had lost herself in the beauty of the unmasked youth, with his thick, masculine eyebrows, smooth bridge of a nose, and tightly drawn lips that manifested the iron strength of his will. Set amid stern features shared only by those who had come through the numerous battles of a grief-ridden world, his eyes harbored sorrow even as they sparkled. That final touch made this crystallized beauty the image of youth incarnate, chiseled, as it were, by nature itself, perfect and complete. Nevertheless, the girl was shaken back to her senses by something vaguely ominous lurking in the depths of his gaze. It sent a chill creeping up her spine. Giving her head a shake, the girl asked, "So, how about it? Will you come with me?"

"You said you were knowledgeable about Vampire Hunters. Are you also aware of the fees they require?"

Scarlet tinged the girl's cheeks. "Uh, yeah..."

"Your offer being?"

The more powerful the supernatural beasts and monsters a Hunter specialized in, the more expensive their fees. In the case of Vampire Hunters, they got five thousand dalas a day minimum. Incidentally, a three-meal pack of condensed rations for travelers was about a hundred dalas. "Three meals a day," the girl said, as if she'd just settled on it.

The youth said nothing.

"Plus..."

"Plus what?"

"Me. To do with as you please."

A faint smile played across the youth's lips, as if mocking her.

"The Kiss of the Nobility is probably preferable to being bedded by the likes of me."

"The hell it is!" Suddenly tears glittered in the girl's eyes. "If it comes down to that or becoming a vampire, I have no problem with someone havin' his way with me. That doesn't have anything to do with a person's worth anyway. But if you must know, I'm ... no, forget that, it doesn't matter. So, how about it? Will you come with me?"

Watching the girl's face for a while as anger and sorrow churned together, the youth quietly nodded. "Very well then. But in return, I want to be clear on one thing."

"What? Just name it."

"I'm a dhampir."

The girl's face froze. This gorgeous man couldn't be ... But come to think of it, he was *too* gorgeous ...

"Is that okay? If you wait a while longer, another Hunter may come by. You don't have to do this."

Swallowing the sour spit that filled her mouth, the girl offered a hand to the youth. She attempted a smile, but it came out stiff.

"Glad to have you. I'm Doris Lang."

The youth didn't shake her hand. Just as expressionless and emotionless as when he first appeared, he said, "Call me 'D.'"

D oris' home was at the base of a hill about thirty minutes at a gallop from where the pair happened to meet. The two of them rode at a feverish pace and arrived there in less than twenty minutes. The second she wrapped up her discussion with D, Doris put the spurs to her horse, as if pushed by the encroaching twilight. Not only vampires, but also all the most dangerous monsters and supernatural beasts waited until complete darkness fell before they became active. There wasn't cause to be in such a hurry, but D remained silent and followed his attractive employer.

Her home was a farm surrounded by verdant prairies that were most likely rendered permanently fertile by the Great Earth Restoration Project three millennia earlier. At the center was the main house. Constructed of wood and tensile plastics, the house was surrounded by scattered stables, animal pens, and protein-synthesizing vegetation in orchards consisting mainly of thermo-regulators fastened to reinforced sheets of waterproof material. The orchards alone covered five acres, and second-hand robots were responsible for harvesting the protein produced there. Hauling it away was a job for the humans.

When Doris had tethered her horse to the long hitching post in front of the main house, the reason for her hasty return threw the door open and bounded out.

"Welcome home," a rosy-cheeked boy of seven or eight called down from the rather lofty porch. He hugged an antiquated laser rifle to his chest.

"This is my little brother Dan," Doris said to D by way of introduction, and then in a gentle voice she asked, "Nothing out of the ordinary while I was gone, was there? Those mist devils didn't come back now, did they?"

"Not at all," the boy replied, throwing out his chest triumphantly. "Don't forget, I blasted four of the buggers just the other day. They're so scared they wouldn't dare come back again. But just supposing they do, I'll fry 'em to a crisp with this baby here." That said, his expression suddenly grew sullen. "Oh, I almost forgot … That jerk Greco came by again. Carrying some bunch of flowers he says he had sent all the way from the Capital. He left 'em here and asked me to pass them along to my 'lovely sister when she gets home.'"

"So what happened to the flowers?" Doris asked with obvious interest.

The boy's mouth twisted into a delighted grin.

"Chopped 'em up in the disposal unit, mixed in some compost, and fed it to the cows!"

Doris gave a deep, satisfied nod. "Good job. Today's a big day. We've got company, too."

The boy, who'd been sneaking peeks at D even as he spoke with his sister, now smiled knowingly at her. "Say, he's a looker, ain't he? So, this is how you like 'em, eh, Sis? You said the robots were in such lousy shape you were going out to look for someone to replace them, but it looks to me like you went out hunting for a man."

Doris flushed bright red.

"Oh, don't be ridiculous. Don't talk that foolishness. This is Mr. D. He'll be helping us out around the farm for a while. And don't you be getting in his way now."

"There's nothing to be bashful about," the boy chuckled. "I know, I know. One eyeful of him, and old Greco don't look much better than a man-eating frog. I like him a heck of a lot better, too. Pleased to meet you, D."

"The pleasure's mine, Dan."

Showing no signs of being bothered by the emotionless tone D used even when addressing a child, the boy disappeared into the main house. The pair followed him inside.

"I'm sorry, he must have really gotten on your nerves," Doris said in an apologetic tone when dinner was finished and she'd finally managed to drive Dan off to his bedroom, ignoring the boy's protests that he wasn't sleepy yet.

D passed the sword he normally wore on his back from his right hand to his left as he stood at the window gazing at the darkness beyond. Thanks to the clear weather that had persisted the past four or five days, the solar batteries on the roof were well charged and glittering light showered generously on every corner of the room from lighting panels set in the ceiling.

Apparently there was something about the inhospitable stranger the boy liked, and he'd planted himself by the man's side and wouldn't leave, imploring him to talk about the Capital, or to tell him about any monsters or supernatural creatures he might have slain in his travels. Then, to top it all off, he created quite a commotion when he said his sister was being a pest and grabbed D by the arm to try and bring him back to his room where they could talk man-to-man all night long.

"You see, he gets like that because travelers are so rare. And we don't usually have much to do with the folks in town, either."

"It doesn't bother me. I take no offense at being admired."

As he spoke, he made no attempt to look at Doris sitting on the sofa, wearing the shirt and jeans she'd changed into earlier. His tone was as cold as ever. Closing his eyes lightly, he said, "It's now nine twenty-six Night, Frontier Standard Time. Since it has already fed once on the person it's after, I don't imagine it'll be in that much of a hurry, so I suppose after midnight will be the time to watch. In the meantime, could you tell me everything you know about the enemy? Don't worry; your brother is already asleep. I can tell by his steady breathing."

Doris' eyes went wide. "You can hear something like that through the door and everything?"

"And the voice of the wind across the wilderness, and the vengeful song of the spirits wandering the forest shade," D murmured, then he came to stand at Doris' side with the smooth strides of a dancer.

When she felt that cold and righteous visage peering down at the nape of her neck, Doris shouted, "Stop!" and pulled away without thinking.

Though the abhorrence was quite evident in her voice, D's expression didn't change in the least. "I'm just going to have a look at your wounds. To get a general idea of how powerful a foe I'm up against."

"I'm sorry. Go ahead, take a look," she said, turning her face away and exposing her neck. Even if the slight trembling of her lips was a remnant of her reaction seconds earlier, the redness of her cheeks was caused, no doubt, by the embarrassment of a virgin having her flesh scrutinized by a wholly unfamiliar young man. After all, in her seventeen years, she hadn't so much as held hands with a boy before.

Seconds later, D's expression had a distant air to it. "When did you run into *him*?"

Doris breathed a sigh of relief at the sound of his voice, which was entirely without cadence. But why was her foolish heart pounding so? Unaffected by her racing pulse, and gazing raptly at D's face all the while, she began to recount the tale of that terrible night in the most composed tone she could muster.

"It was five nights ago. I was chasing a lesser dragon that'd slipped onto the farm while we were fixing the electromagnetic barrier and killed one of our cows, and when I finally thought I'd finished it off, it was already pitch-black out. To make matters worse, it was near *his* castle. I was all set to hightail it home when what should happen but the dying beast suddenly spits fire and burns the back half of my horse to a cinder. I'm thirty miles from home, and the only weapons I've got to speak of are the spear I use to kill lesser dragons and a dagger. I ran as fast as I could. I must've run for a good thirty minutes when I noticed something, like there was someone running along right behind me!"

Doris suddenly fell silent, not only because the memory of that terror had become fresh again, but also because a fiendish howl had just pierced the darkness from somewhere very close. The breath was knocked out of her as she turned her beautiful face in that direction, but soon enough she realized it was only the sound of some wild animal. Her expression became one of relief. Though rather dated, an electromagnetic barrier that had cost them a pretty penny sealed the perimeter of the farm, and within it they had a variety of missile weapons set up.

She resumed the account of her horrid experience. "At first I thought it was a werewolf or a poison moth man. But there was no sound of footsteps or wings flapping, and I couldn't even hear it breathing. Yet I just knew there was someone right behind me, no more than a foot away, and moving at exactly the same speed I was. I finally couldn't take it any more and I whipped around—and there was nothing there! Well, there was for a fraction of a second, but then it circled around behind me again."

Memory was sowing terror across the girl's face. She gnawed her lip and tried to force her trembling voice out. D said nothing, but remained listening.

"That's when I started shouting. I told whoever it was to stop hiding behind me and come out that instant. And when I'd said that, out he came, dressed in a black cape just like I'd always heard. When I saw the pair of fangs poking over his mean, red lips, I knew what he had to be. After that, it's the same old story. I got my spear ready, but then my eyes met his and all the strength just drained right out of me. Not that it mattered much, because when that pasty face of his got closer and I felt breath as cold as moonlight on the base of my neck, my mind just went blank. The next thing I knew it was daybreak and I was lying out on the prairie with a pair of fang marks on my throat. That's why I've been down at the base of that hill each and every day, morning till night, looking for someone like you." Her emotional tale over at last, Doris slumped back onto the sofa exhausted.

"And he hasn't fed on you again since?"

"That's right. Though I do wait up for him every night with a spear ready."

D's eyes narrowed at her attempt at levity. "If we were merely dealing with a blood-starved Noble, he'd be coming every night. But, you see, the greater the interest they take in their victim, the longer the interval between attacks so they can prolong the pleasure of feeding. But the fact that it's been five days is incredible. It seems he's extremely taken with you."

"Spare me the damn compliments!" Doris cried. No trace of the spitfire who had challenged D to battle at twilight remained now. She sat there, a lovely seventeen-year-old girl trembling in fear.

As D surveyed her coolly, he added words that only made the hair on her neck stand higher. "The average interval between attacks is three to four days. More than five is extremely rare. He'll come tonight without a doubt. From what I can tell from your wounds, he's quite powerful, as Frontier Nobility go. You said something about 'his castle.' His identity is clear to you, is it?"

Doris gave a little nod. "He's been lord over this region since long before there was any village of Ransylva. His name is Count Lee. I've heard some say he's a hundred years old, while others say he's ten thousand."

"Ten thousand years old, eh? The powers of a Noble grow with the passing years. He could prove a troubling adversary," D said, though his tone didn't sound particularly troubled.

"The powers of a Noble? You mean things like the power to whip up a gale with a wave of the arm, or being able to turn into a fire dragon?"

Ignoring Doris' query, D said, "There's one last thing I need to ask you. How does your village handle those who've been bitten by vampires?"

The girl's face paled in an instant.

In many cases those who'd felt the baleful fangs of a vampire were isolated in their respective village or town while arrangements were made to destroy the culprit, but if they were simply unable to defeat the vampire, the victim would be driven from town or, in the worst cases, disposed of. This was the custom because a night fiend, crazed with rage at not being able to feed on the one it wanted, would attack anyone it could get its hands on. More towns and villages than anyone could count had been wiped out for just that reason. Ransylva had similar policies in effect. That was the reason Doris hadn't asked anyone else for help, but had privately sought a Vampire Hunter. Her failure to confide in her brother was for fear that his conduct might tip off the villagers if they happened to go into town. Had she no younger brother to consider, she'd surely have gone after the vampire on her own, or done away with herself.

Vampires dealt with their victims in one of two ways. Either they drained all the blood from their prey in one feeding and left them a mere corpse or, through repeated feedings, they turned the individual into a companion. The key point in the latter was not the number of times the vampire fed but rather something D had touched on earlier: whether or not the vampire took a liking to its victim. Sometimes a person joined their ranks after a single bite, while other times they might share the kiss of blood for months only to die in the end. And it went without saying that those transformed into vampires had to bear their destiny as detestable demons, wandering each night in search of warm human blood, living in darkness eternal. For Doris, and for every other person in this world, that was the true terror.

"Everywhere it's the same, isn't it," D muttered. "Accursed demons, ghouls from the darkness, blood-crazed devils. Bitten once and you're one of them. Well, let them say what they will. Stand up, please," he said to Doris, who was caught off-guard by the one remark meant for her. "It looks like the guest we were expecting has come. Let me see the remote control for your electromagnetic barrier."

"What, he's here already? You just said he'd be here after midnight."

"I'm surprised, too."

But he didn't look it in the least.

D oris came back from her bedroom with the remote control and handed it to D.

In order to keep all kinds of strange visitors from sneaking onto the farm while both Lang children were away, they had to have some way to erect the force field from the outside. Acquired secondhand off a black market in the Capital shortly after their father's death four years ago, the barrier was their greatest treasure except, of course, for the rare occasions when it broke down. Their losses to the wraiths and rabid beasts that wandered the night were far less than those of other homes on the periphery; to be more exact, their losses were practically nonexistent. But the purchase came with a price. After they bought it, they were left with less than a third of their father's life savings.

"How are you gonna fight him?" Doris inquired. It was a question that sprung from the Hunter blood flowing in her veins. The fighting techniques of Vampire Hunters, who were rare even out on the Frontier, were rumored to be gruesome and magnificent, but almost no one had ever witnessed them firsthand. Doris herself had only heard of them in tales. And the youth before her now was completely different from the rustic Hunter image conjured up by those stories.

"You should see for yourself, and I wish I could let you, but I need you to go to sleep."

"What—?"

The youth's right hand touched Doris' right shoulder, which was taut with swells of muscle while still retaining some delicacy. Whatever the technique or power he now employed, as soon as Doris noticed the frightening cold charge coursing through her body from her shoulder she lost consciousness. But just before she did, she glimpsed something eerie in the palm of D's left hand, or at least she believed she did. She thought she saw something small, of a color and shape she couldn't discern, but whatever it was it clearly had eyes and a nose and a mouth, like some sort of grotesque face.

Apparently confident in the efficacy of his actions, D didn't even bother to check if Doris was actually unconscious before leaving the room with his sword over his shoulder. The reason he'd put her to sleep was to prevent her from interfering in the battle that was about to begin. No matter how firm their resolve, anyone who'd felt the vampire's kiss once could not help but heed the demon's commands. Many were the Hunters who had been shot from behind or had their hearts pierced by the very women they sought to save from cursed fangs. To guard against that, veterans would give the victims a sedative or confine them in portable iron cages. But the extraordinary skill D had just displayed with his left hand would have been viewed by even the most veteran of Hunters as impossible in all but dreams cast by the Fair Folk.

Once out in the hall, D opened the door to Dan's room. The boy snored away peacefully, oblivious to the deadly duel about to ensue. Quietly shutting the door, D slipped through the front hall and down the porch steps onto the pitch-black earth. No trace of the midday heat remained now. The green grass swayed in a chilled and pleasant night breeze.

It was around September. It was to the great credit of the Revolutionary Army that they hadn't destroyed the dozen weather controllers buried beneath the seven continents. If not by day then at least by night the most comfortable levels of heat and humidity for both the Nobility and humans were maintained all year round. There were, however, still the occasional violent thunderstorms or blizzards, written into the controller's programs by some uniformity-hating Nobles to recreate the unpredictable seasons of yore.

With a graceful stride that was a dance with the breeze, D passed through a gate in the fence and went another ten feet before coming to a stop. Before long there came from the depths of the darkness, from the far reaches of the plain, the sound of horse hooves and wagon wheels approaching. Could it be that D had heard them even as he talked with the young lady in that distant room?

A team of four horses and a carriage so black it seemed lacquered with midnight appeared in the moonlight and halted about fifteen feet ahead of D. The beautifully groomed black beasts drawing it were most likely cyborg horses.

A man in a black inverness cape was seated in the coachman's perch, scrutinizing D with glittering eyes. The black lacquered whip in his right hand reflected the moonlight. By the light of the moon alone D could make out a touch of beast in his face and the terribly bushy backs of his hands.

The man quickly alighted from the driver's seat. His whole body was like a coiled spring; he even moved like a beast. Before he could reach for the passenger door, the silver handle turned and the door opened from the inside. A deep chill and the stench of blood suddenly shrouded the refreshing breeze. As D caught a glimpse of the figure stepping down from the carriage the slightest hue of emotion stirred in his eyes. "A woman?"

Her dazzling golden hair looked like it would creep along the ground behind her. If Doris was the embodiment of a sunflower, then this woman could only be likened to a moonflower. Her snow-white dress of medieval styling was bound tight at her waist, spreading in bountiful curves reaching to the ground. The dress was certainly lovely, but it was the pale beauty unique to the Nobility that made the young lady seem an unearthly illusion, sparkling as she did like a dream in a shower of moonlight. But the illusion reeked of blood. The flames of a nightmare crackled in her lapis-lazuli eyes, and her beckoning lips were red as blood as they glistened damply in D's night-sight, calling to mind a hunger that would not be sated in all eternity. The hunger of a vampire.

Gazing at D, the young lady laughed like a silver bell. "Be you some manner of bodyguard? Hiring a knave like you for protection is just the sort of thing a lowly human wretch would do. Having heard from Father that the girl who lives here is not only of a beauty unrivaled by the humans in these parts, but that her blood is equally delectable, I came to see her for myself. But as I expected all along, there is no great difference between these foolish, annoying little pests."

Ghastliness rushed into the girl's face. The pearly fangs that appeared without warning at the corners of her lips didn't escape D's notice.

"First I shall make a bloody spatter of you, and then I'll drain the humble blood from her till not a drop remains. As you may well know, Father is inclined to make her part of our family, but I will not stand by while the blood of the Lee line is imparted to a good-for-nothing that would stoop to a trick of this sort. I shall strike her from the face of the earth into the waiting arms of the black gods of hell. And you shall accompany her."

As she spoke, the young lady made a sweep of her slender hand. Her driver stepped forward. Murderous intent and malevolence radiated from every inch of him like flames licking at D's face.

You lowly worms have forgotten your station, his mien seemed to say. *Turncoat scum you are, forgetting the debt you owe your former masters, rebelling against them with your devious little minds and weapons. Here's where you learn the error of your ways.*

The transformation had begun. The molecular arrangement of his cells changed, and his nervous system became that of a wild beast born to race across the ground at great speeds. The four limbs clutching at the earth began to assume a shape more befitting a lower animal. A prognathous jaw formed, and revealed rows of razor-sharp teeth jutting from a crescent-moon mouth that split his face from ear to ear. Jet-black fur sprouted over every inch of him.

The driver was a werewolf, one of the monsters of the night resurrected from the dark depths of medieval legend along with the vampires. D could tell just by watching the transformation, which some might even term graceful, that the driver was not one of the genetically engineered and cybernetically enhanced fakes the vampires had spread across the world.

A throaty howl blazing with the glee of slaughter split the wordless void. With both eyes glittering wildly, the inverness-wearing wolf lurched up onto his hind feet. This was exactly what made the werewolf a lycanthrope among lycanthropes, for despite its four-footed form, a werewolf's speed and destructive power were greater when it stood erect.

Perhaps taking the fact that the youth had stood stock still and not moved a muscle since their arrival to mean he was paralyzed with fright, the black beast crouched ever so slightly. Trusting its entire weight to the powerful springs of its lower body, it leapt over fifteen feet in a single bound.

Two flashes more brilliant than the moonlight split the darkness.

D didn't move. The werewolf, dropping down on D from above with every intention of sinking its iron-shredding claws into his skull, changed course in midair. It sailed over D's head as if poised to make another jump, and landed in the bushes a few yards behind the Hunter.

Staged completely in midair, a jump like that was a miraculous maneuver only possible by coordinating the power of the lungs, the spine, and extremely tenacious musculature for a split second, and it was something werewolves alone could do. Even groups of seasoned Werewolf Hunters occasionally fell victim to attacks like this because the attack was far more terrible than any rumors the Hunters might have heard, and they weren't prepared to counter the real thing. These demonic creatures could strike at their prey from angles and directions that were patently impossible as far as three-dimensional dynamics were concerned and the attack was entirely silent.

However, moans of pain spilled from the beast's throat as it huddled low in the brush. Bright blood welled from between the fingers pressed against its right flank, soaking the grass. Its eyes, bloodshot with malice and agony, caught the blade glittering with reflected moonlight in D's right hand as the Hunter stood facing it silently. Just as the werewolf was ready to drive its claws home, D had drawn the sword over his shoulder with ungodly speed and driven it into his opponent's flank.

"Impressive," one of them said. Strangely, that someone was D, who'd been under the impression that he had cleanly bisected the werewolf's torso. "Until now, I'd never seen what a true werewolf was capable of."

His low voice sowed the seeds of a new variety of fear in the heart of the demonic beast where it lay in the bushes. The beast's legs could generate bursts of speed of three hundred and seventy miles per hour—almost half the speed of sound. There had been less than a fiftieth of a second between the time it jumped and its attack on D, which meant the youth had been able to swing his sword and split its belly open even more quickly. Worse yet, the werewolf's wound wouldn't close! That wouldn't be so unusual when it was human, but once it assumed the beastly form, the cells of a werewolf's flesh were like single-cell organisms, giving it the regenerative power of a hydra. Cells created more cells, closing wounds instantly. But the blade the werewolf had just tasted made regeneration impossible, though it was probably not due to the blade but rather the skill of the youth who wielded it. Skin and muscle tissue that could reject bullets weren't showing any signs of regenerating!

"What's wrong with you, Garou?" the young lady shouted. "In wolf form, you should be unstoppable! Do not make a game of this. I demand you tear this human apart immediately!"

Though he heard his mistress scolding him, the werewolf Garou didn't move, partly because of the wound but also because of the youth's divine skill with a sword. What really tapped the wellspring of horror was the lurid will to kill that gushed from every pore of the youth just before the werewolf could unleash its deadly attack. That hadn't come from anything human!

Is he one of those? A dhampir?

Garou realized he'd finally run into a real opponent.

"Your guard is wounded," D said softly, turning to the young lady. "If he doesn't come at me again, he might live to a ripe old age. You might, too. Go home and tell your father a dangerous obstacle has cropped up. And that he'd be a fool to attack this farm again."

"Silence!" the young lady screamed, her gorgeous visage becoming that of a banshee. "I am Larmica, daughter of Count Magnus Lee, the ruler of the entire Ransylva district of the Frontier. Do you think I can be bested by the likes of you and your sword?"

Before she'd finished speaking, a streak of white light shot toward her breast from D's left hand. In fact, it was a foot-long needle he'd taken out at some point and thrown faster than the naked eye could follow. It was made of wood. As it traveled at that unfathomable speed, the needle burned from the friction of the air, and the white light was from those flames.

But something odd had happened.

The flames had come to a stop in front of D's chest. Not that the needle he'd thrown had simply stopped there. The instant it was about to sink into Larmica's breast, it had turned around and come back, and D had stopped it with his bare hand. Or to be more accurate, Larmica had caught the needle with superhuman speed and thrown it back just as quickly. The average person wouldn't even have seen her hand move.

"If the servant is no more than a servant, still the master is a master. Well done," D murmured, heedless of the flaming needle in his hand or the way it steadily scorched his naked flesh. "For that display of skill you get my name. I'm the Vampire Hunter D. Remember that, should you live." As he spoke, D sprinted for the young lady without making a sound.

Terror stole into Larmica's expression. In a twinkling, the distance between them closed to where she was within sword's length of him, and then—

"Awooooooooooh!"

A ferocious howl shook the night air, and an indigo flash of light shot from the coachman's perch on the carriage. D dove to the side to dodge it, only able to escape the beam because his superhuman hearing had discerned the sound of the laser cannon on the perch swiveling to bear on him. The beam pierced the hem of his overcoat, igniting it in pale blue flames. Presumably, the cannon was equipped with voice recognition circuits and an electronic targeting system that responded to Garou's howls. Avoiding the flashes of blue that flew with unerring accuracy to wherever he'd gone to dodge the last, D had no choice but to keep twisting through the air.

"Milady, this way!"

He heard Garou's voice up in the driver's seat. There was the sound of a door closing. As D attempted to give chase, another blast from the laser cannon checked his advance, and the carriage swung around and was swallowed by the darkness.

"I'll settle with you another day, wretch, mark my words!"

"You'll not soon forget the wrath of Nobility!"

Whether he was pleased at having staved off the enemy or perturbed he hadn't managed to put an end to the vampiress, D wore no emotion on his face as he rose expressionless from the bushes, the malice-choked parting words of the pair circling him endlessly.

People on the Frontier

CHAPTER 2

T he year is A.D. 12,090.

The human race dwells in a world of darkness.

Or perhaps it might be more accurate to call it a dark age propped up by science. All seven continents are crisscrossed by a web of super-speed highways, and at the center of the system sits a fully automated "cyber-city" known as the Capital, the product of cutting-edge scientific technology. The dozen weather controllers manipulate the climate freely. Interstellar travel is no longer a far-fetched dream. In vast spaceports, hulking matter-conversion rockets and ships propelled by galactic energy stare up at the empyrean vault, and exploration parties have actually left their footprints on a number of planets outside our solar system—Altair and Spica, to name just two.

However, all of that is a dream now.

Take a peek at the grand Capital. A fine dust coats the walls of buildings and minarets constructed from translucent metal crystal; in places you'll find recent craters large and small from explosives and ultraheat rays. The majority of automated roads and maglev highways are in shambles, and not a single car remains to zip from place to place like a shooting star.

There are people. Tremendous mobs of them. Flooding down the streets in endless numbers. Laughing, shouting, weeping, paying their respects to the Capital, the melting pot of existence, with a vitality that borders on complete chaos. But their garb isn't what you'd expect for the masters of a once-proud metropolis. Men don shabby trousers and tunics redolent of the distant Middle Ages, and threadbare cassocks like a member of a religious order might wear. Women dress in dim shades and wear fabric rough to the touch, completely devoid of flamboyance.

Through the milling crowd of men armed with longswords or bows and arrows comes a gasoline-powered car most likely taken from some museum. Trailing black smoke and popping with the firecrackers of backfires the vehicle carries along a group of laser-gun toting lawmen.

A dreadful scream rises from one of the buildings and a woman staggers out. From her inhuman cry people instinctively know the cause of her terror, and call out for the sheriff and his men. Before long, they race to the scene, ask the wailing woman where the terror is located, and enter the building in question with faces paler than the bloodless countenance of the witness herself. They ride an independently powered elevator down five hundred stories.

In one of the subterranean passageways—all of which had supposedly been destroyed ages ago—there's a concealed door, and beyond it a vast graveyard where the Nobility, blood-craving creatures of the night, slumber as in days gone by in wooden coffins filled with damp soil.

The sheriff and his men soon go into action. Fortunately, it seems there are no curses or vicious beasts here, no defense system of lasers or electronic cannons. These Nobles were probably resigned to their fate. The lawmen hold rough wooden stakes and gleaming metal hammers in their hands. Their expressions are a pallid blend of fear and sinfulness. The mob of black silhouettes encircles a coffin, someone's arm rises toward the heavens then knifes back down. There's a dull thud. A horrifying scream and the stench of blood fill the graveyard.

The anguished cry grows thinner and dies out, and the group moves on to the next coffin.

When the lawmen leave the graveyard not long after that, their faces are adorned with crimson beads of blood and a shade of sinfulness much deeper than the one they wore before this mission.

Though the Nobility was nearly extinct, the feelings of pride brought on by the awe humanity held toward them had seeped into their very blood over the course of ten long millennia and would not be shaken off so easily. Because they had indeed reigned supreme over the human race. And because the automated city—now populated by people who couldn't fathom its machinery or receive the tiniest fraction of the benefits it might provide—and everything else in the world that could be called civilization was something they had left behind. They—the vampires.

This strict stratification of vampires and humanity came about when one day in 1999 mankind's history as lords of the earth came to an abrupt end. Someone pushed the button and launched the full-scale nuclear war that the human race had been warned about for so long. Thousands of ICBMs and MIRVs flew in disarray, reducing one major city after another to a white-hot inferno, but the immediate fatalities were far outstripped by the wholesale death dealt by radiation more potent than tens of thousands of x-rays.

The theory of a limited nuclear war, where sensible battles would be fought so the winners might later rebuild and rule, was obliterated in a split second by a million degrees of heat and flame.

The survivors barely made it. Their numbers totally insignificant, they shunned the surface world and its toxic atmosphere and were left with no choice but to live in underground shelters for the next few years.

When they finally returned to the surface, their mechanized civilization was in ruins. With no way of contacting survivors in other countries, any thoughts these isolated pockets of humanity might have had of things returning to the way they'd been before the destruction, or even of rebuilding to the point where it could be called a civilization, were flights of fantasy, and nothing more.

The regression began.

With generation after generation striving merely to survive, memories of the past grew dim. The population increased somewhat after a thousand years, but civilization itself plunged back to the level of the Middle Ages. Dreading the mutant creatures spawned by radiation and cosmic rays, the humans formed small groups and moved into plains and forests that over the years had gradually returned to verdure. In their struggles with the cruel environment, at times they had to kill their newborn babies to keep what little food they had. Other times the infants went toward filling their parents' empty bellies.

That was the time. In that pitch-black, superstitious world they appeared. How they—the vampires—kept themselves hidden from the eyes of man and lived on in the luxuriant shadows was unclear. However, their life form was almost exactly as described in legend and they seemed the best suited to fill the role of the new masters of history.

Ageless and undying so long as they partook of the blood of other creatures, the vampires remembered a civilization the human race could not, and they knew exactly how to rebuild it. Before the nuclear war, the vampires had contacted others of their kind who lurked in dark places around the globe. They had a hidden super-power source that they'd secretly developed in fallout shelters of their own design, along with the absolute minimum machinery required to reconstruct civilization after the absolute worst came to pass.

But that's not to say they were the ones who caused the nuclear war. Through cryptesthesia, the black arts, and psychic abilities mankind never guessed they'd cultivated, the vampires simply knew when the human race would destroy itself and how they, the vampires, could restore order to the world.

Civilization was rebuilt and the tables were turned for vampires and humans.

How much friction and discord that course created between the two sides was soon apparent. Within two thousand years of stepping onto history's great stage, the vampires gave the world a sprawling civilization driven by super-science and sorcery, dubbed themselves the "Nobility," and subjugated humanity. The automated city with its electronic brain and ghostly will, interstellar spaceships, weather controllers, methods of creating endless quantities of materials through matter-conversion—all this came into being through the thoughts and deeds of them and them alone.

However, who could have imagined that within five short millennia of this golden age they would be treading the road to extinction? History didn't belong to them after all.

As a species, the vampires possessed an underlying spark to live that was far less tenacious than that of humans. Or perhaps it would be better to say that their life held an element that ensured their future destruction. From the end of the fourth millennia A.D., the vampire civilization as a whole started to show a phenomenal decline in energy, and that brought on the start of mankind's great rebellion. Though they had an expertise in the physiology of the human brain, and had developed the science of psychology to such extremes they could manipulate the human mind in any way they chose, in the end they found it impossible to eradicate the innate urge to rebel that lurked in the depths of the human soul.

Weakened by one great uprising after another, the Nobility entered dozens of armistices with the humans, each of which maintained the peace for short periods. But before long the Nobles faded away, like gallant nihilists who realized their destiny.

Some took their own lives, while others entered a sleep that would last until the end of time. Some even headed off into the depths of space, but their numbers were extremely few; in general the vampires had no wish to establish themselves in extraterrestrial environs.

At any rate, their overall numbers were on the decline; ultimately they scattered before mankind's pursuit. By the time A.D. 12,090 arrived, the vampires served no purpose beyond terrorizing the humans on the Frontier. Yet, precisely because this was their sole purpose, the humans felt a special terror of them that shook their very souls.

To be honest, it was miraculous that mankind was able to plan and execute a rebellion no matter how utterly desperate they might have been.

The horror all felt for vampires—who slept by day and awoke at night to suck the lifeblood from humans and ensure their own eternal life—became part of the vampire mythology, right along with the ancient legends of transformations into bats and wolves, and their power to control the elements. As a result of clever psychological manipulation that continued throughout this mechanized age, the horror laid roots down into the deepest layers of the human psyche.

It is said that the first time the humans signed an armistice with the vampires—their rulers—all the representatives on the human side save one were shaking so badly their teeth chattered. Even though vampires could no longer be found in the Capital, it had still taken the humans nearly three hundred years to check every street and building.

Given how much strength the vampires had in their favor, why hadn't they set about exterminating the human race? That is the eternal question. It couldn't be that they were simply afraid of destroying their source of the blood, since they had mastered a method of perfectly synthesizing human blood in the first stage of their civilization. As far as manual labor went, they had more than enough robots to bear the load by the time the revolution broke out. In fact, the reason why they allowed humans to continue to exist in the first place, even in their role as subordinates, is a mystery. Most likely it was due to some sort of superiority complex, or out of pity.

Vampires were rarely seen by humans any more, but the fear remained. On very rare occasions, they appeared from the depths of the darkness and left their vile bite on the pale throats of their victims; sometimes a person would seek them out with wooden stake in hand like a man possessed, while at other times the humans would drive the victim out from their midst, earnestly praying they wouldn't receive another visit from the vampires.

The Hunters were a product of the people's fear.

Being nearly indestructible themselves, the vampires weren't so eager to exterminate the mutant creatures humanity feared so much in the years just after the war. Quite the contrary, the vampires loved the vicious beasts, nurtured them, and even created others like them with their own hands.

Thanks to their unparalleled knowledge of biology and genetic engineering, the vampires unleashed one legendary monster after another into the world of man: werewolves, were-tigers, serpent men, golems, fairies, mer-creatures, goblins, raksas, ghouls, zombies, banshees, fire dragons, salamanders resistant to flames, griffins, krakens, and more. Though their creators neared extinction, the creatures still ran rampant on the plains and in the mountains.

Working the land with the scant machinery the Nobility allowed them, defending themselves with replicas of old-fashioned gunpowder weapons or homemade swords and spears, the humans studied the nature of these artificial monstrosities for generations, learning their powers and their weaknesses. In time, some people came to work exclusively on weapons and ways to kill these things.

Of those people, some specialized in producing more effective weaponry, while those of surpassing strength and agility trained themselves to use those weapons. These exceptional warriors were the first Hunters.

As time went by, Hunters became more narrowly focused, and specialists like the Were-tiger Hunter and Fairy Hunter were born. Of them all, Vampire Hunters were universally recognized as possessing strength and intellect beyond the rest, as well as an ironclad will impervious to the fear their former rulers inspired in others.

The next morning, Doris was awakened by the shrill whinny of a horse. White light speared in through her window, telling her it was a fresh day. She was lying on the bed dressed just as she was when D knocked her out. Actually, D had carried her to the bed when his first skirmish was over. Her nerves had been frayed with worry after her vampire attack, and she was incredibly tense from her search for a Hunter, but when the power of D's left hand put her to sleep she was totally at peace and had slept soundly till morning.

Instinctively reaching for her throat, Doris recalled what had happened the night before.

What happened while I was asleep? He said we had company, and that had to be him. I wonder how D made out? As she sprung out of bed in a panic, her expression suddenly grew brighter. She was still a little lethargic, but physically nothing else seemed out of the norm. D had kept her safe. Remembering that she hadn't even shown him where his room was, she pawed at her sleep-disheveled locks and hurried out of her bedroom.

The heavy shades in the living room were fully drawn; at one end of the murky room sat a sofa with a pair of boots hanging off the end.

"D, you really did it, didn't you? I knew hiring you was the right thing to do!"

From beneath the traveler's hat that covered his face came the usual low voice.

"Just doing my job. Sorry, it seems I forgot to put the barrier back up."

"Don't you worry about that," Doris said animatedly, checking the clock on the mantle. "It's only five past seven in the morning. Get some more sleep. I'll have your breakfast ready in no time. And I'll make it the best I can."

Outside a horse whinnied loudly again. Doris was reminded she had a visitor.

"Who the hell would be making such a racket at this hour?" She went over to the window and was about to raise the shade when a sharp "Don't!" stayed her hand.

When Doris turned to D with a gasp, her face was twisted by the same terror that had contorted it the night before when she tried to escape his approach. She remembered what the gorgeous Hunter really was. And yet she reclaimed her smile soon enough; not only was she stouthearted, but she also had a naturally fair disposition. "Sorry about that. I'll fix you up a room later. At any rate, get some rest." As soon as she'd said that she went ahead and grabbed a corner of the shade anyway, but the moment she lifted it and took a look outside, her endearing face quickly became a mass of pure hatred. Returning to her bedroom for her prized whip, she stepped outside indignantly.

Astride a bay in front of the porch was a hulking man of twenty-four or twenty-five. The explosive-firing, ten-banger pistol he was so proud of hung from the leather gun-belt that girt his waist. Below a mop of red hair, his sly eyes crept across every inch of Doris' frame.

"What's your business, Greco? I thought I told you not to come around here no more." Her tone just as commanding as it had been in her search for the Hunter, Doris glared at the man.

For a brief instant, anger and confusion surfaced in his cloudy eyes, but a lewd smile soon spread across the man's face and he said, "Aw, don't say that. I come out here all worried about you and this is the thanks I get? Seems you been looking for a Hunter now, haven't you? Couldn't be you've gone and got attacked by our old lord, could it?"

In a heartbeat, vermilion spread across Doris' face, the result of the anger and embarrassment she felt at Greco hitting it right on the mark. "Grow up! If you and your trashy friends in town go around spreading wild stories about me just because I won't have nothing to do with you, I'll teach you a thing or two!"

"Come on, don't get so worked up," Greco said, shrugging his shoulders. Then his gaze became probing as he said, "It's just, the night before last there was this drifter in the saloon blubbering on about how he got himself challenged to a test of skill out at the hill on the edge of town by a right powerful girl, then got his ass handed to him before he could even draw his sword. So I buy him a drink to hear all the details and it turns out looks-wise and build-wise, the girl sounds like the spitting image of you. The frosting on the cake was he said she's damn handy with a weird kind of whip, and there ain't no one in these parts that could be besides you, missy." Greco's eyes were trained on the whip Doris had in her right hand.

"Sure, I was out looking for someone. Someone good. You should know as well as anyone how much damage mutants have been causing around town lately. Well, things are no different out here. It's more than I can take care of all by my lonesome."

On hearing Doris' reply, Greco smiled faintly. "In that case, all you'd have had to do was go ask Pops Cushing in town, seeing how he's in charge of scouting new talent. You know, five days back, one of the hands at our place seen you chasing a lesser dragon toward the lord's castle right around dusk. Now, on top of that, you've got this need for hired help you don't want anyone in town to know about." Greco's tone of voice changed entirely. He threateningly suggested, "Let's see you take that scarf off your neck."

Doris didn't move.

"Can't do it, can you," he laughed. "I figured as much. I think I'll go into town and have a few words with … well, I don't think I have to tell you the rest. So, what do you say? Just be sensible and give me your okay for what I've been asking you to do all along. If we got hitched, you'd be the mayor's daughter-in-law. Then no one in town could lay a stinkin' finger on you or—"

Before his vile words were done, a snap rang through the air and the bay reared up with a whinny of pain. Doris' whip had stung the horse's flank with lightning speed. In a heartbeat, Greco's massive frame was thrown out of the saddle and crashed to the ground. Hand pressed to his tail, he groaned in pain. The bay's hoofbeats echoed loudly as it fled the farm, heartlessly leaving its master behind.

"Serves you right! That's for all the filthy things you've gotten away with by hiding behind your father's power," Doris laughed. "I never cared too much for your father or anyone in cahoots with him. And if you got a problem with that, you bring your daddy and your buddies out here any time. I won't run or hide. Of course, the next time you show that ugly, pockmarked mug of yours around here, you'd better be ready to have me flay the skin right off it!"

Color rose in the big man's face as words so rough you had to wonder where a beautiful young lady kept them shot at him like flames.

"Bitch, you fucked up real good …" As he spoke, his right hand went for his ten-banger. Once again, a surge of black split the sunlight-soaked air, and the pistol he'd tried to draw was thrown into the bushes behind him. And he could draw in less than half a second.

"Next time I'll send your nose or one of your ears flying."

The man knew there was more to her words than empty threats. With no parting quip, Greco scurried off the farm, rubbing his backside and right wrist by turns.

"That scumbag's nothing without his daddy behind him." After she spat the words, Doris turned and froze on the spot.

Dan stood in the doorway, still dressed in his pajamas and armed with a laser rifle. His big, round eyes were brimming with tears.

"Dan, you … you heard everything then?"

The boy nodded mechanically. Greco had been facing toward the house and he hadn't said anything about Dan, so the boy must've stayed behind the door. "Sis … were you really bit by a Noble?" The boy lived in the wilds of the Frontier. He was well aware of the fate of those with the devil's kiss on their throat.

The young beauty who had just sent a brute twice her size packing with a crack of her whip was now rooted to the spot, unable to speak.

"No, it can't be!" The boy suddenly ran over and threw his arms around her. The sorrow and concern he'd been wrestling with surged out in a tidal wave, soaking Doris' slacks with a flood of hot tears. "You can't be, you just can't! I'd be all alone then … You can't be!" Though he didn't want it to be true, he had no idea what he could do about it, and his sorrow sprung from his helplessness.

"It's okay," Doris said, patting her brother's tiny shoulder as she fought back tears of her own. "No lousy Noble's put the bite on me. These are bug bites I've got on my neck. I only hid them because I didn't want you getting all worried."

A ray of light streamed into his tear-streaked face. "Really? Really truly?"

"Yep."

Surely the boy had a heart that could shift from low gear to high on the fly if that was all it took to calm him down. "But what'll we do if the folks in town believe all Greco's fibbing and come busting in here?"

"You know how good I am in a fight. Plus, I've got you here—"

"And we've got D, too!"

At the boy's exuberant words, the girl's face clouded. That was the difference between someone who knew the way Hunters worked and someone who didn't. In fact, the boy hadn't been told D was a Hunter.

"I'm gonna go ask him!"

"Dan—"

Before she could stop him, the boy disappeared into the living room. She hurried after him, but was too late.

In a completely trusting tone, Dan addressed the youth on the sofa. "A guy just came out here trying to get my sister to marry him, and he says he gonna spread the worst kind of lies about her. He'll be back with a bunch of folks from town, I just know it. And then they'll take my sister away. Please save her, D."

Imagining his answer, Doris unconsciously closed her eyes. The problem wasn't the reply itself, but the effect it would have. A cold, adamant rejection would leave a wound on the boy's fragile heart that might never heal.

But this is how the Vampire Hunter replied: "Leave it to me. I won't let anyone lay a finger on your sister."

"Okay!"

The boy's face shone like a sunny morning.

From behind him, Doris said, "Well, breakfast will be ready soon. Before we eat, go have a look at the thermo-regulators out in the orchards."

The boy galloped off like the spirit of life itself. Doris turned to the still prone D and said, "Thank you. I know it's the iron law of Hunters that they won't lift a finger for anything but dealing with their prey. I'd be in no position to complain no matter how you turned him down. You did it without hurting him ... and he loves you like a big brother."

"But I do refuse."

"I know. Aside from your job itself, I won't ask any more of you—what you said to him just now will do fine. I'll handle my own problems. And the sooner you get your work finished the better."

"Fine."

Not surprisingly, D's voice was emotionless and bitterly cold.

As expected, "company" came as the three of them were just finishing a somewhat peculiar breakfast. What made it peculiar was that D only ate half as much as young Dan. The menu consisted of ham and eggs on a colossal scale—mutant-chicken eggs a foot across on an inch-thick slab of light, homemade ham—along with preservative-free black bread hot out of the oven, and juice from massive Gargantua grapes cultivated right on their own farm. Of course, the juice was freshly squeezed and the three large glasses were filled from a single grape. And those were just the main dishes; there was a gigantic bowl of salad and fragrant floral tea, too. Only a farm like the Langs' could offer a rich menu like this, and the freshness of the ingredients alone should have been enough to make a good-sized man take seconds or thirds on the ham and eggs. The refreshing morning sunlight and giant lavender blossoms that adorned the table were in essence part of a sacred ritual to give all those gathered around it the strength to fight the cruel Frontier for another day.

And yet, D quickly set down his fork and knife and withdrew to the room in the back Doris had just given him.

"That's weird. I wonder if he ain't feeling too good?"

"Yes, I'm sure it's something like that." Though she pretended nothing was wrong, Doris pictured D back in his room now taking his own kind of breakfast, and started to feel ill.

"Not you too, Sis! What's the matter? I know you like him and all, but don't get sick just because he does."

Doris was about to lay into Dan for his teasing remarks when tension suddenly flooded her face.

Outside, a thunder of hoofbeats drew closer. Lots of hoofbeats.

"Damn it, here they come," Dan shouted, dashing over to where a laser rifle hung on the wall.

He started to call out for D, but Doris' quick hand silenced him.

"But why not? It's gotta be Greco and his thugs," he said with disgust.

"Let's see if the two of us can't handle it first. If that doesn't work, maybe then …" But she was perfectly aware that no matter what was going to happen to the two of them, D wouldn't do anything.

Armed with a whip and a rifle, the pair stepped out onto the porch. She let her little eight-year-old brother join her because the law of the Frontier was that if you and your family didn't defend your own lives and property, no one else would. If you always relied on others, you wouldn't last long against the fire dragons and golems.

In no time, a dozen men on horseback formed up in front of them.

"Dear me, the cream of local society is out in force. A no-account little farm like this don't deserve such distinguished guests." As Doris greeted them in a calm tone, her eyes were cautiously trained on the men in the second and third ranks. In the foremost rank were prominent villagers like Sheriff Luke Dalton, Dr. Sam Ferringo, and Mayor Rohman—this last was Greco's father, whose face was unusually oily for a man nearing sixty. There was no reason to worry about any of those three suddenly trying anything funny, but behind them was a mob of brutal hooligans just itching to make a statement with the Magnum guns and battered heat-rays they wore on their hips should the opportunity arise. They were all hired hands from Mayor Rohman's ranch. Doris glared at each of them in turn without a trace of fear until she came across a familiar face at the very tail of the mob, and her gaze became one of pure contempt. When it looked like trouble was brewing, it was just like Greco to shut his big mouth, find the safest possible place, and try to look like he didn't have the faintest idea what was going on.

"So, what's your business?"

Apparently by mutual consent, Mayor Rohman spoke first.

"As if you don't know. We're out here on account of the marks you've got under that scarf. You show them to Doc Ferringo now, and if they're nothing then fine. But if they're ... well then, unfortunately we'll have to put you in the asylum."

Doris snorted in derision. "So you believe the nonsense that damn fool son of yours been talking? He's been out here five time asking me to marry him and I've turned him down every time, so he's stuck with some pretty damn sour grapes. That's why he's spreading these stories when they ain't true. You keep spouting that filth and you won't like what happens, mayor or not."

The bluff rolled from her so fluently the mayor couldn't get a word in edgewise. His bovine countenance flushed with rage.

"That's right! My sister ain't been bit by no vampire! So hit the road, you old pervert," Dan shouted from his sister's side, pushing the mayor over the edge.

"What do you mean by calling me an old pervert? Why, you ... you little bastard! To say something like that about the mayor even in jest ... A pervert of all things! I'll have you know ... "

The old man had lost all control. He might hold all the real power in town, but he was still just the mayor of one tiny village. Simply touch on one of his sore spots, and his emotional restraints would burst. In that, he wasn't so different from the thugs behind him.

From the back, Greco bellowed, "They're making fools of us! C'mon boys, don't pay them no nevermind. Let's grab them and burn the damn house down!"

Cries of "Hell yeah!" and "Damn straight!" resounded from the rowdies.

"Hold everything! You pull any of that crap and you'll answer to me!"

The rebukes flew from Sheriff Dalton. For a moment, Doris' expression was placid. Though still under thirty, the sincere and capable sheriff was someone she was willing to trust. The hoodlums stopped moving, too.

"Are you with them, Sheriff?" Doris asked in a low voice.

"I need you to understand something, Doris. I've got a job to uphold as sheriff in this here village. And checking out your neck is part of it. I don't want things getting out of hand. If it's nothing, then one peek will do. Take your scarf off and let Doc have a look."

"He's right," Dr. Ferringo said, rising in his saddle. He was about the same age as the mayor, but thanks to his studies of medicine in the Capital, he had the intelligent look of a distinguished old gentleman. Because Doris and Dan's father had been a student of his at the education center, this good-natured man worried about their welfare on a daily basis. Before him alone, Doris couldn't hold her head up. "No matter what the result may be, we won't do wrong by you. You leave it to me and the sheriff."

"No way, she goes to the asylum!" Greco's spiteful words came from the back. "In this village, we got a rule that anyone that gets bit by a Noble goes to the asylum, no matter who they are. And when we can't get rid of the Noble … heh heh … then we chuck them out as monster bait!"

The sheriff whipped around and roared, "Shut up, you damn fool!"

Greco was shocked into an embarrassed silence, but he drew power from the fact that he was surrounded by his hired hands. "Well, put a badge on you and you get pretty damn tough. Before you give me any more back talk, check out the bitch's neck. After all, that's what we're paying you for, isn't it?"

"What'd you say, boy?" The sheriff's eyes had a look that could kill. At that same moment, the hoods were going for their backs and waists with their gunhands. An ugly situation was developing.

"Stop it," the mayor barked bitterly at the entire company. "What'll we prove by fighting among ourselves? All we have to do is take a look at the girl's neck and we'll be done here."

The sheriff and the hoods had no choice but to begrudgingly go along with that. "Doris," the sheriff called out to her in a gruffer tone than before, "you'd best take that scarf off."

Doris tightened her grip on the whip.

"And if I say I don't wanna?"

The sheriff fell silent.

"Get her!"

With Greco's cry, the mounted thugs raced right and left. Doris' whip uncoiled for action.

"Stop!" the sheriff shouted, but it looked like his commands would no longer do the trick, and just when the battle was about to be joined—

The toughs all stopped moving at once. Or to be more accurate, their mounts had jerked to a halt.

"What's gotten into you? Move it!"

Even a kick from spurred heels couldn't make the horses budge. If the men could've looked into their horses' eyes, they might have glimpsed a trace of ineffable horror. A trace of overwhelming terror that wouldn't permit the horses to be coerced any further, or even to flee. And then the eyes of every man focused on the gorgeous youth in black who stood blocking the front door, though no one had any idea when he'd appeared. Even the sunlight seemed to grow sluggish. Suddenly, a gust of wind brushed across the fields and the men turned away, exchanging uneasy looks.

"Who the hell are you?" The mayor tried his level best to sound intimidating, but there was no hiding the quiver in his voice. The youth had about him an air that churned the calm waters of the human soul.

Doris turned around and was amazed, while Dan's face shined with delight.

Without a word, D stopped Doris from saying whatever she was about to say and stepped in front of the Langs as if to shield them. His right hand held a longsword. "I'm D. I've hired on with these people."

He looked not at the mayor, but at the sheriff as he spoke.

The sheriff gave a little nod. He could tell at a glance what the youth before them really was. "I'm Sheriff Dalton. This here's Mayor Rohman, and Dr. Ferringo. The rest back there don't count for much." After that reasonable introduction, he added, "You're a Hunter, aren't you? I see it in your eyes, the way you carry yourself. I seem to recall hearing there was a man of unbelievable skill traveling across the Frontier, and that his name was D. They say his sword is faster than a laser beam or some such thing." Those words could be taken as fearful or praising, but D was silent.

The sheriff continued in a hard voice. "Only, they say that man's a Hunter, and he specializes in vampires. And that he's a dhampir himself."

There were gasps. The village notables and hoods all froze. As did Dan.

"Oh, Doris! Then you really have been ..."

Dr. Ferringo barely squeezed the hopeless words from his throat.

"Yes, the girl's been bitten by a vampire. And I've been hired to destroy him."

"At any rate, the mere fact that she's been bitten by a vampire is reason enough not to let her remain at large. She goes to the asylum," the mayor declared.

"Nothing doing," Doris shot back flatly. "I'm not going anywhere and leaving Dan and the farm unattended. If you're hellbent on doing it, you'll have to take me away by force."

"Okay then," Greco groaned. The girl's manner and speech, defiant to the bitter end, reawakened his rancor at being spurned.

He gave a toss of the chin to his thugs, whose eyes burned with the same shadowy fire as a serpent's.

The rowdies were about to dismount in unison, but at that moment their horses reared up simultaneously. There was nothing they could do. Each gave their own cry of "Oof" or "Ow," and every last one of them was thrown to the ground. The sunny air was filled with moans of pain and the whinnying of horses.

D returned his gaze to the sheriff. Whether or not the sheriff comprehended that a single glare from the Hunter had put the horses on end was unclear.

An indescribable tension and fear flowed between the two of them.

"I have a proposal." At D's words, the sheriff nodded his assent like he was sleepwalking. "Hold off on doing anything about the girl until I've finished my work. If we come out of it okay, that's fine. If we don't ..."

"You can rest assured I'll take care of myself. If he's beaten by the lord, I'll drive a stake through my own heart." Doris gave a satisfied nod.

"Don't let her fool you! This jerk's in league with the Nobility. You shouldn't be making deals with him—he's out to turn every last person in Ransylva into a vampire, I'm sure of it!" Having been thrown to the ground for the second time that day, Greco was still down on all fours, screaming. "Let's do away with the bitch. No, better yet, give her to the lord. That way, he won't go after any of the other women."

With a *pffft!* a four-inch-wide pillar of flame erupted from the ground right in front of Greco's face. The earth boiled from a blast of more than twenty thousand degrees, and the flames leapt to Greco's greasy face, searing his upper lip. He tumbled backwards with a beastly howl of agony.

"Say anything else bad about my sister and your head'll be next," Dan threatened, perfectly aligning the barrel of his laser rifle with Greco's face. Though it's true the weapon had no kick, it was still unheard of for a child a good deal shorter than the weapon's length to be skilled enough to hit a target dead-on.

Far from angry, the sheriff wore a grin that said, "You done good, kid."

D addressed the sheriff softly.

"As you can see, we have a fierce bodyguard on our side. You could try and plow through us, but a lot of people will probably get hurt unnecessarily. Just wait."

"Well, some of them could do with a little hurting if you ask me," said the sheriff, glancing briefly at the hoodlums moaning behind him. "What do you make of this, Doc?"

"Why don't you ask me?!" the mayor screamed, veins bulging. "You think we can trust this drifter? We should send her to the asylum, just like my boy says! Sheriff, bring her in right this moment!"

"The evaluation of vampire victims falls to me," Dr. Ferringo said calmly, and then he produced a cigar from one of his inner pockets and put it in his mouth. It wasn't a cheap one like the local knock-off artists hand rolled with eighty percent garbage. This was a high-class cigar in a cellophane wrapper that bore the stamp of the Capital's Tobacco Monopoly. These were Dr. Ferringo's treasure. He gave a little nod to Doris.

Her whip shot out with a wa-pish!

"Oof!" The mayor gave an utterly hysterical cry and grabbed his nose. With one slight twist of Doris' wrist, her whip had taken the cigar from the doctor's mouth and crammed it up one of the mayor's nostrils.

Ignoring the mayor, whose entire face was flushed with rage, the doctor declared loudly, "Very well, I find Doris Lang's infection of vampirism to be of the lowest possible degree. My orders are rest at home for her. Sheriff Dalton and Mayor Rohman, do you concur?"

"Yessir," the sheriff replied with a nod of satisfaction, but suddenly he looked straight at D with the intimidating expression of a man sworn to uphold the law. "Under the following conditions. I'll take the word of a damn-good Hunter and hold off on any further discussion. But let me make one thing crystal clear—I don't want to have to stake you folks through the heart. I don't want to, but if that time should come, I won't give it a second thought." And then, throwing the Lang children a look of pathos, he bid them farewell. "I'm looking forward to the day I can enjoy the juice of those Gargantua-breed grapes of yours. All right, you dirty dogs, mount up and make it snappy! And I'm warning you, any of you so much as make a peep about this back in town, I'll throw you in the electric pokey, mark my words!"

The crowd disappeared over the hill, glancing back now and then with looks of hatred, compassion, and, from some, encouragement. D was about to go into the house when Doris asked him to wait. He turned to her coolly, and then she said, "You sure are strange for a Hunter. You might've taken on some work you didn't have to, and I can't pay you for it."

"It's not about work. It's about a promise."

"A promise? To who?"

"To your little bodyguard over there," he said with a toss of his chin. Then, noticing Dan's stiff expression, he asked, "What's wrong? You hate me because I'm supposedly 'in league with the Nobility'?"

"Nope."

As he shook his head, the boy's face suddenly crumpled in on itself and he started to cry.

The young hero who'd put Greco in his place minutes earlier now returned to being an eight-year-old boy. He blubbered away as he threw his arms around D's waist. This child had rarely cried since the death of his father three years earlier. As he watched his sister struggling along as a woman on her own, the boy had secretly nurtured his own stores of pride and determination in his little heart. Naturally, life on the Frontier was hard and lonely for him too. When his youthful heart felt he might be robbed of his only blood relative, he forgot himself and latched onto not his sister, but rather to the man who'd only arrived the day before.

"Dan ..."

Doris reached for her brother's shoulder with one hand, but D gently brushed it away. Before long, the boy's cries started to taper off, and D quietly planted one knee on the wooden floor of the front porch, looking the boy square in his tear-streaked face.

"Listen to me," he said in a low but distinct voice. Noticing the unmistakable ring of encouragement in his voice, Doris opened her eyes in astonishment.

"I promise you and your sister I'll kill the Noble. I always keep my word. Now you have to promise me something."

"Sure." Dan nodded repeatedly.

"From here on out, if you want to scream and cry, that's your prerogative. Do whatever you like. But whatever you do, don't make your sister cry. If you think your crying will set her off too, then hold it in. If you're being selfish and your sister starts to cry, make her smile again. You're a man, after all. Okay?"

"Sure!" The boy's face was radiant. It glowed with an aura of pride.

"Okay, then do your big brother a favor and feed his horse. I'll be heading out on business soon."

The boy raced off, and D went into the house without another word.

"D, I ..." Doris sounded like something was weighing greatly on her.

The Vampire Hunter ignored her words, and said simply, "Come inside. Before I head out, I want to put a little protective charm on you." And then he vanished down the dark and desolate hall.

The Vampire Count Lee

From the farm he rode hard north by northwest for two hours, until he came to a spot where a massive ashen citadel towering quietly atop a hillock loomed menacingly overhead. This was the castle of the local lord—the home of Count Magnus Lee.

Even the shower of midday sunlight changed color here, and a nauseating miasma seemed to come from the morbid expanse of land surrounding the castle. The grass was green as far as the eye could see, and the trees were laden with succulent fruit, but not a single bird could be heard. Still, as one would expect around noon on a sunny day, there were no signs of life in the vampire's castle. Constructed to mimic the castles of the distant middle ages, the walls were dotted with countless loopholes. The dungeon and courtyards were surrounded by broad, stone stairways that linked them together, but there was no sign of android sentries on any of them. The castle was, to all appearances, deserted.

But D had already sensed the castle's bloodied nocturnal form, and the hundreds of electronic eyes and vicious weapons that lay in wait for their next victim.

The surveillance satellite in geo-stationary orbit 22,240 miles above the castle—as well as the uncounted security cameras disguised as fruit or spiders—sent the castle's mother-computer images so detailed that an observer could count the pores of the intruder's skin. The photon cannons secreted in the loopholes had their safety locks switched off, and they were drawing a bead on several hundred points all over the intruder's body.

As the Nobility was fated to live by night alone, electronic protection during the day was an absolute necessity. No matter how much mystic-might the vampires might wield by night, in the light of day they were feeble creatures, easily destroyed by a single thrust of a stake. It was for precisely this reason that the vampires had used all their knowledge of psychology and cerebral biology in their attempts to plant fear in the human mind throughout the six or seven millennia of their reign. The results of this tactic were clear: even after the vampire civilization had long since crumbled—it was rare to catch even a glimpse of one about—they could take residence in the midst of their human "foes" and, like a feudal lord, hold complete mastery over the region.

According to what Doris told D before he set out, the villagers in Ransylva had taken up sword and spear a number of times in the past, endeavoring to drive their lord off their lands. However, as soon as they set foot within the castle grounds, black clouds began swirling in the sky above, the earth was rent wide, lightning raged, and not surprisingly, they were ultimately routed before they even reached the moat.

Not giving in so easily, a group of villagers made a direct appeal to the Capital and succeeded in getting the government's precious Anti-Gravity Air Corps to execute a bombing mission. Because the government was afraid of depleting its stores of energy or explosives, however, it wouldn't authorize more than a single bombing run. The defense shields around the castle prevented that single attack from accomplishing much before it was forced to return home. The following day, villagers were found butchered with positively unearthly brutality, and, by the time the villagers had seen the vampires' vengeance play out, the flames of resistance were utterly snuffed.

Home to the feudal lord who would taste D's blade, the castle the Hunter approached was the sort of demonic citadel that kept the world in fear of the now largely legendary vampires.

Perhaps that was what brought a haggard touch to D's visage. No, as a Vampire Hunter he should've been quite familiar with the fortifications of the vampires' castle. As proof, he rode his horse without the slightest trace of trepidation to where the drawbridge was raised. But against the lord and his iron-walled castle, crammed with most advanced electronics, what chance of victory did a lone youth with a sword have?

Blazing-white light could have burnt through his chest at any moment, but a tepid breeze merely stroked his ample black hair, and soon he arrived at the edge of a moat brimming with dark blue water. The moat must have been nearly twenty feet wide. His eyes raced across the walls as he pondered his next move, but when he put his hand to his pendant the drawbridge barring the castle gate amazingly began to descend with a heavy, grating noise. With earth-shaking force, the bridge was laid.

"It is a great pleasure to receive you," a metallic voice called out from nowhere in particular. It was computer-synthesized speech— the ultimate in personality simulation. "Please proceed into the castle proper. Directions shall be transmitted to the brain of milord's mount. Please pardon the fact no one was here to greet you."

D said nothing as he urged his horse on.

Once he'd crossed the bridge, he entered a large courtyard. Behind him came the sounds of the drawbridge being raised again, but he advanced down the cobblestone way toward the palace without a backward glance.

The orderly rows of trees, the marble sculptures glittering in the sunlight, stairways and corridors leading to places that couldn't be guessed—all gave the feeling of scrupulous upkeep by machines. Though no one could say how many millennia ago they'd been planted or sculpted, they looked as fresh and new as if they'd been placed there only yesterday. But there were no signs that life went on here. The machines alone lived, and their mechanical eyes and fiery arrows were trained on D.

When his horse halted before the palace gates, D quickly slipped out of the saddle. The thick doors dotted with countless hobnails were already open wide.

"Enter, please." The same synthesized voice reverberated from the dark corridor.

A hazy darkness bound the interior. Not that the windowpanes were dampening the sunlight—this effect was a result of the artificial lighting. In fact, the windows in the vampire's palace were no more than ornamentation, impervious to the slightest ray of light.

As he walked down the corridors guided by the voice, D noticed that each and every window was set in a niche in the wall. It would take two or three steps up the scaffolding to climb to the window from the hallway: one couldn't walk over to the window, but would rather pop up in front of it. The design had been copied from German castles in the middle ages.

The predominant element of vampire civilization was their love of medieval styles. Even in their superiorly advanced, tech-filled Capital, the designs of many of the buildings closely resembled those of medieval Europe. Perhaps something in their DNA cried out for a return to the golden age that lived on in their genetic memory, a time when superstition and legend and all manner of weird creatures prevailed. Maybe that explained why so many detestable monsters and spirits had been resurrected by their super-science.

The voice led D to a splendid door of massive proportions. At the bottom of the door there was an opening large enough for a cat to come and go as it pleased. This door opened without a sound as well, and D set foot into a world of even deeper darkness. His haggard air was gone in an instant. His nerves, his muscles, his circulation—every part of him told him the time he had known had suddenly changed. The instant he smelled the thick perfume wafting throughout the room—which appeared to be a hall—D knew the cause. *Time-Bewitching Incense. I've heard rumors about this stuff.* When he sighted the pair of silhouettes hazily sketched by wispy flames at the far end of the vast hall, his suspicion became conviction.

The silhouettes gave off a ghastly aura that made even D's peerless features stiffen with tension. Beside a slender form—which he knew at a glance to be female—stood a figure of remarkable grandeur dressed in black. "We've been waiting for you. You are the first human to ever make it this far in one piece." From the corners of the vermilion lips that loosed this solemn voice poked a pair of white fangs. "As our guest, you deserve an introduction. I am the lord of this castle and administrator of the Tenth Frontier Sector, Count Magnus Lee."

Time-Bewitching Incense could be called the ultimate chemical compound born of the vampires' physiological needs.

For the most part, the information and rumors people passed along about the physiology of these fiends—the various stories told since time immemorial—were essentially true. Outlandish tales about transforming into bats, turning themselves into fog and billowing away, and so on—stories that there were vampires who could do such things and others who couldn't were taken as fact. Just as in human society ability varied according to an individual's disposition, so too among the vampires there were some demons who freely controlled the weather, while other fiends had mastery over lower animals.

Many aspects of the vampire's fantastic physiology, however, remained shrouded in mystery.

For example, the reason why they slept by day but awoke at night remained unclear. Even enveloped by darkness in a secret chamber that blocked out all possible light, a vampire's body grew rigid with the coming of that unseen dawn, their heart alone continuing to beat as they fell into death's breathless slumber.

Despite a concerted effort at explanation spanning thousands of years and investing the essence of every possible field of science—ecology, biology, cerebral physiology, psychology, and even super-psychology—the damned couldn't shed a bit of light on the true cause of their sleep. As if to say, those who dwelt in the darkness were denied even the rays of hope.

Born of the vampires' desperate research, Time-Bewitching Incense was one means of overcoming their limitations.

Wherever its scent hung, the time would become night. Or rather, appear to be night. In a manner of speaking, normal temporal effects were so altered by this chemical compound, the incense made time itself seem hypnotized. In the glistening sunlight of early afternoon, the night-blooming moonlight grass would open its gorgeous white flowers, people would doze off and remain asleep indefinitely, and the eyes of vampires would shine with a piercing light. Due to the extreme difficulty of finding and combining the components, the incense was very hard to come by, but rumors spread to every corner of the Frontier about Hunters who forced their way into a vampire resting place when the sun was high only to be brutally ambushed by Nobles who just happened to have some on hand.

There, in the false night, D faced the dark liege lord.

"Did you come here expecting to find us asleep, foolish one? As you managed to stop my daughter, I believed you to be a more stalwart opponent than the usual insects, and I allowed you this meeting. But, where you sauntered into the blackest hell without even suspecting the danger awaiting you, I may have erred gravely in my assessment."

"No," said a voice he'd heard before. The figure at the Count's side was Larmica. "This man doesn't exhibit the least trace of fear. He's a thoroughly exasperating and deliciously impudent fellow. Judging by the skill he demonstrated this past evening when dealing Garou a grievous wound, he could be nothing save a dhampir."

"Human or dhampir, he remains a traitor. A bastard spawned by one of our kind and a mere human. Tell me, bastard, are you a man or a vampire?"

To this scornful query, D gave a different answer. "I'm a Vampire Hunter. I came here because the walls opened up for me. Are you the fiend that attacked the girl from the farm? If so, I'll slay you here and now."

For a moment, the Count was left speechless by the gleaming eyes that bored through the darkness at him, but an instant later he seemed indignant. He laughed loudly. "Slay me? You forget your place. Do you not realize the sole reason I allowed you to come this far is because my daughter said it would be a shame to kill a man such as yourself, that we should persuade you to join us in the castle and make you one of our kind? I have no idea which of your parents was of our kind, but judging by the speech and conduct of their son, it was obviously a buffoon without an inkling of their own low station. This is a waste of time. Dhampir, shame of our race, prepare to meet your maker." Having roared these words, the Count raised his right hand to strike, but was stopped by Larmica's voice.

"Please wait, Father. Allow me to speak to him."

Fluttering the train of a deep blue dress quite unlike the one she wore the previous night, Larmica stepped between the Count and D.

"You spring from the same noble blood as our family. Regardless of what Father said, no son of a humble-born vampire could ever possess such skill. When I caught the missile you hurled at me, I thought my blood would freeze."

D said nothing.

"What say you? Will you not apologize to Father for your boastful speech and join us here in the castle? What reasons have you to dog us? Is being a Hunter a job worth wandering the untamed plains in such shabby apparel? And what of the human wretches you've protected—what manner of treatment have you received from the humans who should be grateful to you? Have they accepted you as their fellow man?"

In the unknowably deep twilight of the hall, the voice of the beautiful young woman flowed without hesitation. Her haughty and domineering mien was unchanged from the night before, but one had to wonder if D noticed the faint shadows of entreaty and desire that clung to her.

Dhampir—a child born of the union between a vampire and a human. There could be no existence more lonely or hateful than that. Normally, dhampirs were no different from humans, relatively free to work by the light of day. When angered, however, they lashed out with the unholy power of a vampire, killing and maiming at will. Most detestable of all were the vampire urges they inherited from one of their parents.

Based on their innate and intimate knowledge of vampires' strengths and weaknesses, many chose to become Vampire Hunters in order to make a living in human society. The fact was, they demonstrated a level of ability head and shoulders above merely human Hunters, but outside of hunting, they were nearly completely ostracized by humanity and kept their distance. Occasionally, their vampire nature would awaken so powerfully they themselves couldn't suppress it, causing them to crave the blood of the very people that depended on them.

As soon as a dhampir finished a job, the people who barely tolerated him while he went about his mission would chase him off with stones, their gaze full of malice and contempt. With both the cruelly aristocratic blood of the Nobility and the brutally vulgar blood of the humans, dhampirs were tormented by the dual destinies of darkness and light; one side called them traitors while the other labeled them devils. Truly, the dhampirs—like the Flying Dutchman cursed to wander the seven seas for all eternity—led an abominable existence.

And yet, Larmica was saying all she could to get him to join them. Still she spoke.

"You can't possibly have a single pleasant reminiscence from your life as a Hunter. Of late, the insects in the village have been rather boisterous. At some point they will no doubt send in an assassin like yourself. If Father and I were to have a stalwart individual like you acting as a sort of guard when they do, we would feel most secure. What say you? If you are so inclined, we may even make you truly one of us."

The Count was ready to explode with rage at the words his daughter—gazing with sleepy, painfully lustful eyes at motionless D—had said. But before he could, he heard a low voice.

"What do you plan to do with the girl?"

Larmica laughed charmingly. "Do not overreach your bounds. The woman shall soon belong to Father, soul and all." And then, staring fixedly at her father with a cutting and highly ironic gaze, she said, "I believe Father wishes to make her one of his concubines, but I cannot allow it. I shall drain her of her very last drop of blood, then leave her for the human worms to rip apart and put to the torch."

Her words suddenly stopped. The Count's eyes gave off blood light. The fearsome night-stalking father and daughter surmised through their supernaturally attuned senses that the trivial opponent before them—the youth who was trapped like the proverbial rat—was rapidly transforming. That he was becoming the same thing they were!

"Still you fail to comprehend this," Larmica scolded. "What can come of this obligation you have toward the human worms? Those menials spared no pains in exterminating each and every living creature on the face of the earth besides themselves, and managed to nearly wipe themselves out through their own carelessness. They only continued living through the charity of our kind, yet the first time our power waned, the insurgents were all too happy to fly the flags of revolt. They, not we, are the creatures that should be expunged from this planet and from all of space."

At that moment, the Count thought he'd heard a certain phrase, and his brow knit. The muttered words had clearly come from the young man before him, but he promptly dredged the same phrase from the depths of distant, half-forgotten memories. Reason denied the possibility of such a thing.

Impossible, he thought. *Those are the very words I heard from his highness. From the great one, the Sacred Ancestor of our species. That filthy whelp couldn't possibly know such things.*

He heard D's voice. "Is that all you have to say?"

"Fool!"

The screams of both father and daughter resounded through the vast chamber. Negotiations had fallen through. The Count's lips warped into a cold-blooded and confident grin. He gave a crisp snap of the fingers on his right hand, but a rush of consternation came into his pale visage a few seconds later when he realized the countless electronic weapons mounted throughout the hall weren't operating.

The pendant on D's chest emitted a blue light.

"I don't know what you have up your sleeve, but the weapons of the Nobility don't work against me." Leaving only his words there, D kicked off the ground. Lightning fast, there would be no escaping him. Drawing his sword in midair, he pulled it to his right side. Just as he landed, his deadly thrust became a flash of silver that sank into the Count's chest.

There was the sound of flesh striking flesh.

"Eh?!"

For the first time, a look of surprise surfaced in D's handsome but normally expressionless countenance. His longsword was stopped dead, caught between the Count's palms about eight inches from the tip. Moreover, from their respective stances, D was in a far better position to exert more force upon the sword, but though he put all his might behind it, the blade wouldn't budge an inch, just as if it was wedged in a wall.

The Count bared his fangs and laughed. "What do you make of that, traitor? Unlike your vulgar swordplay, this is a skill worthy

of a true Noble. When you get to hell, tell them how surprised you were!" As he said that, the figure in black made a bold move to the right. Perhaps it was some secret trick the Count employed in the timing, or the way he put his strength into the move, but for whatever reason, D was unable to take his hand off the hilt. He was thrown along with the sword into the center of the hall.

However …

The Count quite unexpectedly found his breath taken away. There were no crunching bones to be heard; the youth somersaulted in midair like a cat about to land feetfirst on the floor with the hem of his coat billowing out around him. Or rather, he was ready to land there. With no floor beneath his feet, D kept right on going, falling into the pitch-black maw that opened suddenly beneath him.

As he heard the creaking of trapdoors to either side of the massive thirty by thirty-foot pit swinging back up into place, the Count turned his gaze to the darkness behind him. Larmica appeared from it. "It's a primitive trap, but it was fortunate for us we had it put there, was it not, Father? When all your vaunted atomic armaments were useless, a pitfall of cogs and springs rid us of that nuisance."

At her charming laughter, the Count made a sullen face. He had reluctantly allowed this trap to be installed due to Larmica's entreaties. *There's no way she could have foreseen this day's events*, the Count thought, *but this girl, daughter of mine though she may be, seems on occasion to be a creature beyond imagining.*

Shaking off his grimace, he said, "At the same instant I hurled him, you pulled the cord on the trapdoor—who but my daughter would be capable of as much? But is this for the best?"

"Is what for the best?"

"Last night, when you returned from the farm and spoke of the stripling we just disposed of, the tone of your voice, the manner of your complaints—even I, your own father, cannot recall ever hearing you so indignant, yet your indignation held a feverish sentiment that was equally new. Could it be you're smitten with the scoundrel?"

Unanticipated though her father's words were, Larmica donned a smile that positively defied description. Not only that, she licked her lips as well.

"Do you believe I could let a man I loved drop *down there*? Father, as its architect you know far better than anyone what a living hell that subterranean region is. Dhampir or not, no one could come out of that benighted pit alive. But …"

"But what?"

Here Larmica once again made a ghastly smile that even caused Count Lee, her own father, to flinch.

"If he can escape from there with naught but a sword and the power of his own limbs, I shall devote myself to him body and soul. By the eternal life and ten thousand bloody years of the history of the Nobility, I swear I love him—I love the Vampire Hunter D."

Now it was the Count's turn to smile bitterly. "It is hell for those you despise, and a worse hell for those you desire. Though I don't believe there is anything in this world that can face *the three sisters* and live to tell the tale."

"Of course not, Father."

"However," the Count continued, "should he survive and you meet him again, what will you do should he spurn your affections?"

Larmica responded in a heartbeat. Flames of joy rose from her body. Her eyes glittered wildly but were moist with hot tears, her crimson lips parted slightly, and her slick tongue licked along her lips as if it possessed a will of its own. "In that case, I will deal the deathblow to him without fail. I shall rip out his heart and lop off his head. And then he shall truly be mine. And I shall be his. I will taste the sweet blood as it seeps from his wounds, and after I have kissed his pale and withered lips, I shall tear open my own breast and let the hot blood of the Nobility course down his gaping throat."

When Larmica had taken her leave, following her incredibly gruesome yet fervent declaration of love, the Count's expression was a mixture of anger and apprehension, and he turned his gaze to the pit. He pressed one hand against the left side of his chest through his cape. The fabric was soaking wet. With blood. Though he seemed to have masterfully caught D's blade, more than an inch at the tip had sunken into his immortal flesh. Some trick with the sword may have been involved, for, unlike any wound he'd heretofore taken in battle, the gash still hadn't closed, and the warm blood that was the fount of his life was flowing out. *Now there is a man to be feared. He might even have ...*

The Count erased from his mind all thoughts of what might happen should he face the youth again in a battle to the death. Considering the *things* that awaited the whelp in the subterranean world, D didn't have one chance in a million of returning to the surface.

Turning his back to the hall, the Count was about to walk back to his dark demesne when the words the youth had whispered flitted through his brain. Words the Count had heard from *that august personage*. A phrase that could render the faces of every Noble, extinct or still living on, melancholy every time it was recalled. How could that stripling know those words?

Transient guests are we.

The Demons' Weakness

"**S**is, you sure we don't need more fertilizer than this?" Dan's apprehensive tone as he took the last plastic case and set it down in the bed of their wagon stabbed into Doris' breast. This was right about the time D was passing through the gates of the vampires' castle.

The pair had gone into Ransylva to do their shopping for the month. However, the results were something pitiful. Old Man Whatley, proprietor of a local store, had always been kind enough to bring things out from the storeroom that he didn't have displayed, but today he coldly refused as he'd never done before. As Doris named off necessities, he replied with apparent regret that they were either sold out or on back order. And yet, behind the counter and in the corner Doris saw he had stacks of them. When asked, however, he fumbled to say that the merchandise was already spoken for.

Doris caught on quickly enough. There was only one person low enough to cause her such grief.

Still, she didn't have time to waste arguing with Whatley, so she choked back her rage, swung by the home of an acquaintance, and somehow managed to get what she needed for the time being. At present, every minute from sunrise to sunset was as precious as a jewel to Doris. At night, her ghastly life-or-death battle with the demon awaited. No matter what happened, she had to get home before nightfall—that was the message D had drilled into her before he set out. Well, she knew that, but ... Once she'd loaded the last package of dried beef into the wagon bed, Doris gnawed her lip. The uncharacteristically forlorn expression Dan wore back there in the wagon became a smile the second his face turned toward her. The boy was doing all he could to keep her from worrying on his account. Because she understood that, Doris' heart was filled with a concern, a sorrow, and an anger that would not be checked. One of her hands reached over and unconsciously tightened around the handle of the whip she had tucked in her belt. There was only one place to direct her rage.

"Darn it, I forgot to swing by Doc Ferringo's place," she said with feigned agitation. "You wait here. It wouldn't do to have our goods get swiped, so don't you leave the wagon."

"Sis ..."

Her brother's word seemed to cling to her, as if he sensed something, but Doris replied, "Hey, a big boy like you should be ashamed to make a face like that. D would laugh if he could see how down in the mouth you look. Stop your worrying. As long as I'm around, everything'll be fine. Ain't that the way it's always been?" Speaking gently but firmly, and giving him no chance to disagree, she quickly set off down the street, thinking, *At this hour, I figure those scumbags'll be in the Black Lagoon or Pandora's Hotel. I'll learn them a thing or two!*

Her supposition proved correct. The second she opened the batwing doors of the saloon, Greco and his gang smirked and stood up from their table in the back. Quickly counting their number at seven, Doris narrowed her eyes suddenly when she saw what Greco was wearing.

His whole body was sparkling. From the top of his head to the tips of his feet Greco was covered by metallic clothing—actually, a kind of weapon called a combat suit. Doris had never seen one before, but her amazement soon faded, and with a scornful expression that said, *looks like that frivolous fool has jumped a new fashion bandwagon*, she laid into him. "You were all hot under the collar about what happened this morning, so you went and leaned on Old Man Whatley so he wouldn't sell us nothing, didn't you? And you call yourself a man? You're the lowest of the low!"

"What the hell are you yammering about?" Greco smiled mockingly. "I don't have to take that off no one who's about to be some vampire's fun toy. You should thank your lucky stars we didn't let that little tidbit out. You'd better get it into your head that it's gonna be the same thing next month and the month after. Looks like you probably managed to scrape something together today, but how long'll that pitiful amount keep your orchards going and your cows fed? Maybe two weeks, if you're lucky. Of course, that's supposing you're still walking around and throwing a shadow that long. Well, you'll be okay because pretty soon you won't have to eat anything to survive, but what'd you have planned for your poor little brother?"

Before his snide comments had ended, the whip streaked from Doris' hand. It wrapped around the helmet portion of his combat suit and she channeled her power into toppling him. But her recklessness was born of her ignorance. Greco—or rather, his combat suit—didn't budge an inch. He pulled the end of the whip with his right hand, and with one little tug, the whip flew into his hands.

"How many times did you think I was gonna fall for that, bitch?"

Shocked though she was, Doris was indeed the daughter of a Hunter, and she leapt back almost six feet. As she jumped, eyes that sparkled vulgarly with the light of hatred, lust, and superiority followed her.

"Don't forget it's my daddy that runs the show in town. There's nothing to keep us from seeing to it you and your stupid little brother starve to death."

Doris was a bit shaken, and it showed on her face—she knew the truth of what he'd just said.

A committee generally governed village operations, but the ultimate authority in town was the mayor. Under the harsh conditions of the Frontier lands, time-consuming and half-hearted operating procedures like parliaments and majority rule would bring death down on the villagers in no time. Monsters, mutants, bandits—the hungry eyes of outside forces were focused relentlessly on Ransylva. And naturally, village operations included the buying and selling of goods. It would be a piece of cake to come up with some reason to suspend a shop from doing business. When it came to the life or death of his business, Old Man Whatley had no choice but bow under duress. For Doris, a hard two-day ride to go shopping in Pedros, the nearest neighboring village, was out of the question under the present conditions. Anyway, it was clear Greco and his cronies would try to stop her.

"You have a lot of nerve, saying a despicable thing like that. I don't care if you are the mayor's son ..." Doris' voice trembled with rage.

Ignoring that, Greco said, "But if you'd be my wife, all that'd be different. We've got it all set up so when my daddy retires, the folks with pull in this town will see to it I'm the next mayor. So, what do you say? Won't you reconsider? Instead of busting your ass on that rundown farm, you could have all the fancy duds you could ever wear and all you could eat of the classiest fixin's. Dan would love it, too. And we could run off that creepy punk because I'd protect you from the vampire. If we put the money out there, you'd be surprised how many Hunters'll show up. What do you say?"

In lieu of an answer, Doris drew closer. *Well, look at that—no matter how tough she tries to act, she's still a woman after all*, Greco thought for a split second before a mass of liquid spattered against the helmet's smoked visor. Doris had spat on him.

"You—you crazy bitch! I try and treat you nice, and you pull this shit!" Greco wasn't accustomed to using the suit, and his right hand clanked roughly as it mopped his faceplate clean. But then he grabbed at Doris with incredible speed. He had hold of her torso before she had a chance to leap away. He pulled her into him. Purchased mere hours earlier from a wandering merchant, the combat suit was second-hand and of the lowest grade, but the construction—an ultra-tensile, steel armor built on a base of reinforced, organic, pseudo-skin over an electronic nervous system—increased the wearer's speed three-fold and gave him ten times his normal strength. Now that Greco had Doris, there was no way she could get away.

"What are you doing? Let go of me," she screamed, but she only succeeded in hurting her own hand when she slapped him.

Greco had no trouble whatsoever restraining both of Doris' hands with one of his own, and he hoisted her a foot off the ground. The helmet split down the middle with a metallic rasp. The face peering out at her was that of bald-faced, fiendish lust. A thread of drool stretched from the corner of his lips, which held a little smirk. Doris glared at him indignantly, but he said, "You're always putting on the airs. Well right here, right now, I'm gonna make you mine. Hey, dumbass, don't do anything funny and just stay the hell out of this!" With that last remark—roared at the middle-aged bartender who had left the counter to try and break things up—the bartender returned to his post. After all, he was up against the mayor's son. Eyes bloodshot with lust, Greco's filthy lips drew close to the immobilized young beauty. Doris turned her face away.

"Let me go! I'll call the sheriff!"

"That ain't gonna do much good," he laughed. "Hell, if it came right down to it, he likes his neck a little too much to stick it out. Hey, the bar is closed now! Someone stand guard so no one comes in."

"You got it." One of Greco's lackeys headed for the door, but then halted abruptly. Suddenly, there was a wall of black in front of him, blocking his path. "What the hell do you—"

His shout was truncated almost immediately, and a split second later, the lackey flew through tables and chairs, crashed into two of his cohorts, and smacked headfirst into the wall. Not that he was thrown at it. The black wall had merely given the man a light push backwards. But his strength must have been inhuman: both the lackey that had gone flying and also the two others he'd hit were all laid out cold on the floor, and some of the plaster had been knocked out of the wall.

"You bastard! What the hell do you think you're doing?" As the thugs grew pale and reached for the weapons at their waists, the black wall looked at them and shrugged casually.

Easily over six-and-a-half-feet tall, he was a bald giant. Arms, knotted like the roots of a tree, protruded from his leather vest. He must have weighed three hundred and fifty pounds if he weighed an ounce. Judging from the well-worn, massive machete hanging from his belt, the thugs realized their foe had more than just size on his side, and their expressions grew more prudent.

"Please forgive us. My friend here is wholly unfamiliar with the concept of restraint."

Wriggling in Greco's embrace, Doris forgot her struggles for a moment and turned toward the newcomers only to have her eyes open wide with surprise. The voice had been beautiful, but the man himself positively sparkled.

His age must have been around twenty. He had gorgeous black hair that spilled down to his shoulders, and deep brown eyes that seemed ready to swallow the world, leaving all who beheld them feeling gloriously drunk. The youth was an Asian Apollo. He, along with the giant and two other companions, seated himself at a table.

The only other people in the Black Lagoon aside from Greco and his gang, the newcomers began to amuse themselves with a game of cards. If the keen glint in their eyes was any indication, they had to be traveling Hunters of some confidence.

"What the hell are you fools supposed to be," Greco asked, still holding Doris.

"I am Rei-Ginsei, the Serene Silver Star. My friend here is Golem the Tortureless. We're Behemoth Hunters."

"The hell you are," Greco bellowed, as he looked the four of them over. "You're telling me you hunt those big ol' behemoths with so few people? A baby behemoth can't even be killed without ten or twenty guys." He laughed scornfully. "Granted, you've got that big bastard, but that still leaves you with a sissy boy, a pinhead, and a fucking hunchback. So please help me out here—how exactly does a bunch of rejects like you hunt anyway?"

"We shall show you—here and now," Rei-Ginsei said with his sun-god smile. "But before we do, kindly release the young lady. If she were ugly, it might be another matter, but to treat a beautiful woman in such a manner is a grave breach of etiquette."

"Then why don't you make me stop, you big, bad Hunters?"

The vermilion lips that framed his pearly white teeth bowed with sorrow. "So that's how it's to be then? Very well ..."

"Okay, come on then!"

Greco was used to getting into fights, but the reason he forgot the power of his combat suit and threw Doris aside with all his might may have been because he had some inkling of how the coming battle was going to end.

Unable to prepare for her fall, Doris struck her head on the edge of a table. When she regained consciousness she was held in a pair of powerful arms, and matters had already been settled. "Ow, that hurts," she said, rubbing her forehead.

Rei-Ginsei gave her a gentle smile and swept her up off the floor. "We dealt with those ruffians. I'm not completely clear on the situation here, but I think leaving before the sheriff is summoned might avoid complications."

"Um, yeah, you're right." Due to her throbbing headache her answer was muddled, but Doris noticed the sharp squeak of wood-on-wood behind her and turned around in time to be utterly astonished. Every last one of Greco's hoodlums was laid out on the floor. Despite the pain in her head, Doris was still sharp enough to notice something strange about them almost instantly.

The arms and legs of the two sprawled closest to her on the floor had been bent back against the elbow and knee joints and were twisted into horrific objets d'art. Most likely, the hoodlums had fallen victim to Golem's monstrous strength, but what caught Doris' eye were the remnants of a longsword and a machete lying near them. She wasn't sure about the machete, but the longsword was definitely a high-frequency saber with a built-in sonic frequency wave generator, able to cut through iron plate. Both weapons were shattered down to the hilt as if they'd tried to chop through a block of steel.

Just behind one of the round tables squirmed Greco's right-hand man, O'Reilly. He was known for his skill with a revolver; once, Doris saw him knock a bee out of the air from fifty yards with his quick draw. When she'd seen him last, he was already going for his gun. When one of the four came at him, the barrel of his weapon should have spit flame in less than three-tenths of a second. Yet here he was, sprawled face-down on the floor with his hand still locked around the pistol grip. But what truly made Doris shudder was the location of the wound that felled him. The back of his head was split open. One of the four—well, perhaps not Golem but one of the other three—had got behind him and dealt the blow without giving him the three-tenths of a second he needed to work his quick draw.

Diagonally across from O'Reilly someone else raised his head. Doris felt as if all the blood had drained from her body. The first three thugs who'd been slammed into the wall were still unconscious, and they could be considered lucky for that. The remaining man's face looked like it'd been stung by vicious killer bees—his skin was swollen with dark red pustules that dripped a steady stream of discharge onto the floor. Though Doris didn't notice it at first, at that very moment a black insect crawling across the floor stopped at her feet, scurried a little closer, and then walked right past her as if someone was calling it back. It was a tiny spider. It went from the leather sandals of the hunchback to his leg, then climbed farther up his back to a massive hump, covered by a leather vest. Both the vest and the hump split right down the middle, and the spider disappeared into the fissure. The fissure closed promptly.

"Surprised? I fear it may be too much of a shock for a beautiful young woman like yourself ..."

Doris heard Rei-Ginsei's voice as if from a distance, like the pealing of a bell, for her soul had been stolen when she saw the most frightening outcome of the whole unearthly battle: she saw Greco, the only one unharmed, still seated in his chair with his hands locked around the armrests and the expression of a dead man on his face. The squeak of wood-on-wood she had heard was the sound of his trembling body rattling the legs of the chair against the floor. Whatever he'd witnessed from the safety of his combat suit, it had thrown his eyes wide open, and they reflected nothing but paling terror.

"What'd you guys do?" Doris asked in a firm voice when she finally looked back at Rei-Ginsei and slipped from his arms.

"Not a thing." Rei-Ginsei made a mortified expression. "We simply finished what they started—in our own inimitable style, of course."

"Thank you," Doris said gratefully. "I truly appreciate your help. If you're going to be in town a while, I'd like to do something to thank you later."

"Don't trouble yourself about it. There is nothing in this world more profane than the ugly making the beautiful submit by force. They merely got a taste of heaven's wrath."

"You flatter me, but would you have done the same for another girl if she was being treated the same way?"

"Of course I'd come to her aid. Provided she was beautiful."

Doris averted her eyes from the calmly smiling face of the gorgeous man. "Well, thank you again. Now if you'll excuse me."

"Yes, allow us to take care of this mess. We're well accustomed to it." As Rei-Ginsei nodded jovially, something black gushed into his gaze. "I'm quite sure we'll meet again."

A few minutes later, Doris had the wagon racing back toward the farm.

"Did something happen back there, Sis?"

Her distant expression didn't change at the concerned query from Dan, who rode shotgun. The anxieties running amuck in her mind wouldn't allow her a smile.

She could only expect that Greco would make things even harder for her now, and on top of that she had no guarantee D would be back tonight. She just knew she should've stopped D when he told her he was going into the lord's castle during the day to take advantage of the dhampirs' ability to operate in daylight. If he didn't make it back, they would be left helpless and alone before the Count's next onslaught. She had no proof the Count would come tonight, but she was pretty sure of it. Doris shook her head unconsciously. No, that would mean D was dead.

I know he's coming back, she thought.

Her right hand brushed the nape of her neck. Moments before he'd set out, D had put what he said was a charm on the fang marks there. The charm was disappointingly simple, consisting merely of a light press of the palm of his left hand to the wound; he hadn't even explained what effect it was supposed to have, but it was all Doris had to rely on now.

Another face formed in her mind. That dashing young man in the saloon could also be considered her savior in a way, but Doris felt an ominous shadow fall across her heart. When he'd lifted her from the floor and she saw his handsome visage up close, she had in truth swooned. But her virgin instinct had caught the sickly sweet smell of rotting fruit that lingered around his gorgeous face.

No, most likely it wasn't her instinct that caught it, but rather the work of something firmly etched in a deeper part of her: the visage of a young man more beautiful and more noble than Rei-Ginsei. Doris had a foreboding that the handsome new arrival would prove a greater danger to her than Greco had. That was another of her concerns.

Come back. I don't care if you can't beat the Count, just come back to me.

That these thoughts had nothing to do with her safety was something the seventeen-year-old had not yet noticed.

For the past few minutes, the tepid, waist-deep water had been growing warmer, and the mist licking its way up the stony walls had become denser. He had been walking for thirty minutes now. The drop from the great hall must have been around seventy feet. A vast subterranean aqueduct brimming with water had awaited D. As the water only came up to his chest, it didn't matter much that he'd fallen feet first—what had saved D from a brutal impact was his inhuman skill, and the indisputably superhuman anatomy all dhampirs possessed.

Vampire anatomy—primarily their bones, muscles, and nerves—allowed them to absorb impact and recover from damage hundreds of times better than humans could. While it naturally varied from individual to individual, dhampirs inherited at least fifty percent of those abilities. From a height of seventy feet, a dhampir could probably hit solid ground and survive. It would be nigh impossible to keep from breaking every bone in their body and rupturing some internal organs, but even then some of the faster dhampirs would be able to heal completely in about seventy-two hours.

At any rate, D hadn't been hurt in the least, and he stood chest-deep in the black water surveying his surroundings. This was most likely a pre-existing subterranean cavern that had been buttressed through later construction. Places here and there on the black, rock walls to either side showed signs of being repaired with reinforced concrete. The water throughout was lukewarm, and a pale, white mist lent the air an oppressive humidity. The aqueduct itself was roughly fifteen feet wide. It seemed to be a natural formation, and an odor peculiar to mineral springs had reached D's nostrils even as he was falling into the pit. All around him stretched a world of complete darkness. Only his dhampir eyesight allowed him to distinguish how wide the aqueduct was. He turned his gaze upward, but, not surprisingly, he was unable to discern the trapdoor seventy feet above. As the doors had long since been reset, it was only natural he couldn't see them. And of course there was no means of egress to be seen on the rock walls that boasted mass beyond reckoning.

"What to do, what to do ...," D muttered this rare comment in a deep voice, yet started walking purposefully in the direction from which the water all around him flowed, though the flow was soundless and so gentle as to be imperceptible. Hard and even, the bottom of the aqueduct seemed to be the work of some external force. That wasn't to say that he had merely to walk long enough and far enough for an exit to present itself. He was unaware of *the three sisters* the Count had mentioned so ominously in the chamber far above.

Something was waiting for him.

D was cognizant of that much. And he knew that his thrust had dealt a wound to the Count. There was no way the vampire lord would let such a fearsome opponent just drop into the subterranean waterway and then sit idly by. D was positive some sort of attack was coming. And yet, as he walked along, there was no hesitation in the legs that carried him across the firm bottom of the aqueduct, and no hint of tension or fretfulness in the shining, handsome face that seemed to make the darkness retreat. And then he halted.

About twenty-five feet ahead, the aqueduct grew wider and a number of eerily shaped stones jutted from the water's surface. There alone the mist was oddly thick—or rather, it hung so heavily it seemed to rise from the very waters, twisting the stones into far more outrageous and disturbing shapes and sealing off the waterway. The air bore a foul stench of decay. D's eyes saw a film of oily scum covering the water and white things concealed in the recesses of the stones. Bleached bones. Deep in the mist there was a sharp splash, like a fish flicking its tail up out of the water.

There was something here. Its lair was beyond the eldritch stones.

Still, D showed no sign of turning back, and he continued walking calmly into the mist at the center of the stones. Once inside, the space between the stones looked like a sort of pool or a fishpond. The stones formed rows to either side that completely enclosed the waterway. The water sat stagnant there, blacker than ever, and the white mist eddied savagely. It seemed the source of the mineral springs wasn't too far off. The more he advanced, the greater the number of eldritch stones, and, as the number of bones multiplied, the stench grew ever more overpowering. Most of the bones were from cattle and other livestock, but human remains were also evident. There was a skeleton that, judging from the quiver on his back, looked to be a huntsman, a woman's skull resting in the tattered remnants of a long dress, and the diminutive bones of a child. Many of them hadn't had time to be denuded; dark red meat and entrails hung from their bones, rife with maggots. In this vile, disturbing scene—a scene that would make the average person go mad or stop, paralyzed with fear—D noticed the spines and ribs of all the stark skeletons had been pulverized. This was not the

result of being gnawed by tenacious fangs and jaws. They'd been crushed. Like something had squeezed them tight and twisted them ways they were never meant to go.

Once again, D halted.

There was another splash, this time much closer. The whine of a blade leaving its sheath rose from D's back. At the same time, ripples formed on the surface a few yards ahead of him, and a white mass bobbed to the surface. And just after that, another one bobbed to the right. Then one to the left. Unearthly white in the darkness—they were the heads of carnal, alluring women.

Perhaps D had lost his nerve, because he stood stock-still instead of holding his sword at the ready. The women gazed at him intently. Their facial features were distinct, but all were equally beautiful, and the red lips of the three women twisted into broad grins. Far behind them there was another sharp splash. Perhaps these three swam this way to escape whatever was chasing them? If that was the case, the way they kept all but their heads submerged after meeting D was quite out of the ordinary. And the grins they wore were so evil, so enticing. He looked at them and they at him for a few seconds. With the sound of a torrent of drops, the three women rose in unison. Their heads came up to the height of D's. And then above his—far above.

Who in the human world could imagine such an amazing sight? Three disembodied but beautiful heads smiling down charmingly at him from a height of ten feet. These women had to be the three sisters the Count had mentioned.

At that point, D said softly, "I've heard rumors about you. So you're the Midwich Medusas I take it?"

"Oh, you know of us, do you?" The head in the middle, which would be the eldest sister, wiped the smile from her face. Her voice was like the pealing of a bell, but it also dripped with venom. However, it wasn't the fact that the dashing young man before them seemed to recognized them for what they truly were that gave her voice a ring of surprise, but rather because there wasn't a whit of fear in his words, so far as she could detect.

The Midwich Medusas. These three women—or these three creatures—were supernatural beasts of unrivaled evil that fed on the lust of young men and women. They had devoured hundreds of villagers in a part of the Frontier known as Midwich. Years earlier, they'd supposedly been destroyed by the prayers of an eminently virtuous monk passing through the region, but, unknown to all, they had escaped. After a chance encounter with Count Lee, they agreed to take up residence far below his castle on the condition they received three cows per day. Unlike the faux monsters the Nobility engineered, nothing could be more difficult to destroy than a true demon like this one. The Medusas had survived tens of thousands of years and had even outlived their own legend. Like the hydra of ancient myth, the three heads of the Medusas, which appeared to be separate, were in fact joined a few yards down in a massive pillar of a torso clad with scales of silvery gray that remained sunken in the water. The splashing sounds to their rear came from the end of the torso—a tail that thrashed in delight at finding prey.

But D could only see the women's heads. The reason he knew what they really were was because he'd recognized the heads of three beautiful women as the objects of one of the many bizarre rumors out on the Frontier. But the real question was, why did they melt into the darkness below the neck?

"He's a fine specimen, sisters." The whispers from the head on the right sounded deeply impressed, and she licked her lips. Her red flame of a tongue was slim, and the tip was forked. "At long last, we have a man worthy of our pleasuring. And not just a pretty face, either—look at how muscular he is."

"Sisters, you can't have him first," the third head—the one on the left—declared. "Just five days ago, the two of you fed on the huntsman who wandered in here while I was asleep. This time I shall be first. First to take him to the heights of rapture, and first to taste his blood when he hits that peak."

"The nerve of you! We are your elders," the head on the right—and apparently the second-in-command—bellowed.

"Stop your sibling quarrels," the middle head scolded them, turning to the head on the left. "You may be the first to drink of his blood. However, the three of us shall pleasure him together."

"Yes."

"I'm amenable to that."

Without another word the three heads nodded in agreement. Little flame tongues flicking in and out and the women fondled every inch of D with smitten eyes.

"But be on guard," the oldest sister said quite plainly. "This man does not fear us."

"Rubbish! Could anyone know what we are and not tremble? When we grew angry at our meager repasts and bared our fangs, did not the Count himself beat a hasty retreat, never to return to our realm again?" asked the second sister.

"Even supposing that he is not afraid, what could he do? Manling, can you move?"

D remained silent. In truth, he couldn't move. From the first moment he laid eyes on the women's heads, his whole body had been gripped by countless hands.

"Do you comprehend, manling," the second sister went on. "That's our hair at work."

Exactly. The reason why the necks and torso of the Midwich Medusas melded with the darkness was because everything below their jaws was hidden by black hair that fell in a cascade of tens of thousands of strands, shrouding the rest completely. However, this was no ordinary hair. Once on the water's surface, the strands spread out like tentacles, drifted about, and when they felt the movement of something in the lair, in accordance with the will of the three sisters, they would lure the prey into the center. Then, when the appropriate time came, they could wrap around the victim's limbs in a split second and rob the victim of his freedom with the strength of piano wire.

And that wasn't all. The truth was, it wasn't water that was in the three sisters' stone-bordered den. The eldritch stones diverted the aqueduct and sent the water flowing around either side, while their lair was actually filled with a secretion from the hair itself. The liquid flowed subtly to complement the gently swaying movements of the hair, swirling it around, and even D—with a sense of touch far more sensitive than that of humans—hadn't been alerted to the presence of the strands. Unbeknownst to D, the hair had crept up from his waist and wrapped itself around his wrists and upper arms, as well as his shoulders and neck, completely restraining his limbs.

Even more disturbing, the rest of those countless hands—nay, tentacles—had started slipping in through the cuffs and seams of his clothes, creeping across him, rubbing against his naked flesh, teasing him, plotting to make D a slave of inflamed desire. No matter how resolute their will, a person's reason would dissolve after a few seconds of these delicate movements, reducing them to lust-driven mindlessness—this was the Midwich Medusas' obscene torture, and no one could resist it.

"Well, have you come to crave us?" the oldest sister asked. "Ordinarily, we would take your life at this point. Like so." With her words as their signal, the three heads twisted through the air to part their locks. The black cataract changed its course, and three lengthy necks striped with black and blue, as well as the massive torso that supported them, came into view. The torso was so thick, two grown men would have trouble reaching around it. The long necks swooped down at D, wrapping around and around the powerfully built man held captive by the bonds of their black hair. For its part, the hair continued its tiny wriggling movements below D's clothes.

"We can break your bones whenever it suits us," the oldest sister said, her red eyes ablaze as she stared at D's face. The fire in her eyes was an inferno of lust. "But you're such a gorgeous man. Such a well-proportioned man." Her tongue licked D's cheek.

"Verily. Lo these past three centuries we've not seen one so beautiful." The moist lips of the second sister toyed with D's earlobe from behind. Her hot, rank breath blew into his ear.

"But we won't kill you. The three of us will see to it you taste more than your share of unearthly rapture, and then drain you to the marrow." The youngest sister fairly moaned the words.

The source of the Midwich Medusas' life was not only the energy they derived from the consumption of living organisms. With bizarre abilities only demons possessed, they reduced strapping men and lovely women in the bloom of youth to wanton creatures aching with desire, then imbibed the aura of pure rapture the victims' radiated at their peak—this was the secret of the three sisters' immortality, and this was how they had lived on since before the vampires, since the ancient times when humans ruled.

Of course, that wasn't to say they would feed on just anyone. The sisters were gourmands in their own way. Though the Count had sent hundreds of people into the subterranean world, and still others had wandered in from various entrances, the sisters hadn't tasted pleasure like this for centuries, and had devoured their victims' flesh greedily but joylessly year after year. Now the time had come for pleasure to burn through their shared body once again. A heady blush tinged the three beautiful faces, their eyes danced with flames, and the hot breath spilling from their vermilion lips threatened to melt D's frostily gorgeous visage.

"Well now," the oldest sister fairly moaned. Three sets of damp, bewitching lips closed in on the firm iron gate that was D's mouth.

The instant their lips met his, the sisters saw it. They saw the crimson blood-light glinting from D's eyes. It dealt a mysterious blow to their wicked minds. In that instant, the three sisters felt a sweet thrill racing through their body, the likes of which they'd never experienced before.

"Oh, those lips," the oldest sister said in a husky voice.

"Show me your throats," a low, rusty voice commanded.

Without time to comprehend it was D's voice they heard, the sisters raised their necks as one and brought the slick white base of their throats to D's lips. Something told them there was no other way to snuff the feverish excitement gnawing its way through their bodies. The Midwich Medusas' wits were no longer functioning properly.

"Undo your hair."

D's limbs were immediately set free. His right hand returned his sword to its sheath while his left scooped up a fistful of hair.

"A trap baited with pleasure—but who caught whom?" Before his muttered words had faded, D dropped the strands he held and pulled the three lengthy necks to himself with both arms. "I don't like doing this, but it's the only way to find a way out of here. Someone's waiting for me." As he spoke, his eyebrows suddenly rose and his eyes rolled back. His lips spread wide, exposing a pair of fangs. Brutal and evil, his visage was that of a vampire.

There in the darkness, what happened in the moments that followed?

The cries of the women melded with the repeated splash of their tail beating the water's surface, suggesting unearthly delights had just taken mastery of them. It was the sisters who had blundered into the pleasure-baited trap. Before long, there was the sound of something heavy dropping into the water three times in succession, and then D quickly gave the command: "Arise."

Twisting their torso and serpentine necks, the three sisters rose again. A hollow shadow clung to their countenances, and their bloodshot eyes were as damp as the mist, as desire choked the vitality from them. And it was truly eerie how their glistening, greasy faces were completely bloodless, with a luster like paraffin.

At the base of each of the three necks a pair of deep red dots could be seen. Fang marks.

Who could have known the demonic blood slumbering within D would awaken at the last possible second? He wiped his mouth with the back of his hand. Now, as his gorgeous countenance returned to the cool mountain spring it always was, he commanded the three sisters to lead him to an exit in a voice that resembled a moan of pain.

The three heads bobbed wordlessly in midair, then moved off into the darkness. As D followed them and vanished into the darkness also, a taunting voice could be heard from around his waist. "No matter how you hate it, you can't fight your blood. That's your destiny—and you know it deep in your bones."

In a split second came the response. "Silence! I don't remember telling you to come out! Get back in there!"

The angry shouts clearly belonged to D. So, who had been speaking before ? What could D have meant by those strange expressions? And most of all, why had his ice-cold exterior shattered, even if only for a moment?

While the edge of the plains swallowed the last bit of afterglow from the sunset, and Doris continued waiting for D, Dr. Ferringo's buggy pulled up to her house. Doris was somewhat embarrassed, and tried to get the doctor to leave. Doctors were far too precious on the Frontier for her to put one in such danger. After all, this fight was hers and hers alone. She'd mixed a sedative in with Dan's dinner and he was already fast asleep. That was probably the best thing to do with him, since a Noble stalking their prey wouldn't even spare a glance at anyone who wasn't in their way.

"Um, Doc, I'm a little busy today with stuff here on the farm," Doris called preemptively from the porch.

But the doctor responded, "That's quite all right, I don't mind. I was just out on a house call—could I trouble you for a glass of water?" Dispelling her objections with a wave of his hands, he went ahead and opened the door, trotted into the living room, and installed himself on the sofa.

He'd been a friend of her late father, he'd brought Doris and Dan into the world with his own two hands, and since the death of their parents to this very day, he'd helped them in countless ways. Because of this, Doris couldn't very well toss him out on his ear. To make matters worse, for some reason he began to recount his youthful adventures battling supernatural creatures—or "the damned things," as he liked to call them—and Doris had no recourse but to sit and listen attentively. He must've been aware the Noble would most likely be coming for her, so she had to wonder why he seemed so dead set on hanging around.

Night rolled closer with each passing minute, and D wasn't back yet. The moment the sun set, Doris resolved to fight alone. All the armaments and traps spread across the farm had been double-checked, but she only grew more afraid. And now she had not only herself but the physician to worry about as well.

No matter what happens to me, I've got to protect Doc at all costs. Please, don't let him strike till after Doc has gone. As she made this wish, another concern annoyingly crept up on her.

No matter what happens, I can't let myself think about that. If he makes me one of them, what'll happen to Dan? He can't live the rest of his life knowing his only blood relative is one of the Nobility—that's just too big a burden to carry. Nothing doing, Doris. Get your arms and legs ripped off trying if you have to, but fight that bastard off. The bravery she mustered only lasted a heartbeat before sinking into the shadow of her fears. Coupled with centuries of psychological conditioning, the horror of actually falling victim to the pernicious fangs of the Nobility had more than enough dark power to daunt a young girl of seventeen, no matter how distinguished a fighter she may have been.

When the hands on the clock indicated nine thirty Night, Doris finally came out with it. "Well, Doc, I think I'm gonna turn in now." *So please hurry up and go home*—this much Doris implied, but Dr. Ferringo showed no signs of rising. Instead, he said something that shocked her senseless.

"You'll have a dangerous customer paying you a call real soon."

"That's right, Doc, so you'd best be on your way—"

"My, but you are a sweetie," the elderly physician said, showering her with a gaze of boundless affection. "But there's a time and a place for restraint. You don't have to be that way with me. Seventeen years ago, I brought you into this world with my own two hands, and you've always been like a daughter to me, haven't you? Now this old fool ain't the sort to just stand by while a young lady does battle with a demon straight from hell." As Doris stood at the door to the living room watching the old man, her eyes glistened softly with tears. "Don't look so down in the mouth," the old man said jovially. "I may not look it, but it was yours truly that taught your father the tricks of the Werewolf Hunting trade."

"I know that. It's just—"

"If you know it, then why don't you stop your blubbering? Of course, it is interesting to see a little spitfire like you squirt a few tears from time to time. Anyway, where's that young fellow? You hired him for protection, but when night started coming on, he probably took to his heels, I suppose. He was a spooky character, that one, but he turned out to be a worthless drifter, did he?"

"No, he didn't!" Up to that point Doris stood silently, touched by his words and nodding in agreement, but this sudden about-face, and her exclamation, made the elderly physician jump in his seat. "That's not the sort of man ... uh, I mean, he's not the kind to do that. No, sir. The reason he's not here tonight is because he went into the Count's castle alone. And he hasn't come back yet. I just ... Something's happened to him, I just know it ..."

An ineffable light sparked in Dr. Ferringo's eyes. "So you were kind of ... Now I see ... I didn't know you felt that way about him."

Doris regained her composure and hastily wiped at her tears. "What do you mean by that? It's not like I ... I mean ..."

The physician grinned at the young girl as a rosy blush suffused her face. Then he made a gentle wave of his hands. "Okay, okay. My mistake. If you think that much of him, then we needn't worry about him. I'm sure he'll be back soon. Until he does, what do you say to working up the nerve to capture the Count?"

"Sure," Doris said with a cheery nod, then suddenly, with great apprehension, she asked, "How are we gonna do that?"

There was no precedent for a human capturing a member of the Nobility—a vampire. Battles between the two species were normally a matter of kill or be killed. It went without saying that one side ended up dead more often than not. Particularly when doing battle at night, in the Nobility's element, the respective weapons and abilities of the combatants made the outcome painfully obvious.

"With this." The elderly physician produced a small glass bottle from his faithful medical bag. It was filled to its corked neck with yellowish granules.

"What in the world is that?" Doris' tone was a jumble of expectation and misgivings.

Dr. Ferringo didn't answer, but rather pulled a battered envelope from the same bag and unfolded the letter it contained. He held it out to Doris.

The second she laid eyes on the characters scrawled in sap-based ink on the yellowed paper, Doris turned to the physician with a perplexed expression. "This handwriting ... My father wrote this ..."

His hoary head bobbed in agreement. "Your dear father used to send me these while he was out on the road honing his fighting skills, back before your brother and you were born. But this was the last of them. If you read it, you'll see that it relates an encounter between your father and a vampire."

"My father and a vampire?" Doris forgot everything else and began poring over the letter. The first sentence or two informed the reader he'd arrived at his lodging. Then, the very characters themselves became jumbled with excitement and fear.

I've found it. The bastard's weakness is a t ...

That was all there was. After the last character, the rest of the sheet was just a lonely expanse of rough, yellowed paper. Doris fixed a confused gaze on the elderly physician. "Why didn't my father finish what he was writing? Was there anything in any of his other letters?"

The physician shook his head. "While your father was writing that letter in his lodgings, he was attacked by a vampire, but he fended it off. There can be no doubt your father somehow discovered some weakness of theirs. That much he stated plainly in another letter. The point is, he fought off the fiend, put his mind to order, and had just taken up a pen to record his discovery when he realized he'd completely forgotten what that discovery was."

"Are you serious? How could that happen?"

"I'll address that later. At any rate, less than five minutes after the danger had passed, your father found himself standing like a zombie with a pen in his hand. Like a man possessed, he sifted through his memories, wracked his brain, and eventually even tried to reenact his own half of the engagement, but all his efforts were for naught. The vampire appeared and they scuffled. Then, when all hope seemed lost, he narrowly managed to make his foe take flight—that much he could clearly recall, but the form of that decisive attack and manner in which he'd learned it were completely expunged from his memory."

"But why? How did that happen?"

Ignoring the same question from Doris a second time, the physician went on. "We had that last little 't' as a hint, but your father never did figure out what that was supposed to stand for. He wrote again about how the situation developed in another letter and sent it along to me, entrusting me to make something out of it. Unfortunately, I failed to live up to his expectations ..."

"Well if that's the case," Doris said, completely forgetting the danger creeping steadily closer and whipping herself into a frenzy, "all we have to do is solve the mystery of the little 't' to find out what the Nobility's weakness is, right?" Her voice trembled with expectation, but it quickly withered. She recognized that the shadow clinging to the face of the elderly physician said that the situation was not merely grave, but close to hopeless.

In the past, attempts to learn a definitive way to protect themselves from vampires had been tried time and again, but all of them had proved fruitless. Though humans must have had ample opportunity to learn that secret in the countless conflicts that raged ever since their species lost the right to rule the world, not one such method had been passed down to posterity. Now, ages had passed since anyone had even tried to discover them.

"The Nobility is going to beat us after all, aren't they? I mean, if they don't have any weaknesses ... "

As Dr. Ferringo heard Doris' words crawling across the floor like a beaten dog, he shook his head and stated firmly, "No. If that were the case, we wouldn't have these rumors being passed down all these years that there are things that can hurt them. Didn't your own father state he managed to drive a vampire off in some manner or other? Your father wouldn't have lied to save his own life. I've heard tell of knights and travelers who've had experiences similar to his, and I've even spoken to a few in person."

"And did you find out anything?"

"No, all of them had the same thing happen that your father did. They escaped the loathsome fangs of the fiend by some means ... or rather, they forced the fiend to escape. And yet, despite that, not one of them could recall anything at all about what they'd done."

Doris was speechless.

"More recently, I've been tempted to view these rumors of a weakness in the Nobility as legends born of wishful thinking, but I plowed through a mountain of records, and based on the actual cases I could assemble, I'm positive that a weakness does in fact exist. People simply can't remember what it is. In my view, it's a kind of manipulation of our memories."

"Manipulation of our memories?" Doris knit her brow.

"To be more precise, perhaps we could call it a selective and automatic editing of our memories. To wit, our minds have been programmed to automatically erase all memories of a certain kind."

"You mean, memories of their weaknesses? Of weapons that can drive them off?" Unconsciously, Doris was trying to peek inside the old man's head. Was that what the powder in the bottle really was?

Watched by eyes that were a battlefield between hope and uncertainty, the physician went on undeterred. "Remember, we're talking about the bastards who ruled the world for ten thousand years. I'm sure it would be mere child's play for them to alter human DNA and reprogram our minds to selectively weed out any memories of those sorts. That's a theory that's been around for quite some time, and based on my own research, I've taken up with that camp. I'm not usually the type to go along with theories when I don't know the folks behind them, but what's right is right. That being the case, the rest is simple."

"The rest being?"

"All we have to do is bring those memories back."

Doris gasped. "Can you really do that?"

The physician looked very pleased with himself as he rolled the bottle in question in the palm of his hand. "Here we have the fruit of that very endeavor. I hypnotized a dozen of the men and women I interviewed, and tried to regress them with the help of reenactment-stimulating drugs I procured from the Capital. What I have here is something two of them mentioned. You see, even with all their science, the creatures of the night couldn't completely erase our memories."

Doris noticed that the physician seemed to hesitate at the last sentence, but couldn't fathom why. She pursued a different matter instead. "But if what you say is true, Doc, won't the two of us lose all memory of that powder soon?"

"No, I've been fine so far. Again, this is purely a hypothesis, but the loss of memory only occurs when the subconscious mind has actual proof that we've discovered a weakness of the damned Nobility. In our heart of hearts, neither you nor I completely believe in the efficacy of this powder. As a result, the enemies' programming hasn't gone into action, either."

"Then why don't we just write it down somewhere?"

"That wouldn't do any good. On reading it, even the person who wrote it would take it as the deluded ravings of a madman."

A somewhat deflated Doris changed her tack. "So is that powder the same little 't' thing that was in my father's letter?"

Once again the physician shook his head. "I'm afraid not. I've given the matter much consideration, but I simply can't connect the powder with that initial. Some might say your father, overwhelmed by the excitement of this great discovery, miswrote it, but I don't believe that's the case. The reason I don't is because most of the other interviewees failed to mention the powder as well. I think it's safe to assume the letter 't' refers to something else entirely."

"But if some of them could remember the powder, why didn't they remember the other thing?"

Dr. Ferringo faltered. And then he began to speak in the gravest tone Doris had ever heard. "I've always felt there was something somewhat ironic about human/Nobility relations—in the Nobility's view of humanity, to be specific. In your present circumstances, I can't expect you to appreciate this, but they may well feel a kind of affection toward us."

"What the hell! The Nobles think they're our friends? That's ridiculous!"

Rougher than her tone was the way Doris' hand tugged at the scarf around her neck. For the first time in her life, she glared at the elderly physician. "I don't care who you are, Doc, that's ... I just don't have the words ... "

"Don't pull such a face." The physician waved his hands in an attempt at placating her. "By no means is that to say all of the Nobility feel that way. Any examination of the historical facts will show that, in the preponderance of cases, they don't demonstrate affection, but rather act as if human beings were lower than machines. Emotionally speaking—if we assume for a moment that they indeed have emotions—as much as ninety-nine percent of them are no different from the lord who attacked you. But it's very difficult to discount the possibility that the other one percent exists. I'll have to relate all the facts I've unearthed to you another day ..."

Am I gonna see another day? Doris wondered. Beyond the window, something evil was on its way, tearing through the pleasantly sweet air of the spring-like evening.

Dr. Ferringo wasn't looking at Doris any longer. His eyes seemed nailed to a spot on the floor as he continued to expound on long-held suspicions. "For example, why would they make distinctions between their weaknesses and the weapons that exploit them? Why did some memory of this powder remain when it could've been erased as completely as whatever the 't' stands for? My guess is that compared to this 't' thing, the powder is a minor hindrance, at best. Could it be the bastards are just teasing us? Is this our masters saying, 'Let them have a minor weakness like this,' as they throw us a bone? If that's the case, then why not make it common knowledge from the start?" Here

Dr. Ferringo's words trailed off. Pausing a beat, he added, "This is the conclusion I've come to after a humble little investigation that's occupied half this old fool's sixty years—I take this as a challenge from a race that reached the pinnacle and now slides toward extinction. It's a challenge being offered to us humans, a race that can't even begin to be measured against them. But we may eventually rise to their level, or perhaps even surpass them. And I believe this is what they say: 'If you humans want to inherit our throne, then try to beat us into submission by your own power. If you have the powder, then try to solve the mystery of the 't' thing. And when you've solved it, try to prevent it from being shrouded again in the mists of forgetfulness.'"

"That's impossible ..." To Doris, the words spilling from her own lips sounded a million miles away. "That'd make them just like an instructor breaking in a Hunter trainee ..."

Though he gave a slight nod, it was unclear if the elderly physician truly fathomed Doris' words. His gaze didn't deviate in the least as he said, "This isn't something the Lesser Nobility would be capable of. It may well be ..."

"It may well be what?"

"Him. All the true Nobility in the world were united under the thousand Greater Nobility, the seven Kings, and the legendary dark lord who ruled them all—the great vampire, the king of kings, Dra—"

At that moment, a wave of tension swept into Doris' countenance. "Doc!" she shouted, but it sounded more like a cry for help than a warning. Snapping back to reality, the physician turned his head to follow Doris as she made for the living room window.

The light of the moon on the cool plains showed no signs of anything on the move, but the ears of both caught the sounds of wagon wheels and hooves pounding distant terrain.

"Looks like he's coming."

"I've got a hell of a welcome party set up for him." Though she'd reclaimed the stalwart mien of an Amazon, in her heart of hearts the girl let a plaintive cry escape.

You didn't make it back in time after all, D.

The black cyborgs seemed to run on unearthly clouds, and, when their hoofbeats echoed so close that it was impossible Doris was mistaken, she went to the other side of the living room and twisted one of the silver ceremonial masks adorning the wall to the right.

With a dim sound, part of the floor and wall rotated and pulled out of sight. In a matter of seconds, a wooden control-console and armchair appeared. Though the control console itself was wood, the switch- and lever-dotted top was iron, with a riot of colored lamps and gauges adding to the confusion. This was a combat control center—Doris' father had summoned a craftsman all the way from the Capital to install it. Every weapon on the farm could be controlled from here. As far as being prepared for the attacks by the creatures that ran rampant in the wild, this was about as good as money could buy. A full-field prismatic scope lowered from the ceiling.

"Ha! Back in those days, I asked your father what kind of work he was having done, and he told me he was having a new solar converter put in. Your father was a sly one to even keep this from me."

There wasn't time to respond to the recollections of the still-easygoing physician. The prismatic lens of the view scope showed a black carriage drawn by a team of four horses coming down the road to the farm at full speed. Doris' hand reached for one of the levers. The view scope doubled as a targeting system.

"Steady," Dr. Ferringo told her as he peered out the window, the little bottle in his hand. "You've still got the electromagnetic barrier." Before he had finished speaking, the triple-barred, wooden gate opened without a whisper. As the black carriage was about to sprint through the gate with a gust of wind, it was enveloped by a blinding flash of light.

Powerful enough to char a lesser dragon through tough scales otherwise impervious to blades, the electromagnetic barrier set off a shower of sparks that turned blackest night to brightest day for a fleeting moment. Bursting through a giant, white-hot blossom of fire, the ball of white light forced its way onto the farm. The horse, the driver, the wagon wheels—white flames clung to them all. It was an outlandish sight, like a carriage from hell that had suddenly appeared on earth.

"They're through. What in the world?..." Doris' puzzled exclamation came as she watched the cyborg horses—as soon as they'd broken through the barrier, she'd expected the four of them to tear right into her front yard like a veritable hurricane, but not a single hoof was out of step as they executed a brilliant stop right on the spot.

The magnetic flames swirling around them quickly dispersed. The enemy was protected by a more powerful barrier.

"Not yet. Look! He's getting out!" Once again, her hand was checked by the physician's hopeful command, but in his voice Doris caught a ring of both tension and fear that outweighed the former emotion by far. Embodiment of courage and intellect that the elderly physician was, the damage of scores of centuries of brainwashing by the Nobility had seeped well into his subconscious.

The black door opened, and a massive figure garbed in sable trod down steps that automatically projected onto the ground.

"He must be some kind of idiot—look at him, jumping out like he doesn't have a care in the world."

Ostensibly encouraged, Doris' voice still lacked strength. Her foe knew that any defenses she might be ready to spring on him would pose no threat. When the villain that had left his filthy mark on her neck bared his pearly fangs in a grin and started toward the house alone, Doris pulled the lever.

All over the farm there was the sound of one spring releasing after another. Black chunks flew through the air toward the Count, only to bounce back inches shy of him. What fell to the ground were boulders a good four feet in diameter. Fired in rapid succession, all of the rocky missiles were robbed of their kinetic energy by an invisible barrier, falling around the calmly advancing Count.

"Just as I thought—he's no pushover." Doris pulled a second lever. This time it was steel javelins the launchers disgorged. All of the first ten bounced off him, but the eleventh and final javelin pierced the Count's abdomen.

"I got him!" Doris exclaimed, squeezing the lever so hard she threatened to break it. What froze her smile was the way the temporarily motionless Count gave a horrible grin before he resumed his deliberate stride, the steel javelin still protruding from his stomach and back.

The bastard's trying to tell me he doesn't even need his force field to stop my attacks!

It felt like an icy paw of fear was stirring her brains as Doris suddenly realized that there was no need for a vampire to "go get" a former victim. For those who'd felt the kiss of blood on their neck but once, a single word from a fiend outside their door would suffice to call them out into the waiting arms of Death. That was precisely the sort of thing D was guarding against when he rendered her unconscious the first time she had unwanted guests.

"He's toying with me!" Doris pushed and pulled levers like a woman possessed. So long as nothing pierced its heart, a vampire would not die. Though undoubtedly aware of this immutable fact, seeing the fearsome power in action with her own two eyes had completely robbed the girl of the cool judgment the daughter of a skilled Hunter should possess. She was robbed of her reason by the same fear that slumbered in all mortals, the fear of unknowable darkness.

Machine guns concealed in the shrubbery spat fire, and explosive-tipped arrows set aflame by a lens on the solar storage unit fell like rain.

Through the oily smoke, the fiery explosions, and the deafening roar that surrounded him, the Count grinned. It was clear this was the stiffest resistance humanity could currently offer. Their kind remained on earth, tough as cockroaches, while his species slid silently and inevitably toward extinction, dwindling like the light of the setting sun.

Suddenly, his anger flared, consuming all the admiration he'd felt for the resistance his prey offered. His eyes became flame. As he gnashed his naked fangs together, the Count dashed to the porch, took the stairs in a single leap, yanked the javelin from his abdomen, and heaved the weapon at the door. The door burst off its hinges and toppled into the house. Beyond the door hung a black, iron netting. The instant he heedlessly thrust the steel javelin into it to sweep it out of his way, there was a flash at the point of contact, and the Count felt a violent burning sensation flowing into his body through the hand he had around the weapon. For the first time, the flesh beneath his black raiment shuddered in agony, and his hair stood on end. The vampire's accursed regenerative abilities did their best to counteract the vicious electric shock, and then set to adjusting the molecular arrangement of the cells that needed to be removed. The shock he received came from a transformer that converted energy collected in the solar panels on the roof by day into a high-tension load of fifty-thousand volts. Even as he felt his cells charred and nerves destroyed by the precipitous electrical shock, the Count swung the javelin. With a parting gift of fresh agony and a shower of sparks, the conductive net of interlaced wire tore and fell to the floor.

"Well done for a lone woman," the Count muttered with admiration, his eyes bloodshot. "She's every bit the fighter I thought she'd be. Child, I must have your blood at all costs. Wait for me."

Doris knew she had exhausted all means at her disposal. As the monitor was switched to the interior of the house, the visage of a thirsting demon filled the screen. Suddenly the living room door was knocked back into the room. Doris leapt up from the control console and stood in front of Dr. Ferringo to shield him.

"Child," the figure in the doorway said, "while you fight admirably for a woman, the battle is done. You must favor me with a taste of your hot blood."

The snap of a whip split the air.

"Come," the Count commanded in a penetrating voice.

The tip of her whip lost its impetus in midair, and the weapon fell to the floor in coils. Doris began walking with the shaky steps of a marionette, but the elderly physician grabbed her shoulder. His right hand covered her nostrils, and the young woman slumped to the floor without a sound. The physician had kept a chloroform-soaked cloth concealed in his hand all along.

"So you intend to interfere with me, old fool?" the Count asked in a stark, white voice devoid of all emotion.

"Well, I can't stand back and do nothing," the old man responded, stepping forward with his left hand clenched. "Here's something you hate—garlic powder."

A wave of unrest passed across the Count's face, but he soon gave a broad grin. "You should be complimented on your discovery—but you truly are foolish. True enough, I am powerless against that scent. You may slip through my grasp this night. But the instant you confirm how effective it is against me, that confirmation shall cost you all memory of the very thing you hold in your hand. And tomorrow evening I shall come again."

"I'm not gonna let you do that."

"Oh, and what shall you do?"

"This old fool had a life once, too. Thirty years back, Sam Ferringo was known as something of an Arachni-man Hunter. And I know a thing or two as well about how to do battle with your kind."

"I see." There was a glint in the Count's eyes.

The elderly physician gave a wave of his hand. Powder and a strange odor swirled through the air.

Gagging, the vampire reeled back with his cape over his nose and mouth. He was struck with a horrible urge to vomit. He felt utterly enervated, as if his brains were melting and life itself was draining from his body. The cells in his sinus cavity—the olfactory nerves that make the sense of smell possible—were dealt a devastating blow by the allicin that gives garlic its distinctive aroma.

"Your kinds' days are over. Back to the world of darkness and destruction with you!" At some point, Dr. Ferringo had pulled out a foot-long stake. With the rough wooden weapon in his right hand, the physician advanced. Right before his eyes, a black bird snapped its wings open. It was the Count's cape. Like a sentient being, it wrapped around the elderly physician's wrists, then swept around wildly to hurl the man clear across the room—all without the Count appearing to lift a finger. This was one of the secret tricks of the Nobility. The Count had learned it from no less than the Sacred Ancestor of his race.

Scrambling desperately to rise from the floor, the elderly physician was horrified to see the still wildly coughing Count climbing onto Doris.

"Wait!"

The Count's face eclipsed part of the girl's throat.

What the physician saw astonished him.

The Count fell backward, his face pale. Perhaps no one had ever seen a Noble wear such an expression of stark terror as the elderly physician now witnessed. Ignoring the awestruck physician, the figure in black disappeared through the door, his cape fluttering behind him.

When the elderly physician finally got to his feet, rubbing his hip all the while, he could hear the echo of wagon wheels fading into the distance. *Somehow or other, it looks like we're out of the woods for now.* Just as this tremendous feeling of relief welled up inside him, Dr. Ferringo suddenly got the feeling he'd forgotten something important and cocked his head to one side. *What in the blazes is that smell? And why did that bastard take to his heels?*

Soaring Shrike-Blades of Death

As soon as the sun was up the next morning, Doris entrusted the still slumbering Dan to the elderly physician and left the farm. "Are you dead set on going? Even supposing he's still alive, you've got no idea whether or not you'll find him." Doc was referring to D, of course. Doris kept her silence and smiled. It wasn't a disheartened smile. She'd save him all right, even if it killed her. That was the conviction that bolstered her smile.

"Don't worry, we'll be back for sure. Take care of Dan for me." And with that, she wheeled her horse around toward the vampires' castle.

She was scared. She'd already felt the vampire's baleful fangs once, and had nearly been attacked again scant hours earlier. And she'd already lost all memory of the effectiveness of garlic. Having heard from Dr. Ferringo that the Count had run off for some unknown reason, Doris assured herself the powder really had worked. As soon as she came to believe it, however, every memory of the powder was purged from her brain. In its place, Doris remembered how the previous night, the fearsome Noble dealt with every attack she threw at him like it was mere child's play. The memory of it was etched vividly in her mind.

She couldn't beat him. There was no way to stop him.

While she raced across the plains with a display of equestrian skill that would put any man to shame, her heart was poised to drop into a pit of the darkest despair until the innocent face of her brother Dan caught her and pulled her back. *Don't worry, your big sister ain't about to let that bastard get the best of her. I'll bring D back, and then we'll get rid of the lot of them*, she thought.

Beyond Dan's face, another face flickered. Colder than that of the Count, a visage so exquisite it gave her goose bumps.

Be alive. I don't care how bad you're hurt, just please still be alive.

E ven after the weather controller's "comfort-control time" was over, the chill-laden morn on the prairie was so beautiful and charged with vitality that the green of the landscape took on a deeper hue. A dozen men on horseback, looking like they'd ridden hard all night, kicked up a cloud of dust as they came to an abrupt halt on a road traversed only by a pleasant morning breeze. The road ran on into the village of Ransylva, stitching its way between prairies of waist-high grass. Seventy feet ahead, four figures had sprung from the undergrowth and now stood in the middle of the road, blocking the traveler's way.

"What the hell are you trying to prove?!"

"We're the Frontier Defense Force, dispatched on orders from the Capital. Out of our way!" The eyes of the second man to shout narrowed cautiously. The outlandish appearance of this foursome touched on remembered dangers.

"A girlish little punk, a big freaking bastard, a bag of bones with a pointed head, and a hunchback—you pricks wouldn't happen to be the Fiend Corps would you?"

"An excellent deduction," Rei-Ginsei said with a grin wholly befitting the lush, green morning. With that gem of a smile, it was hard to imagine this dashing youth as the head of the brutal bandit gang that had terrorized the northern part of the Frontier. "We came down here to make a little money after our faces got a wee bit too well known up north, but before we can even get started, it comes to our attention you boys are going from village to village posting warrants for us, so we decided to wait for you out here. Kindly refrain from doing anything untoward."

To the man, the members of the FDF were enraged by his insolent tone. The solemn-faced man who was apparently their commander barked, "Shut your damn flap! We made double-time to Pedros after we got word you pricks had been seen in town there, but we just barely missed you, much to our regret. I can't believe our luck. You clowns just jumped into our laps. We're busting you right here. I don't care if you're the meanest bandits to ever walk the earth, you've all gotta be soft in the head. You know, we're the fucking Frontier Defense Force, dumbass!" His self-confidence wasn't a bluff. Dispatched by the Capital at regular intervals to police the entire Frontier, the FDF had been trained to combat all manner of beasts and creatures. They were equipped with serious firepower, and in a fight, each and every one of them was worth a platoon of normal men.

Heavy metallic clinks echoed from the saddles of the squad members serried behind him. That was the sound of shells being automatically fed into the recoilless bazookas each man was issued. The squad members already had Rei-Ginsei and his group in the unswerving sights of their laser rifles. No matter how the bandits' battle in the saloon the previous day had defied imagining, it seemed unlikely that mortal men like themselves could weather the FDF's assault.

"How does this strike you—since you went to all the trouble of turning yourselves in, we'll let you throw down your weapons, okay? That way you'll at least get to go on living till they get you up on the hangman's scaffold," said the commander.

"I don't fancy that."

"Why, you little punk!"

"By all means, shoot me if it'll make you feel any better. But before you do, there's one thing you seem to be forgetting."

The commander knit his brow in consternation. "The Fiend Corps is not a quartet," Rei-Ginsei said in an exquisite voice.

"What?!"

A stir ran through the FDF members. At some point, the foursome had taken their eyes off the FDF and turned them straight to the side.

"We have a guardian angel the rest of the world knows nothing about." Still looking off to the side, Rei-Ginsei pulled the corner of his lips up sharply. His was the devil's own smile. "Oh, here it comes now!" When an unremitting source of terror to the human body and soul appeared right in front of them, the degree of shock each of the victims felt seemed to be directly dependent on their proximity to it.

The instant *the thing* materialized from thin air, hovering over the commander's horse, the leader died of shock, and the five FDF members within ten feet of him went insane. And that wasn't all. Apparently even animals could see the thing, or perhaps they could sense its troubling presence; the lead horses forgot all about running away, but instead dropped to a spasming heap on the ground, frothing from the nose and mouth. The rest of the steeds reared up.

Most likely, the FDF members who fell from their mounts as a result didn't cry out because part of their psyches had already been shattered. Some of them had their heads staved by the hooves of the rampaging horses, while others seemed frozen as they watched it coming closer and closer.

The thing leisurely made its way from one survivor to the next, touching each of the members in turn.

The Capital's greatest fighting men quietly died of madness, powerless to stop it.

"Well, what do you think? The fifth member of the Fiend Corps is quite the looker, isn't it?"

The last member of the FDF was crawling across the ground, but as he listened to Rei-Ginsei's sardonic laughter *the thing* suddenly vanished without a trace.

"What the—?!"

As the startled Rei-Ginsei looked over his shoulder, the sole surviving FDF member trained his laser rifle on the bandit's forehead. Thanks to a Spartan training regime, he could still muster murderous intent toward the enemy despite his insanity.

"Boss!"

Before Golem could move, a beam of red light pierced Rei-Ginsei's brow.

However, it was the FDF member who jerked backwards. Incredibly, the laser beam that hit Rei-Ginsei right between the eyes burst out of the back of the other man's head. A stench of seared flesh and brains hung in the otherwise refreshing air.

"Are you okay, boss?" the man with the pointed head asked as he cast a loathsome gaze on the soldiers littering the ground. Not merely his head, but the man's entire frame was streamlined like a shooting-star class rocket. He was called Gimlet.

"I believe I'll survive," Rei-Ginsei laughed, rubbing his forehead. There was a black circle about a quarter inch in diameter scorched right between his eyebrows.

While the others inquired no further after his condition, the four fiends looked at each other with concern over another suspicious occurrence.

"Something must've happened to Witch," said the hunchbacked man.

"Chullah's right," Rei-Ginsei chimed in. "The only reason I made such a blunder is because I never in a million years imagined that *thing* just disappearing in the middle of an operation." He certainly had a strange way of covering his blunders. Turning back to the expanse of prairie to his left, he muttered, "If one of her spells should break at her age, she'll be walking the cold, dark road to hell ..."

"Would you like me to go check it out?" asked Gimlet.

He shook his fine head from side to side. "No, I shall look into this. The rest of you kindly dispose of these unsightly remains. Burn them or eat them, whichever suits your fancy," he said, smiling at his disturbing orders.

And this is what was happening while the gruesome battle neared its conclusion, or rather, to be precise, just before the sudden disappearance of *the thing* that had materialized from thin air.

Racing across the plains, Doris was just about to turn her steed in a new direction when she discovered something unexpected in someplace unimaginable and jerked her horse's reins in the opposite direction instead. The spot was less than a mile and a quarter from Count Lee's castle. Bypassing the more circuitous roads, she'd galloped straight through a hilly region, but from here on out, she'd have to take a somewhat less direct route.

Her father had brought her here just once when she was little and she'd seen it from a distance then, but she'd never seen the place from this close before. Half of her frightened, the other half deadly serious, she took in the mysterious scenery stretching out in the morning light. The villagers called this place The Devil's Quarry. In this part of the endless expanse of prairie, there were countless statues standing like stone forests, or laying on the ground and looking to the heavens. No two had the same face or form, and there wasn't a single statue that didn't have the aspect of some bizarre monstrosity. A sculpture of a baldheaded man with incredibly large eyes, a bust of a creature with dozens of arms baring its fangs, a full-length statue with thousands of beastly bristles each individually carved—all these pieces of incomparably detailed craftsmanship were covered with moss, as were the remnants of stone walls and columns that called to mind the ruins of some ancient citadel. Together, they seemed to form a completely alien dimension. Even the morning sunlight, that should've breathed life into every hill and valley in the world, lent the faces of the sculptures weirder shadows than it might have, as the particles of light were swallowed by the moss and the desolate atmosphere, or sank with leaden weight. Even the air was dank. People said this was the place where the Nobility had once held their wretched ceremonies, or a quarry used in the construction of the castle, but the latter theory was easily dismissed. After all, there wasn't any stone in this whole region to be quarried. At any rate, this was a forbidden area, and no one from the village ever entered.

What had caught Doris' eye was an old woman seated in a deep, bowl-shaped depression near the center of the Devil's Quarry doing the same baffling gestures over and over. Her age was unclear. Judging by her gray hair and the wrinkles creasing her yellowed skin, both of which were obvious even at this distance, she looked to be nearly a hundred, and yet her body seemed strangely imbued with vitality.

What is this? Some old lady lost in her travels, taking a breather?

Even if Doris couldn't bring her all the way into town, she could at least give the woman directions back to the main road. But as Doris was just about to give her mount a flick of the reins, she stayed her hand and quietly slipped down to the ground instead.

Wrapped in a dull gray overcoat, the crone's torso was bent forward at an extreme angle, and there was something about the sight of her—with eyes fixed on her own fingertips as they clutched at nothing—that just felt evil. Of course, Doris was completely unaware that at that very moment on the road a few miles distant, a strange entity that appeared out of thin air was busy delivering death by insanity to the members of the FDF.

Muffling her own footfalls as she led her horse, Doris made her way into the Devil's Quarry, tethered her mount to a nearby pillar, and came up behind the crone. Apparently the old woman didn't notice, as she didn't move at all. As Doris drew closer, she felt goose bumps spread across her flesh.

A poisonous miasma was rising from the crone's vicinity. Clearly she was using some arcane skill toward foul ends. The sound of a low voice chanting a spell reached Doris' ears.

"Stop that!" she shouted despite herself as she took a few steps forward. At that instant, something whizzed out of the bushes and glanced off her cheek. Doris dropped to the ground with lightning speed. Holding her breath and remaining alert, she touched her left hand to her cheek. Warm blood clung to her fingertips.

A spirit beast, eh? Looks like she's got her warded zone set up right around here, Doris thought.

To her left, Doris felt a keen presence. She made a quick combat roll to one side and let fly with the whip in her right hand. Unfortunately, her deadly strike only kicked grass into the air, but she sensed her opponent changing direction to fall back a good distance.

When conjurers and sorcerers worked their art, they established an area around themselves with a radius of ten or so feet in order to have the best chances of success. This was known as their warded zone. Since their concentration might be disturbed, and, in extreme cases, their spell might even lose its efficacy if someone were to step into this zone while they were working, sorcerers conjured up creatures and set them as watch dogs outside the warded zone, ready to attack intruders. The task often fell to massive hounds, poisonous toads, and serpents suckled on pure malice, but this crone used a transparent creature formed of her own force of will—a spirit beast. And a particularly nasty one at that.

Doris was well aware the only thing that had saved her was the superb reflex of a trained Hunter. The average person would've had their throat torn open a few seconds ago. In her heart, she whispered thanks to her father. "It's forty feet to the old lady. Guess this calls for a bit of trickery," Doris muttered to herself. This dangerous gamble was her only choice. She had no idea what kind of misery her opponent could be causing with her spell.

Once again, her whip mowed through open air right toward the crone.

Slashing through the air, the spirit beast attacked Doris. At that moment, her whip snapped back. An instant later, she could feel something in the air rip in half. The air was suddenly flooded with a choking malevolence, but it dispersed quickly enough.

"Waagh!"

The scream that escaped the crone as she doubled over made Doris leap to her feet in the brush. Doris had drawn the spirit beast out by appearing to attack the crone, then used a flick of her wrist to turn the blow on the beast at the last possible second. Of course, if her timing had been off by a split second, Doris would have been the one to die.

Her suicidal gamble had paid off, but it had also had an unforeseen side effect. Because the crone had created the spirit beast with her own sorcery, the destruction of the beast meant a disturbance to her other spell as well. She invested the whole of her life force in performing that spell, and when it was broken, the crone's black heart beat its last. It was at just that moment the outlandish creature bearing down on the last remaining FDF member vanished.

"Hey, lady! C'mon, snap out of it!" Doris raced over and took her in her arms, but the crone's eyes showed dead white, foam spilled from her mouth, and the mortified look on her wrinkled features defied description. There was a pentagram branded on her forehead, the mark of a sorceress. "Oh, crap! This isn't quite what I had in mind ... " Though this was an evil sorceress, and her own actions had clearly been in self defense, the thought that she'd brought about the death of an old woman weighed heavily on Doris' heart.

"I'm sorry, but you'll have to wait here until I can come back. I've got serious business to attend to."

Doris laid the corpse out on the ground, and was about to head back to her horse when she hesitated. She'd already decided that finding out whether or not D was okay was more important than bringing this corpse back to town. She'd come out here aware of all the risks that entailed.

Still, the dark body of the crone looked so terribly sad and forlorn stretched out on the ground. The wind tugged at the sleeves of her overcoat. And a corpse abandoned in the wilds was a tempting target for monsters. It would be bad enough to have them feasting on her, but if one of them *got inside her* that would be yet another threat to humanity. Even in broad daylight, there were probably some creatures around that might risk turning into a ball of flame to slink out and take possession of a corpse that hadn't been disposed of properly.

Doris didn't have any of the gear she'd need to take care of the body. She didn't see a horse or wagon for the crone. On inspection, the inner pocket of the crone's overcoat contained nothing aside from a few suspicious-looking trinkets.

Doris went back to the body and lifted it gently. "I don't really think there are any critters to *take you over* out here, but I'm gonna bring you with me anyway. Of course, I can't offer any guarantees we'll make it back in one piece, either."

Loading the corpse onto the horse behind the saddle, Doris used rawhide lacing to secure its arms and legs around the steed. That was to keep it from falling off, and just to be safe in the event something did possess it. Leave it to the daughter of a Hunter to be accustomed to this sort of work—she had the whole thing done in less than three minutes. Doris got in the saddle. *At any rate, I'll make for the main road.*

When her horse had gone but a few steps, Doris suddenly spun around. At the same moment, she heard a thunk as something heavy buzzed by at neck level. The decapitated head painted a gory parabola as it sailed through the air, and just before it hit the ground, its eyes snapped open. It bared its teeth. They were the eyes of a demon, and the foul fangs of one as well. It flew toward the person responsible for separating it from its body. Black lightning streaked from a mounted figure topping a hill quite some distance off. Split in two from forehead to chin, the crone's head fell to the ground and moved no more.

Doris realized she'd had a very close call.

Right behind her was the decapitated corpse of the crone, frozen in place with its claws a heartbeat away from tearing into the girl's throat. The snapped binding dangled from its wrists. An evil spirit had possessed the corpse before Doris had even touched it. The instant it snapped its bonds to attack Doris from behind, the figure on the distant hill had lopped the head off with consummate skill and speed.

Her horse gave a shake, and the headless corpse dropped to the ground. Doris finally turned to face her savior. "Oh, D, I was … " An elated hue lit up her face, but it was gone all too soon.

While the figure coming down off the hill fresh from his graceful display of skill certainly had beauty on par with D, he was clearly someone else. "I can't believe you picked up on that." As he pulled up along side her on his horse, Rei-Ginsei smiled blindingly. He was referring to how she had sensed a strange presence, and turned around a split second before the possessed corpse attacked.

"That was nothing. It looks like I'm in your debt again. What kind of weapon did you use?"

Rei-Ginsei took a playfully surprised expression at her less than ladylike inquiry. "If you'll forgive my saying so, judging by your clothing and that whip, you appear to be a Hunter."

"My father was. I just sorta play at it," Doris said without embarrassment or modesty, and then she smiled. She wasn't entirely sure why, but her smile felt strangely forced.

Realizing that even after they'd exchanged civilities Doris' eyes were not focused on his face but rather on his weapon-girt waist, the dashing youth smiled grimly.

"What brings you here of all places at this hour of the morning, sir? You been out on the road?"

"Yes, that's it exactly."

"In that case, you suppose you could bring this old lady's body back into town for me? Normally I'd have to go and explain what happened to the sheriff, but the truth is, I'm kind of in a hurry." Doris stopped her horse and proceeded to recount the entire incident.

Listening silently until the end, Rei-Ginsei then muttered, "I see now. So that's what happened to it ... I can take care of the corpse for you. I shall see to it both are disposed of properly."

"Both?" Doris knit her brow, but as the dashing youth's carefree smile struck her, she reflected a smile of her own. "Okay, then. Thanks."

As she was reining her horse around, her arm was grabbed from the side, drawing the lovely young woman into an embrace on horseback. The sweet aroma that lingered around his mouth wasn't what she'd expect from any man.

"What the hell ..."

"I have saved your life, even though it meant slaying one of my four companions. Of course, you're also quite beautiful. And then there's the matter of your rescue yesterday. I hardly think anyone would blame me for taking a little compensation."

"You'd better leave me alone, or else—"

"You've also seen something you shouldn't have. We really can't have you going into town and telling everyone about that. So you'll have to die out here. Why don't we just say I'm avenging my fallen comrade? Don't put up such a fight. You'll live a while longer. Until I've taken my pleasure, at least." The dashing youth's mouth locked over the virgin's lips.

There was a gasp, and Rei-Ginsei quickly pulled back. He pressed his hand to his mouth, and blood spread across the back of it. A bite from Doris had torn his lips open.

"Don't fuck with me! I've got someone I care about. I wouldn't let a creep like you touch me!"

Her tone was awe inspiring. She thought Rei-Ginsei's countenance would flush with anger, but he simply smiled. Only it wasn't the charming smile that people couldn't help but return. It was the satanic grin he'd worn on the main road.

Giving a shudder, Doris lashed her whip at the center of his face. Less than a foot and a half lay between them. It was really too close to swing the whip. And yet the swirl of black from the girl's fist leapt right up at the youth's dashing face. It was about to land there when it disappeared into the black streak of lightning shooting up from her foe's waist. Rei-Ginsei's skill in drawing his bizarre, v-shaped weapon—and slashing off the end of her whip in the blink of an eye—was truly miraculous. And yet, his face had none of the tension of a battle about to be joined, but rather held the same smile as before.

"Hyah!"

Realizing in a heartbeat she didn't stand a chance of victory, Doris reined her horse toward the ruins and took off at full speed.

In her haste to take flight, she forgot the might of her foe's weapon, and the way it had taken off the crone's head from a hilltop over sixty feet away. Rei-Ginsei didn't throw his weapon immediately. As Doris' mount neared the heart of the ruins, he finally let the weapon fly with an underhanded throw. Whirring as it chased down the rapidly dwindling speck of Doris and her steed, it mercilessly slashed through the horse's right-rear leg and right-front leg, turned a graceful loop, and came right back at

them, severing both legs on the left side. As the loss of one leg would've sufficed to prevent the girl's escape, this was a display of sheer brutality. A bloody mist went out as the horse fell.

"Oh! Just beautiful!" As he felt the weight of his weapon returning to his outstretched palm, Rei-Ginsei admired the scene before him.

As the horse toppled over, a lithe body leapt into the air, somersaulted, and landed on the ground with only the slightest break in form.

But Doris' face was deathly pale.

She hadn't forgotten her foe's weapon, or his unholy skill with it. With those very things in mind, she'd had her horse galloping along a zigzagging course. The black weapon seemed to take their movements into consideration nonetheless as it cleanly severed the first two legs. The falling beast threw them into the air as Rei-Ginsei came back and visited a similar fate on the remaining pair.

Doris realized she'd run into a foe that in some ways was even more fearsome than the Nobility. There was a javelin and a longsword strapped to her saddle, but she had the whip in her right hand. Still, the weapon felt strangely light and ineffectual in her grasp.

Rei-Ginsei leisurely rode into the ruins. "After seeing that last display of agility, I find myself even less inclined to kill you soon. Will you not lay with me before you depart this mortal coil?"

"Who'd be low enough to do that? I'd sooner have my head bashed open on one of these rocks than lie down with a self-important snake like you," Doris replied, quickly slipping behind the closest of the massive sculptures. Almost twenty feet high, the statue of a figure with a pair of bared fangs tilted slightly forward, set off balance by the long years and the shifting of the ground. Rei-Ginsei's intimidating, ranged weapon couldn't be expected to do much through this stony shield, but with no way to strike back, Doris remained in the same predicament.

"The stronger the prey, the greater the huntsman's thrill. Even more so when it's such an exquisite beast. Oh, I'm sorry—you're supposed to be a Hunter as well, aren't you?" Rei-Ginsei ended the question with scornful laughter. The second he looked down from that hill, and spotted Doris with Witch's body loaded on her horse, he had decided to kill her. If the connection were made between the disappearance of the FDF squad and the corpse of an old woman who'd been working some sort of sorcery, it would only be a question of time before the name of his gang came up.

Witch had been like a reserve unit no one knew about. Operating independently, her job was to summon a creature more ghastly than the human mind could bear. Her creations left the bandits' foes psychologically devastated. When Rei-Ginsei lopped off the head of the demonically possessed Witch and saved Doris, part of the reason was because of the natural sexual attraction he felt toward the beautiful girl. On the other hand, he'd also intended to get rid of the burdensome old sorceress eventually. Now he had the girl cornered like an animal, she was largely unscathed, and her eyes blazed with animosity as she glared at him from behind the monolith.

"It would be so easy for me to send you into the hereafter, but I fear dispatching you so quickly would leave you ill-equipped to testify to my infamy in the afterlife." The weapon in his right hand glistened in the sunlight. "I believe I shall have to make your frail heart quake a bit more in fear of me. Ah, yes, I recall one of the cardinal rules of the Hunter—first you must flush the elusive prey from its hiding place."

Something howled through the air, and there was an incredible noise from the base of the monolith sheltering Doris. Giving a cry of astonishment, Doris wisely leapt out of the way. Stuck in the ground at an angle, the several tons of sculpted stone didn't look likely to budge an inch, even under a sizable impact, but suddenly its balance seemed to upset, and it started to tilt in her direction.

The weapon that had done this was already back in Rei-Ginsei's hand. It resembled the boomerang the ancient natives of Australia used so effectively. Unlike the boomerang, however, Rei-Ginsei's weapon was razor sharp on both the inner and outer edges. What's more, it was made of iron. Most non-Aborigines had trouble throwing a plain wooden boomerang effectively, yet this handsome youth, as limber as a sapling swaying in the breeze, could throw the iron blades any way he pleased with just one flick of the wrist. His unholy skill lent blades of mere metal the kind of cutting power reserved for magic swords, pushing them through a human body, or the trunk of a tree, or even through stone.

Furthermore, they didn't just strike in a straight line. They could come at the target from the right or the left, from above, even from the feet—there seemed to be nowhere they couldn't go. And while it was impossible to defend oneself from even one of these blades, it seemed unlikely there was anyone in the world that could fend off two or three successive attacks, let alone multiple blades thrown at the same time. The iron blades were liable to slice through any shield as easily as they went through their usual prey. Such were Rei-Ginsei's "shrike-blades."

The ground shook and verdant moss flew everywhere as the monolith fell.

Doris stood at the bottom of a lush green bowl of a depression, stock still with amazement. It was ten feet to the nearest stone wall.

Swaying like a flower in the morning breeze, Rei-Ginsei laughed. "What's wrong? I thought the nature of the beast was to flee when hunted—"

Suddenly, he swallowed his words.

Doris' expression filled with hope, because two things had suddenly changed.

A heavy white mist from nowhere in particular had begun to fill the ruins. It clung to Rei-Ginsei's hand as he held his weapon, and to Doris' cheeks, forming tepid beads. And far off, a horse was whinnying.

Doris made a mad dash for the stone wall. While the fog might protect her from an attack, she didn't think it would blind her foe long enough for her to get away. She would try to get close enough to whoever was riding the horse she'd just heard to call out, and would try to borrow some weapons, though she might lose an arm or a leg in the process. Of course, she didn't think that would be enough to beat him anyway.

Nothing came knifing through the air after her. Leaping over the wall headfirst, she held her breath and tried to judge the distance to the next bit of cover.

The voice that echoed across the distance rendered her determined gaze as lifeless as that of a corpse.

"Boss, I'm gonna help myself to your playmate."

In a dimly lit world, where a dripping, white veil hid the blue of the sky, the shadow of death crept ever closer to the one, lone girl. Rei-Ginsei and his three henchmen—any one of them was more than a match for her.

"What happened to Witch, boss?" another voice inquired.

"She got put down. Lost her head to a pretty little bird."

A low, rumbling stir went through the fog. The voices she heard were choked with blackest rage.

"I'll gouge her eyes out."

"I'm gonna twist the arms and legs off her."

"I'll tear her head off."

Then Rei-Ginsei was heard to say, "And I shall take my pleasure from what remains of her body."

Doris hadn't spoken. She couldn't even be heard to breathe. The men had simply sensed the presence of a girl paralyzed by imminent death. The milky fog reduced everything to vague silhouettes.

Rei-Ginsei held a shrike-blade ready in his right hand. Without a single word of prompting, at that same moment elsewhere in the fog, Golem drew his machete, a bowie knife gleamed in Gimlet's hand, and Chullah's hump split in half.

"Well, now…"

Just as they were about to unleash their murderous assault, Rei-Ginsei suddenly froze.

There's something out there!

Yes, out in the eddying mist, out in the sticky, unsettling fog that steadily gnawed away at their psyches, which soaked through their skin to threaten the flame of life, Rei-Ginsei clearly sensed the presence of something other than his group and their helpless prey. Not only was there something out there, but it was enough to stop a man like him in his tracks. Rei-Ginsei couldn't physically see it, but he felt the presence near the monolith he'd toppled with his lightning-fast throw.

He'd hadn't known anything about this. How could he have guessed the monolith had stood there since time immemorial, blocking an entrance to the subterranean world? The fog around them was one that had risen from the bowels of the earth.

"So, this is the outside world?"

The query came in just the sort of unsettling voice one would expect from a demon of the mists. It had such an inhuman ring to it that Rei-Ginsei and his three brutal henchmen found themselves swallowing nervously. Stranger yet, it was a woman's voice.

"It's so chilly … I like it so much better down below," said another woman.

A third said, "We really must find something to fill our bellies—oh, well, isn't there something right over there? One, two, three, four—five in all."

Rei-Ginsei shuddered, realizing that the three speakers could see perfectly well in the fog that left all others blind. Due to the weirdness of the presence he sensed out there, he'd forgotten all about lowering the shrike-blade he'd raised earlier. He felt there were two things out there. And yet, he couldn't help thinking that one of those was split into three!

"Your guide duties have been fulfilled. Get below again," a rusty but much more human voice commanded. No doubt that was the other presence he felt. But while the voice was more human, the presence itself was far more daunting than the source of the disturbing female voices.

"Oh, you can't ... Look at how handsome he is ... He looks absolutely delicious ..."

Quickly surmising that these plaintive cries referred to himself, Rei-Ginsei got chills.

"No, I forbid it."

He felt extremely thankful for this second command.

"Let us go, my sisters. We have our orders."

"It's such a waste, but I suppose we must."

"But, well ... when shall you visit us again? When will you come to our abode far below, oh beloved one?"

The last voice was entreating.

There was no response, and before long, the strange thing with three voices and one presence moved reluctantly through the fog and disappeared back underground.

The source of the remaining presence spoke.

"I'm not interested in fighting anyone but the Nobility, but if you're hellbent on starting something, then step right up"

He's challenging us! Even with this realization, the quartet found that their will to fight remained weak.

"D ... I know it's you, isn't it?"

Doris sounded on the verge of tears.

"Come to me. Relax. There's no need to hurry."

Out in the fog, there was the sound of teeth grinding together. He said there was no need to hurry because he was sure the quartet wouldn't do a thing to stop him. The gnashing teeth testified to the gang's resentment of his scathing insult.

But the fact of the matter was the unearthly aura radiating from somewhere out in the fog bound the villains tight, preventing them from so much as lifting a finger.

The little bird that had almost been in hand walked over to the source of the voice. Shortly after that, the bandits felt the two of them moving far away.

"Wait ... wait just a minute." At long last, Rei-Ginsei succeeded in forcing words from his mouth. "At least tell me your name ..." Forgetting his customary eloquence, he shouted into the fog, "So, is that your name, asshole? D?"

There was no response, and he felt the pair getting further and further away.

The spell over him was broken.

With a scream, Rei-Ginsei hurled his weapon. Extraordinary in its power, speed, and timing, nothing could stop it; with complete confidence in that fact, he let the shrike-blade fly.

Out in the fog, there was the sound of blade meeting blade. After that there was no sound at all, and silence settled over the white world. All trace of the pair was gone.

"Boss?" Golem inquired dejectedly a few minutes later, but the beautiful spawn of hell-sent supplications just stayed there with his right hand stretched out for a shrike-blade that never returned, his countenance paler than the fog as he sat frozen in the saddle.

A sculpture of a gargoyle with folded wings trained its mocking gaze on the room from its lofty perch. The room was one of many in Count Lee's castle. Completely windowless and far from spacious, it was simple in design, but the robot sentries lined up along one wall, the chair on a dais a step up from the stone floor, the person in black scowling from a colossal portrait that covered much of the wall behind the chair, and the general air of religious solemnity that hung about the room suggested it was a place of judgment—a courtroom of sorts.

The defendant had already been questioned about their crimes, and as the ultimate judge, Count Lee raised his eyebrows in rage.

"I will now pronounce the sentence. Look at me," the Count commanded. He spoke with the dignity of a feudal lord, in a low voice from his place on the dais as he desperately fought back the flames ready to leap from his throat. The defendant didn't move. Brought to the room earlier by the robot sentries, the defendant remained sprawled on the cold stone floor. *Three pairs* of vacant eyes wandered about the room, across the floor, into space, and then up to reciprocate the gaze of the gargoyles near the ceiling. The black hair that reached to the end of the defendant's massive tail made the floor a sea of silky black. It was the three sisters from the subterranean aqueduct—the Midwich Medusas.

"You have forgotten the debt you owe me for sheltering you three long millennia in the waters of the underworld, safe from the eyes of man, and fed to the point of bursting. Not only did you fail to dispatch the worm I sent you, but you even aided his escape. This sort of betrayal is not easily forgiven. And so I condemn you here and now!"

The three heads didn't seem to be shaken in the least by the Count's barrage of abuse as they drifted through space and their eyes seemed to be covered by a milky membrane. Then, all at once, they let out a deep sigh and murmured, "Oh, the divine one ..."

"Kill them!" Before his indignant shout was done—a cry that some might even call crazed—the robot sentries unleashed crimson heat-rays from their eyes, vaporizing the trio of heads. Without so much as a glance at the corpse still smoking and wriggling on the floor, the Count curtly ordered, "Get rid of it," then looked sharply to one side.

He hadn't noticed her entrance, but Larmica stood beside the dais. Even garbed in a snow-white dress, the girl had an air of darkness about her. Returning her father's bloodshot gaze with eyes full of icy mockery, she said, "Father, why have you done away with them?"

"They were traitors," the Count spat. "Of course, there were extenuating circumstances. The stripling drank their blood and made them his slave, and they led him back to the surface. You see, when I awoke, the computers informed me that one of the entrances to the subterranean world had been opened early this morning. My first thought was to have them dragged from their lair for questioning, and they confessed everything. Not that it was difficult—they seem to have been robbed of their souls. They were only too happy to answer my questions."

"And what of the entrance?"

"The robots have already sealed it."

"Then you mean to tell me he made good his escape?"

Averting his gaze from his daughter's face as her expression became ever more fascinated, the Count nodded.

"He got away. But the fact that he beat the three sisters ... not by killing them, but that he bit their throats like one of us and made them do his bidding ... I get the feeling he is no ordinary dhampir ..."

Dhampirs with less self-control fed on human blood from time to time, but there had never been a case where the person they fed on became the same sort of marionette Nobles made of their victims. Being only half-vampire, dhampirs' powers didn't extend that far. Stranger yet, this victim hadn't been a human, but rather a true monster among monsters—the Midwich Medusas.

Larmica's eyes began to sparkle with an ineffable light. "I see. You let him get away from you ... Just like the girl."

Not surprisingly, the Count's visage twisted in rage, and he glared at Larmica.

The girl, of course, was Doris. Larmica referred with sarcasm to how he'd set out flush with confidence to claim his prize, but had been forced to flee after meeting brutal resistance. Even more filled with the pride of the Nobility than her father, Larmica sternly opposed elevating any human to the ranks of her kind, no matter how much her father might be attracted to his prey.

With feigned innocence, she asked, "Will you be sneaking off again this evening to see her? Will you pay another call to that beastly smelling excuse for a farm?"

"No," the Count replied, his voice once again composed. "I believe I'll refrain from that for a while. Now that the stripling is back with her, it might prove difficult to have my way."

"Then you have abandoned your plans for the human girl?"

Now it was the Count's turn to grin slyly. "Again, no. I must pay a call on someone else. Before I had the Medusas executed, the eldest of the sisters made mention of some curious characters."

"Characters? You mean humans, don't you?"

"Yes. Using them, I shall see to it the whelp is destroyed— though you shall have my condolences." There was nothing whatsoever of a consoling nature in his tone.

In a low voice Larmica asked, "Then you will have the girl, come what may?"

"Yes. Such exquisite features, such a fine, pale throat, and such mettle. These last few millennia, I've not seen such a precious female." Here the Count's tone changed. "Seeing the grueling battle she gave me the other night, never giving an inch, has only increased my ardor. Ten thousand years ago, was there not the case of our Sacred Ancestor failing to attain a human maiden of his heart's desire?" As he said this, he gazed with reverence, equal to what any of the Greater Nobility would show, at the colossal painting occupying the wall behind him. "I have heard that the woman our Sacred Ancestor desired was named Mina the Fair, and she lived in the ancient Land of Angels. And it seems our Sacred Ancestor found the blood coursing beneath her nigh translucent skin sweeter and more delectable than any to ever wash across his tongue, though he had already drunk from the life founts of thousands of beauties."

"Because of that woman, our Sacred Ancestor was reduced to dust," Larmica added coldly, giving her father a plaintive look that wasn't at all like her. "Then you won't reconsider this under any circumstances, Father? The proud Lee family has occupied this region of the Frontier for five long millennia, and no human should ever be allowed to join it. All you have ever preyed upon have been drained of blood and left to die, and never have you suggested bringing any of them into the family. So why this one girl? I am certain I'm not alone in questioning this. I have no doubt my late mother would ask exactly the same thing."

The Count gave a pained smile. He nodded, as if acknowledging the inevitable.

"That's the point. I have been meaning to bring this up for some time now, but I intend to take the girl as my wife."

Larmica looked as if a stake had just been pounded through her heart. Nothing shy of that could have delivered the same shock to this proud young woman. After a while, her characteristically pale skin became the color of paper, and she said, "I understand. If you have considered that far ahead, then I will no longer be unreasonable. Do as you wish. However, I believe I shall take my leave of this castle and set off on a long journey."

"A journey, you say? Very well."

For all the distress in the Count's voice, there was also a faint ring of relief. He knew in the very marrow of his bones that his beloved but temperamental daughter would never be able to coexist with the human girl, no matter how he might try to persuade them both.

"So, Father," Larmica asked, her face as charming as if the problem had completely been forgotten, "how exactly do you intend to destroy the young upstart and claim the girl?"

By the time Doris got back to the farm with D, the sun was already high in the sky. Having heard an account of the previous night from his babysitter, Dr. Ferringo, Dan's little heart was steeped in anxiety as he awaited his sister's return. When he saw the two of them return safely he was overjoyed, though his eyes nearly leapt out of his head at the same time.

"What the heck happened to you, Sis? You fall off your horse and bust your behind or something?"

"Oh, you hush up! It's nothing, really. I'm just making D do this to make up for all the worrying he put us through," Doris shouted from her place on D's back. D was carrying her piggyback.

Her nerves had borne her through heated battles with two equally fiendish adversaries—the Count last night and Rei-Ginsei this morning—but the instant she stepped out of the foggy world and heard D tell her, "You're all right now," her nerves had just snapped. The next thing she knew, she was on his broad back and he was treading the road home. "Hey, that's not funny. Put me down," she had cried, her face flushing bright red. D quickly complied, but Doris, seemingly overcome with relief, couldn't muster any strength in her legs. They wobbled under her when they touched the ground, forcing her to sit on the spot. And so he had carried her the rest of the way to the farm.

D carried Doris right on into her room and put her to bed. The second she felt the spring of the mattress beneath her, she dropped off to sleep, but at that moment she got the distinct impression she heard a vulgar voice laugh and say, "She had a nice big butt on her. Sometimes this job has its perks."

When the sun was getting ready to set, Doris awoke. Dr. Ferringo had long since returned to town, and D and Dan were busy repairing the door and hallway damaged in the previous night's conflict. "Don't bother with that, D, we can take care of it ourselves. You've got to be worn out enough as it is."

On the way back to the farm from the ruins, D hadn't really told her the circumstances that had prevented him from returning the night before. He'd simply said, "I blew it."

She understood that he meant he'd failed to destroy the Count. But beyond that, he didn't say anything like, "Sorry I was gone so long," or ask, "Did anything happen last night?" Quite peeved by that, Doris subjected him to a somewhat exaggerated account of the evening's events. She didn't even think it particularly odd that things she'd normally be too terrified to speak of now rolled right off her tongue, simply because D was with her.

Once she'd finished, D said, "Good thing you are all right," and that was the end of it. It seemed a cold and insolent thing to say, but it left Doris thoroughly satisfied nonetheless, and if she was a fool for that, then so be it.

At any rate, she somehow knew D had done battle with the Count, and that, in addition, he'd had some other far from ordinary experience. That was why she said he must be worn out.

"Aw, that's okay," Dan countered. "My big brother D here is great at this stuff. Sis, you and I couldn't have handled all this in a month. Take a gander outside. He took care of everything—he refilled the weed-killers, fixed the fence, and even swapped out the solar panels."

"My goodness," Doris exclaimed in amazement.

Earning premium pay, a Hunter might keep up his own home, but she'd never heard of one helping his employer with repairs. Especially in D's case, where his reward was only… Doris' train of thought got that far before she flushed red. She remembered what she'd promised him before she brought him there to work. "Anyway, sit down over there and have a rest. I'll get dinner going straight away."

"We'll be done soon," D said, screwing the door hinges back into place. "It's been a while since I did this, and it's tougher than I thought."

"Yeah, but you're great at it," Dan interjected. "You tie the knot with him, Sis, and you're set for life."

"Dan!" Her voice nearly a shriek, she tried to smack the boy, but the little figure ducked her hand and scampered out the open door. Only the gorgeous youth and the girl of seventeen remained. The sun stained the edge of the prairie crimson, and the last rays of light spearing through the doorway gave the pair a rosy hue.

"D ..." Doris sounded obsessed as she said his name. "Uh, I was wondering, what were you planning on doing once your work here is done? If you're not in such a hurry, I was thinking ..."

"I'm not in a hurry, but we don't know if my work here will get finished or not."

Doris' heart sank. In her frailty, the girl instinctively reached out for support and piece of mind, only to run into this sledgehammer. There was no guarantee her foe would be destroyed. She'd been lucky to weather two assaults so far, but the battle still raged on.

"D," Doris said once again, the same word sounding like it came from a completely different person this time. "Once you finish up with that, come on back to the living room. I'd like to discuss what kind of strategy we should take from here on out."

"Understood."

The voice that came over his shoulder sounded satisfied.

T heir enemy was extraordinarily quick about making his "visit." That evening, Greco was out carousing with his hoodlum friends, trying to work off some of the rage they still felt from the beating they'd taken at the hands of Rei-Ginsei's gang. He was headed down a deserted street for home when he happened to see a strange carriage stop in front of the inn, and he quickly concealed himself in the shadows.

Stranger than strange, from the time the black carriage appeared out of the darkness till the time it came to a halt, it never made a single sound. The horses' hooves beat the earth clearly enough, and the wagon wheels spun, but not even the sound of the scattering gravel reached Greco's ears.

That there's a Noble's carriage...

This much Greco grasped. His drunken stupor dissipated instantly.

So, this is the prick that's after Doris? Curiosity—and feelings of jealousy toward this rival suitor—held Greco in place. The door opened and a single figure garbed in black stepped down to the ground. By the light of a lamp dangling from the eaves of the inn, the pallid countenance of a man with a supernatural air to him came into view. *I take it that's the lord of the manner then.*

Greco knew this intuitively. Though he'd never seen the man before, he matched the reliable descriptions of the fiend that'd been hammered into his head by village elders when he was still a child. Soon the carriage raced off, and the Count disappeared into the inn. *What the hell brings him into town?* Clouded as they were by low-grade alcohol, his brain cells weren't up to neatly fitting the Count, the inn, and Doris together, but they did manage to give him a push in the right direction and tell him, *Follow him, stupid.*

On entering the inn, Greco found the clerk standing frozen behind the counter. The clerk seemed to be under some sort of spell; his eyes were open wide and his pupils didn't track Greco's hand as he waved it up and down. Greco opened the register. There were ten rooms. All of them were on the second floor. And there was only one guest staying there. The register put him in room #207.

Name: Charles E. Chan. Occupation: Artist.

Careful not to make a sound, Greco padded lightly up the stairs and made his way down to the door of the room in question. Light spilled out through crevasses around the door. *The guest is a guy, so I don't suppose the vampire is here to drink his blood. Maybe he's one of the Count's cronies? I wonder if this clown had to call in help to try and make Doris his own.* Greco pulled out what looked like a stethoscope made of thin copper wire. Hunters swore by this sort of listening device. Quite a while back, Greco had won it in a rigged card game. The gossamer fairy wing, set in a tiny hole in the bell, could catch the voices of creatures otherwise inaudible to human ears, and those sounds were conveyed up the copper wire and into the listener's ears. Ordinarily, the device would be used when searching for the hiding places of supernatural creatures too dangerous to approach, or to listen in on their private conversations, but Greco had made an art out of putting it to the windows of all the young ladies in town. Securing its bell to the door with a suction cup, he put the ear tips in and began to listen. An eerie voice that was not of this world reverberated from the other side of the door. Greco put his eye to the keyhole for good measure.

Rei-Ginsei was astonished when the supposedly bolted door opened without a sound and a figure in black leisurely strolled in. Quickly realizing the intruder was a Noble, he puzzled over the meaning of the visit even as he reached for the shrike-blades on the desk.

The intruder gazed at him with glittering eyes as he made a truly preposterous proposal. "I know all about you and your cohorts," the figure in black said. "That you wiped out a Frontier Defense Force patrol, and that you tried, and failed, to kill a certain young lady. I have business with that particular girl. However, someone remains in my way. That was the person you encountered out in the fog, the one you were powerless to stop."

"What on earth could you be referring to?" Rei-Ginsei asked, with feigned innocence. "I am but a simple traveling artisan. The mere mention of such sordid goings-on is enough to chill my blood."

The black-garbed intruder laughed coldly and tossed a silver badge onto the bed. It had belonged to an FDF patrolman. "I know you believe all the horses and corpses were eaten or burned, and their ashes scattered to the four winds, but unfortunately such is not the case," the voice said coolly. "Monitoring devices in my castle are linked to a spy satellite stationed overhead, and when I awake, it keeps me minutely informed of movements on the Frontier. That badge was reconstructed from molecules of ash recovered at the site, and I also have images of you and yours taken during the attack, and beamed down from the satellite. I needn't tell you what would happen should this information be sent to not only this village, but also every place the lowly human race calls home."

Having heard that much, Rei-Ginsei hurled a shrike-blade. It struck an invisible barrier in front of the fearsome blackmailer's heart and imbedded itself in the floor. In truth, it was then that Rei-Ginsei gave up.

"There is the girl who eludes me to consider as well, " the voice continued. "I shouldn't be surprised if she were to pay a call on the sheriff tomorrow, and I assure you she would tell him all about you and your cohorts. I suppose the reason you've taken up lodging here in town alone is to kill the girl before she can do so, but as long as she has that man by her side, you'll not have an easy time of it. After all, your foe is a dhampir—he has the blood of my kind in him. No matter which course you choose, naught save doom awaits your group."

"Then why would you tell me this? What would you have us do?"

The reason Rei-Ginsei's tone was surprisingly calm was because the intruder had been right on all points but one, and he'd decided that putting up any more of a struggle would be futile.

"I thought I might lend you some assistance," the voice said—a remark that was quite unexpected. "So long as the stripling that's frustrating my efforts is slain, and the girl comes into my possession, I have no interest in what happens in the lowly world of mankind."

"But how?"

A vicious, vulgar light shone in Rei-Ginsei's eyes. He realized he might have a chance now to slay the young punk—his opponent back in the fog. That was the one point on which the

Count had been mistaken. He hadn't left his three henchmen camped in the woods and come into town alone to keep the girl from talking. Well, that had been part of the plan, but his true aim was much more personal. He'd had the little bird where he could rip her wings off, tear her legs off, and wring her dainty neck, and his foe had taken her right out from under his nose. Worse yet, he'd known the humiliation of being paralyzed by a ghastly aura that kept him from lifting a finger against his foe, and he'd had the invincible shrike-blade he prided himself on knocked from the air with a single blow. He'd gone into town to see to it his foe paid for all these things. It was malice. Just as full of hatred and longing for vengeance as he was, his henchmen agreed to his plan. He returned to town alone to be less conspicuous as he looked for the girl and his mysterious foe.

However, wait as he might at the entrance to town, there was no sign of his prey. In asking around, he only managed to learn what the girl's name was and where she lived. Normally he would've gone right out there and attacked her, but the proven strength of this other enemy—who no one in town had been able to identify—was enough to throw cold water on the wildfire that was his malice. He'd left town again briefly to meet with his cohorts and order them to keep an eye on Doris' farm. Then he went back into the village to gather as much information as possible on his enemy for his own murderous purposes. And, while he hadn't exactly gathered any information, he now had a more powerful ally than he ever could've imagined standing right before him.

"How shall we do it?" Rei-Ginsei asked once again.

"This is what you should do."

Discussions between the demon in black and the gorgeous fiend went on for some time.

Presently, the visitor in black dropped something long, thin, and candle-like on the bed.

"That's Time-Bewitching Incense. It's a tool for turning day to night, or night to day. This is an especially potent version. Light it when you're near him, then quickly extinguish it again. That should throw his defenses off. That's when you kill him. However, just to keep you from getting any ideas about other uses you might put this to, it can only be used twice. You have only to give it a good shake and it should light."

"Please, wait a moment," Rei-Ginsei cried out, hoping to stop the departing figure. "I have one additional favor to ask of you."

"A favor?" The shadowy figure sounded both puzzled and angered.

"Yes, sir." With a nod and a smile, Rei-Ginsei made his outlandish request. "I ask that you make me one of the Nobility. Oh, you needn't be so angry about it. Please, simply hear me out. I have to wonder why you bothered selecting me as your partner in this. If this incense alone is enough to do the trick, there must be any number of humans you could have entrusted this to. We live in times where parents will kill their own child for a gold coin and a new spear. And yet, the very fact that you went to all the trouble of coming to see me is proof enough that you need someone of my skill in order to kill the dhampir. I know a thing or two about dhampirs myself. I know they tend to be the very worst sort of enemy you could ever make. And there's something so powerful, so terrifying about the one we're dealing with now, it cuts me to the quick. That is no ordinary dhampir. With all due respect, it's not enough to merely have you overlook my group's misdeeds. I do not ask the same favor for all four of my party—I alone would like to rise to the hallowed ranks of the Nobility."

The shadowy figure fell silent.

Anyone with a heart who heard Rei-Ginsei's overture would've wanted to scream "Traitor!"—to say nothing about what his three henchmen might have done—but then the world has never lacked for turncoats. Even as they hated and feared them like demons from hell, deep in their heart of hearts people looked at the dreaded vampires with a covetous gaze. Power and immortality had such an alluring scent.

"What say you?" Rei-Ginsei asked, pressuring his visitor for a response.

The shadowy figure gave a nod, and Rei-Ginsei nodded in return.

"Then thy will be done."

"See to it."

The shadowy figure left the room. He still had another visit to pay before he returned to his castle. By the guttering lamplight, he failed to notice the other person in the hallway.

The Bloody Battle—
Fifteen Seconds Each

CHAPTER 6

I t was early the next morning that Dan's disappearance came to light.

Weary as she was from her deadly battle the previous night and from staying up almost all night preparing for the Count's attack, Doris failed to notice her younger brother racing out to the prairie at the crack of dawn.

Having told D the details of her run-in with Rei-Ginsei and his gang, Doris had decided to go see the sheriff today to inform him. Though Dan had been told not to leave the farm until they were ready to go into town, the boy was just bursting at the seams with energy. Apparently he'd switched off the barrier and gone out alone with a laser rifle to hunt some mist devils.

Fog-like monsters that slipped in with the morning mist, the creatures were a nuisance on the Frontier mainly because they had a propensity for dissolving their way through crops and the hides of farm animals. They didn't fare well against heat, however, and a blast from a laser beam was enough to destroy them. Being rather sluggish, they posed little threat to an armed boy used to dealing with them.

Hunting mist devils was really Dan's specialty.

Soon after she awoke, Doris realized her brother wasn't on the farm. She raced frantically to the weapon storeroom and saw that he'd taken his rifle, which let her relax for a moment. But when she ran outside to call him back in, she froze in her tracks at the entrance to the farm.

His laser rifle had been left as a paperweight on a single sheet of paper that was lying on the ground, right in front of the gate. The following words were written on the page in elegant lettering:

Your brother is coming with us. The Hunter D is to come alone at six o'clock Evening to the region of ruins where we met the other day. Our goal is simply to ascertain which Hunter has the superior skills, and nothing more. We have no need of observers, not even you, Doris. Until this test of skill has been decided, you are to mention this to no one.

If you deviate from the above conditions in the least, a sweet little eight-year-old will burn in the fires of hell.

—*Rei-Ginsei.*

Doris felt every ounce of strength drain from her body as she returned to the house. She was still trying to decide whether or not she should show the letter to D when D noticed all was not right with her. Trapped in the gaze of his lustrous eyes, Doris finally showed him the letter.

"Well, half of it is true, at least," D said, as if the matter didn't concern him in the least, though it was quite clear he was being challenged to a duel.

"Half of it?"

"If he just wanted to face off against me, all he had to do was come here and say so. Since he took Dan, he must have another aim—to separate the two of us. The Count is behind this."

"But why would he have gone to all that trouble? It'd be a lot faster and easier if he'd said I was the one who had to come alone ..."

"One reason is because the author of this letter wants to settle a score with me. The other—"

"What would that be?"

"Using a child to get you would reflect poorly on the honor of the Nobility."

Doris' eyes blazed with fury. "But he really is using Dan to—"

"Most likely his abduction is the only part of the plan Rei-Ginsei and his gang came up with."

"The honor of the Nobility—don't make me laugh! Even if it wasn't his idea, if he approves of it it's the same damned thing. Nobility my ass—they're nothing but blood-sucking monsters!" After she spat the words like a gout of flame, Doris was shocked at herself. "I'm sorry, you're not like that at all. That was a rotten thing for me to say."

Tears quickly welled in her eyes, and Doris broke down crying on the spot. The recoil from putting all her violent emotions into words had just hit her. Her situation was grim, with one misfortune after another piling onto her as if she was possessed by some evil spirit that drew all these calamities to her. In reality, it was amazing she hadn't surrendered to tears long before now.

As weeping shook her pale shoulders, a cool hand came to rest on them. "We can't have you forgetting you hired a bodyguard."

Even with the present state of affairs, D's voice remained soft. But within the coolly composed ring of his words, the ears of Doris' heart clearly heard another voice propped up by unshakable assurance. And this is what it seemed to say: *I promised to protect you and Dan, and you can be certain I will.*

Doris raised her face.

Right before her eyes was the face of an elegant, valiant young man gazing quietly at her.

It felt as something hot fell onto her full bosom.

"Hold me," she sobbed, throwing herself against D's chest. "I don't care what happens. Just hold me tight. Don't let me go!"

Gently resting his hands on the sob-wracked shoulders of the seventeen-year-old girl, D gazed out the window at the blue expanse of sky and the prairie filling with morning's life.

What was he thinking about? The safety of the boy, his four foes, the Count, or something else? The emotional hue that filled his eyes remained a single shade of cold, clear black. Before long, Doris pulled back from him. With a spent, sublime expression she said, "I'm sorry. That wasn't exactly in character for me. It's just … I suddenly got the feeling you might stay here with me forever. But that's not right. When your job's done, you'll be moving on, won't you?"

D said nothing.

"This is almost over. Something tells me that. But what are we gonna do about Dan?"

"I'll go, of course. I have to."

"Can you take them?"

"I'll bring Dan back, safe and sound."

"Please, see that you do. I feel awful making you look out for him, but I think I'm gonna head into town to hole up. I'll have Doc Ferringo put me up at his place. You know, he saved me the night before last. I'm sure I'll be fine this time, too."

Doris still didn't know that the real reason the Count had run off was the protective charm D had placed on her neck. And most likely the reason D said nothing when the girl told him she was going to the physician's home was because he knew he couldn't guarantee that the charm would ward off someone with the Count's power forever.

When the angle of the sunlight spearing through the window became sharp, the two of them got on their horses and left the farm. Regardless of what D had said, Doris' expression remained dark.

If anyone can bring back Dan, he can—she had no trouble making herself believe this. But she remembered how powerful his enemies were. She could still hear the shrike-blade screaming up behind her in the ruins; the horrid sight of her horse falling over with all four legs cut off was burned deep into her eyelids. Now there were four such fiends out there. A dark spot of despair remained in Doris' heart.

What's more, even if D made it back alive, if the Count were to strike while D was gone, there was no way she could escape him this time. She'd said nothing about it to D, but she still wasn't entirely sure going to Dr. Ferringo's was the right thing to do.

On entering town, countless eyes focused on the pair as they rode down the main street. The looks were colored more by fear than by hate. For people on the Frontier, who lived surrounded by dark forests and monsters, a girl who'd been preyed on by a vampire and a young man with vampire blood in his veins were beyond the normal level of revulsion. Thanks to Greco, everyone had heard what had happened.

A little girl who seemed to recognize Doris said, "Oh, hi," and started to approach, but her mother wasted no time in pulling her back.

Among the men, there were some whose faces showed the urge to kill, and they reached for swords or guns the second they saw D. Not because they'd been told what he was, but rather because of the eerie aura that hung about him. All the women, however, looked like they would swoon as they watched him go by, and given how beautiful he was, that came as little surprise.

And yet, the pair made their way down the street without a single hot-head running out to stop them, and finally they arrived at a house with the sign "Dr. Ferringo" hanging from the eaves.

Doris got down off her horse and rang the bell, and presently the woman from next door, who acted as a nurse and watched the place while Doc was out, answered. Apparently ignorant of Doris' situation, she smiled and stated, "Doc's been out since this morning. It seems there was someone out at Harker Lane's house that needed urgent care and he went off to see to 'em. He left a note saying he'd be back around noon, but where he's still not back yet, he may be dealing with something serious. You know, the lady of the house out there is apt to put anything in season into her mouth, even if it's a numbleberry or a topsy-turvy toadstool." Lane was a huntsman, and his home was out in the middle of the woods, two hours of hard riding from town. "I hate it when this happens. On my own I can't do much besides treat scrapes and hand out sedatives, but since everyone always says that's good enough I've been running myself ragged all morning. Why don't you come in and wait. I'm sure Doc will be back soon, and if you're willing, I could sure use the help."

Uncertain about what to do, Doris looked to D. Sitting on his horse, he gave her the slightest nod.

She decided. Giving a bow to the housewife—who was watching D with starry eyes—Doris said, "It looks like I'll be in your hair until Doc gets back then." She sounded a little tense, but that was unavoidable. While she thought D would come with her, as soon as he saw she'd made up her mind, he started to ride off slowly.

"Dear me, isn't he with you?" the woman asked Doris excitedly. She didn't even try to hide her disappointment. At that point, before Doris could get angry at the thought of a woman of the nurse's age getting all worked up about D, she was sharing the woman's confusion.

"Hold on. Where are you headed?"

"Just taking a look around the perimeter."

"It's still midday. There's not going to be anything out. Stay with me."

"I'll be back soon."

D let his horse go on without once looking back.

After they'd gone a ways he took a left turn. In a needling tone, a voice asked, "Why don't you stick close to her? You mean to tell me you're so worried about that little tike you can't sit still? Or is just that you can't stand to see the suffering on his sister's face? Dhampir or not, seems you're still a little wet behind the ears. Heh heh heh. Or could it be you're in love with the girl?"

"Is that what you think?"

Just whom was D talking to?

The road ahead was a dusty path that continued on between walls of earth and stone. Aside from the lethargic, vexing rays of the sun as it moved past noon, there was no sign of anyone around. And yet, there was still that voice.

"No chance. You're not that kind of softy. After all, you've got *his* blood in your veins. It's perfect, the way you told them to call you D."

"Silence!"

Judging by the way the man in question had roared in reaction to his name, it seemed the voice had touched on a rather sensitive point.

An instant later his tone became soft once again. "You've been full of complaints lately. Would you like to split with me?"

"Oh no!" the voice exclaimed, sounding a touch threatened. But then, as if to avoid showing any weakness, it replied, "It's not like I'm with you because I like it. Well, you know how it goes— give-and-take makes the world go round. Not to change the subject, but why didn't you tell the girl about the mark you put on her neck? Out of loyalty to *your father?* Just a word from you would've put her at ease, I bet. It must be tough having the blood of the Nobility in you."

The voice sounded sincere enough, but the fact that its heart held an entirely different sentiment was made apparent by a burst of derisive laughter.

Still, one couldn't help but wonder if the young man had completely lost his mind to continue a dialogue with an imaginary companion as he sat there on his horse. But because the tone, quality, and everything else about the two voices were completely different, the weird scene only seemed possible through some truly ingenious ventriloquism.

D's eyes sparkled brilliantly, but soon reclaimed their usual, quiet darkness, and the conversation came to an end. Shortly thereafter he took a left at the next corner, came to a similar corner, and once again turned the same way. Eventually, he returned to the front of the physician's home.

"Any strange characters out there?" the voice once again echoed from nowhere in particular.

"None."

Given the way he'd answered, it seemed he had in fact gone off to check the surrounding area for any hint of anything out of the ordinary.

However, he showed no sign of dismounting as he lifted his beautiful visage and grimaced at the sun listing westward from the center of the sky.

"Is that all I can do?" he muttered. Perhaps some vision of the grisly battle to come flitted through his mind; for an instant, a certain expression rose on his oh-so-proper countenance, and then it was gone.

A few horses hitched up across the street suddenly grew agitated, and people walking by shielded their eyes from the dust kicked up by an unpleasantly warm wind blowing by without warning.

The momentary expression on D's face was the same one the Midwich Medusas had seen in the subterranean waterway—the face of a blood-crazed vampire.

Gazing for a brief moment at the closed door to the doctor's home, D reined his horse around and headed out of town. The ruins were two hours away.

"Here he comes. You should see him on top of the hill any minute," Gimlet said, returning with the wind in his wake. When Rei-Ginsei heard this news he pulled himself up off the stone sculpture he'd been leaning against. Gimlet was their lookout.

"Alone, I take it?"

"Yessir. Just like you told him."

Rei-Ginsei nodded, then addressed the other two henchmen who'd been standing there for some time like guardian demons at a temple gate, with their eyes running out across the prairie.

"Everyone is set, I see. Engage him just as we've planned."

"Yessir."

Nodding as Golem and Chullah bowed in unison, Rei-Ginsei walked to the horse hitched up behind him. The place the four of them had chosen for this showdown was the same bowl-like depression where Witch had been killed. Challenging D to a grudge match in the same location where D's aura had battered them and kept them paralyzed was just the sort of thing this vindictive ruffian would do, but consideration had also been given to how useful this location would be for restricting their opponent's movements when they fought him four against one.

Rei-Ginsei squatted next to Dan, who lay behind a rock, gagged and bound hand and foot, and pulled down the cloth covering the boy's mouth. Called a gag rag, the cloth was a favorite of criminals. The fabric was woven from special fibers that could absorb all sound, and its usefulness to kidnappers made it worth its weight in gold.

Still, there was no call for the cruelty displayed by keeping a boy barely eight years old gagged ever since the morning.

"Look, your savior is coming. I put this plan together yesterday after hearing about you and your sister, and I must confess it seems to be going beautifully."

Just as Rei-Ginsei finished speaking, the furious gaze that had been concentrated on him was colored by relief and confidence. Dan looked toward the hills.

Twisting his lips a bit, Rei-Ginsei sneered, "How sad. Neither of you is fated to leave here alive."

"Ha, you guys are the one who won't make it out of here alive." Worried and hungry and looking gaunt, Dan still managed to fling the reply with all his might. He hadn't been given so much as a drop of water since he'd been captured. "You have no idea how tough ol' D is!"

His words were strong, but they were also a childish bluff. He'd never even seen D fight.

Dan thought Rei-Ginsei might fly into a rage, but, to the contrary, Rei-Ginsei only smirked and turned his gaze to his three henchmen standing in the center of the depression. "You may be right. That would certainly mean less work for me."

Dan's eyes opened wide, as if he must have heard that wrong.

But it was true. This gorgeous fiend fully intended to bury his three underlings here along with D. At first he'd only intended to take care of D and Doris, who'd seen his face, but after receiving the Count's oath to turn him into one of the Nobility, Rei-Ginsei's plans had taken a complete turn. The power and immortality of a Noble would be his—he would no longer be a filthy brigand wandering the wilderness.

So, in accordance with the Count's plan, he left Doris for the Noble to handle, while he decided to add three more people to the pair the Count wanted him to kill. In his estimation, if he allowed his henchmen to live, he would come to regret it later.

If D should dispatch them all here, so much the better. But if luck is not with me and some survive, I shall kill them myself.

A solitary rider popped up over the hilltop. He didn't reduce his speed, but galloped toward them at full tilt.

"Well, time to make yourself useful." Grabbing hold of the leather straps that hung around the boy's back, Rei-Ginsei carried Dan over to his horse with one hand, like he was a piece of baggage. The shrike-blades on his hip rubbed together, making a harsh, grating noise. Groping in his saddlebag with his free hand, he pulled out the Time-Bewitching Incense. "That's strange," he said, tilting his head to the side.

"Boss!"

At Chullah's tense cry, Rei-Ginsei whirled around, still gripping the candle.

"D," Dan called out, his shout flying off on the wind.

Rei-Ginsei's sworn enemy had already dismounted and now stood at the bottom of the earthen depression with an elegantly curved longsword across his back.

"Dear Lord ..."

The beauty of his foe left Rei-Ginsei shocked ... and envious.

"I wish I could tell you what an honor it is to have one of my blades knocked down by a man of your kind, but I won't. The fact that you're a miserable cross between a human and a Noble takes the charm out of it."

To Rei-Ginsei's frigid smile and scornful greeting, D softly replied, "And you must be the bastard son of the Devil and a hellhound."

Rei-Ginsei's entire face grew dark. As if his blood had turned to poison.

"Let the boy go."

In lieu of a reply, Rei-Ginsei gave Dan's leather bonds a twist with one hand. An agonized cry split the boy's young lips.

"Ow! D, it really hurts!"

Though they looked like ordinary leather straps, they must have been tied with some fiendish skill, because they started pressing deep into Dan's shoulders and arms.

"These bonds are rather special," Rei-Ginsei said, twisting his lips into a grin and making a small circle with his thumb and forefinger. "Apply force from the right direction and they pull up tight like this. I figure for a child of eight, it should take twenty minutes or so for them to sink far enough into his flesh to choke the life out of him. If you haven't finished us all off by then, this boy will be cursing you from the hereafter. Does that light a little fire under you?"

"D ..."

What an utterly heartless tactic. The bonds had already begun working their way through his clothes. As the boy writhed in agony, D gave him a few powerful words of encouragement.

"This'll just take a minute."

Meaning he would take care of them in fifteen seconds each?

"O … okay."

Unlike the bravely smiling Dan, the four men were livid.

The ring formed by Rei-Ginsei's three henchmen began to tighten like a noose. All of them were painted by the vermilion rays of the setting sun, but the palpable lust for blood rising from each seemed to rob the light of its color.

"Now, let's show him what you can do one by one. Golem, you go first."

As his boss gave him the command, not only Golem but all three henchmen began to look dubious. After all, the initial plan had been for all four of them to attack at once and kill him. But a moment later, Golem's massive brown body raced toward D with the silent footfalls of a cat. The broad blade of his machete glittered in the red light. There was a loud clang! His machete was big enough to chop a horse's head off, but just as it was about to hack into the Hunter's torso, D drew his blade with lightning speed, bringing the tip of it down through Golem's left shoulder. Or rather, it looked like it was going to go right through his shoulder, but it bounced off him.

Golem the Tortureless—a man with muscles of bronze. His body had even proved itself impervious to high-frequency wave sabers.

Once again, Golem's machete howled through the air, and D skillfully dodged it with a leap that carried him yards away in an instant. And once again, the giant went after him, closing on the Hunter.

"What's wrong? You said fifteen seconds each!"

Like a cry to battle borne on the wind, D's angry roar shook the grass and filled the mortar-shaped depression in the earth.

D oris awoke from her nap as someone gently shook her shoulder. A warm, familiar face was smiling down at her.

"Doc! I must've dozed off while I was waiting for you."

"Don't worry about it. I'm sure you're exhausted. It took quite some time to take care of my patient at Harker's, and I've just gotten back here myself. I swung by your place and no one was there, so I hustled back with the sneaking suspicion I might find you here. Did something happen? Where's Dan and that young fellow?"

All her memories and concerns flooding back to her, Doris looked around. After D left, she'd helped the nurse deal with the patients, then she'd stretched out on a sofa in the examination room and fallen asleep.

There was no sign of the nurse, who'd apparently gone home, and the rows of houses and trees beyond the windowpanes were all steeped in red. The curtain was set to rise on her time for terror.

"Well ... the two of them are hiding out in Pedros. I figured I'd join 'em there once I'd paid my respects to you ..."

As she attempted to rise, a cool hand came to rest on her shoulder. Pedros was the name of a nearly deserted village the better part of a day's and a night's ride from Ransylva. Even at that, it was still their closest neighbor.

"Even though you'll have to get through at least one night before you arrive?"

"Uh, yeah."

As he peered at her face with an uncharacteristically hard gaze, Doris unconsciously looked down at the floor.

Giving a little nod, the elderly physician said, "Very well then, I'll press the matter no further. But if you're really going to go somewhere, there's a much better place for you." At these surprising words, Doris looked up at the old man's face. "I found it on my way back from Harker's place when I decided to go through the north woods."

Dr. Ferringo pulled a map out of his jacket pocket and unfolded it. The passing years had dulled his memory, so he often used this map of Ransylva and its surroundings anytime he had to travel far to treat a patient. It had a red mark on it in part of the north woods. It was a huge forest, the thickest in the area, and not a single soul in the village knew their way around the whole of it.

"Part of a stone wall caught my eye, and when I hacked away the bushes and vines covering it I found this place—ancient ruins. It appeared to be the remains of some sort of place of worship. It's pretty large, and I only examined a small portion of it, but I guess you could say luck was with us, because that stone wall was inscribed with an explanation of the site. It seems it was constructed to keep vampires at bay."

This left Doris completely speechless.

Now that he mentioned it, she could recall her father and his Hunter friends gathered around the hearth sharing stories about this place when she was a child. They said that far in the distant past, long before the Nobility rose to power in the world, people who'd been preyed on by vampires were locked up in a holy place and treated with incantations and electronics. Perhaps what Dr. Ferringo had discovered was one such facility.

"Then you mean to tell me if I'm in there, he can't get at me?"

"In all likelihood," Dr. Ferringo replied, smiling broadly. "At any rate, I imagine it's better than trying to reach Pedros now, or holing up here in my house. Shall we go out and give it a try?"

"Yes, sir!"

Less than five minutes later, the two of them were jolting along in Dr. Ferringo's buggy as it hastened down the dusky road to the north woods. They must have rode for nearly an hour. Ahead, tiny walls of trees blacker than the darkness came into view. This was the entrance to the forest.

"Woah!"

Once they were in the buggy, the elderly physician hadn't answered her no matter how she tried to get him to talk, but suddenly he'd given a cry and pulled back on the reins.

A small figure stood at the entrance to the forest. The face was unfamiliar to Doris, but with paraffin-pale skin and ivory fangs poking from the corners of her mouth—it had to be Larmica.

Doris grabbed the doctor by the arm as he prepared to lash the horses again. "Doc! That's the Count's daughter. What in the name of hell is she doing out here? We've got to get out of here, and fast!"

"That's odd," Dr. Ferringo muttered in an uncertain tone. "She shouldn't be here."

"Doc, hurry up and get this thing turned around!"

Seemingly frozen, the doctor didn't move at her desperate cries, while the woman in the white dress standing up ahead came toward them, smoothly gliding through the grass without appearing to move her legs in the least. Doris had already pulled her whip out and was on her feet.

She felt a powerful pull at her hands, and before she knew it her whip had been taken from her. Taken by Dr. Ferringo!

"Doc?!"

"So I was known until yesterday," Dr. Ferringo said, fangs sprouting in his mouth.

Come to think of it, the hand he'd placed on Doris' shoulder back at his hospital had been cold. And he was wearing a turtleneck shirt, which wasn't like him at all! The instant hopelessness and fear were about to wrack her body, a fist sank into the pit of her stomach, and Doris collapsed into the shotgun seat.

"Well done," said the lovely vampire, now hovering beside the buggy.

"Larmica, I presume. You honor me with your praise." With bloodshot eyes and a hunger-twisted mouth, Dr. Ferringo's smiling countenance was now that of a Noble. The previous night, he'd been attacked by the Count and made into a vampire.

The call on Harker's home, and the ancient vampire-proof ruins, were complete fabrications, of course. Taking his orders from the Count, he'd concealed himself in the basement by day, appeared in the evening at a time when D would already have left, and played his part in luring Doris out of town. If separated from D, Doris would surely turn to the doctor—the Count's assessment had been right on the mark.

"You're to bring the girl to my father, are you not? I believe I shall accompany you." Even though she was a fellow vampire, Dr. Ferringo donned a wary expression at Larmica's formal speech and the frigid gaze she turned on him.

He'd been commanded to bring Doris into the heart of the forest and to the waiting Count, but he hadn't heard that Larmica would be coming. And yet she suddenly appeared at the entrance to the forest and said she would go with him. Why wasn't she with her father? But the doctor had only just become the Count's servant, and it would be unpardonable for him to question his master's daughter. Opening the door to the buggy's backseat, he bowed and said, "Be my guest."

Larmica moved into the vehicle like a mystic wind.

The buggy took off.

"Rather fetching for a human, isn't she," Larmica mumbled, peering at the face of the unconscious Doris.

"That she is. When I was human, she was like a daughter to me, and I never had occasion to view her in any other light. But when I look at her now, she's so beautiful it's a wonder I never tried anything with her. To be quite frank, I intend to ask a favor of my lord the Count and see if he won't allow me to partake of a drop or two of her sweet, red blood in return for all my hard work—although I would not be so bold as to seek it from her throat."

These were the words of the kind and faithful old physician? Now he was lost in fantasies of slowly sucking the blood from the very girl who two days earlier he'd risked his life to protect. His teeth ground together greedily.

He heard Larmica's cheery voice behind him. "For the time being, allow me to give you my reward." Without even allowing him time to turn, she took the steel arrow she'd kept concealed and thrust it through the elderly physician's heart, killing him instantly. Tossing his body to the ground, Larmica sailed gracefully through the air, landed in the driver's seat, and quickly brought the horses to a halt. Taking a furtive glance at the woods, she said, "I dare say Father will be furious, but I simply cannot allow a lowly human worm to be made a member of the glorious Lee family—and I most certainly won't welcome one as his bride." When she turned her eyes on the still-sleeping Doris, they had the most lurid light to them. A wolf could be heard howling out on the distant plains.

"Human, I shall show you your place now—as I rip you limb from limb before delivering you to Father." She reached for Doris' throat with both hands. Her nails shone like razors.

In the middle of the wilderness, with no one to protect her, hemmed in by the darkness, the girl remained in her stupor, oblivious to the very real danger she was in.

That was the moment.

A weird sensation shot through every inch of Larmica's body. All her nerves were being pulled out and burned off, each and every cell was decaying with incredible speed. Black ichor squirted out through holes in her melting flesh, and she felt her intestines twist with the urge to vomit, as if the entire contents of her stomach had started to flow in reverse. That's what the sensation felt like.

It was almost as if the night that had just begun had suddenly become midday. A familiar scent struck Larmica's nose.

She had no idea how long it had been there, but a tiny speck of light burned in the darkness to her back. Apparently someone had heard Larmica's anguished cries, and there was the sound of cautious footsteps coming closer through the grass. In its hand, the figure held Time-Bewitching Incense.

Having dodged a third horizontal slash of the machete, D once again took to the air.

To anyone watching, it would have looked like the act of a beaten man. Every time D went on the offensive, the bronze giant kept his eyes—clearly his only weakness—well covered with his massive club of a forearm.

"Give 'em hell, D!"

Golem dismissed Dan's feverish support with a laugh. "Look, you're making the little baby cry—" The sentence went no further.

The four pairs of eyes on the two combatants bulged in their sockets. None of the spectators had any idea what had happened.

D had his right leg out behind him for balance, and his sword ready and pointing down at the ground. The way his blade moved was like a jump cut in a film. The part where it slashed through the air was missing, and it skipped straight to where it went into Golem's mouth, wide with laughter.

Though this freak could control the density of his musculature on the surface, an inch below, his body remained as soft as any other living creature's. D's sword slipped in through the only real opening in his defense aside from his eyes, and drove up to the top of his skull in one smooth thrust.

D must've been aiming for that ever since he discovered the giant's flesh couldn't be cut, but the way he found an opening at the end of the giant's chatter, and made the thrust literally faster than the eye could follow, was nothing short of miraculous.

"Gaaah—"

It was actually rather humorous the way the scream didn't escape the impaled giant until several seconds later. As his massive form dropped backwards, its toughness fading rapidly, D stepped closer and split the giant's skull with one emotionless slash of his sword. This time the giant didn't make a sound. The sight of their staunch friend falling—sending up a bloody mist a shade more crimson than the setting sun—snapped his spellbound compatriots back to their senses.

"Looks like you did it, punk. I'm up next," Chullah said in a voice that sounded crushed to death, but as he stepped forward he was checked by a human awl—Gimlet.

"What speed. Kid, I'm willing to put my life on the line to see which is faster—my legs or that freaking sword of yours." He was in front of D in a flash, like he'd ridden the wind over there, and he had a world-beating grin on his lips. Was it due to self-confidence, or was it the thrill in his bandit blood at meeting his worthiest opponent ever?

D held his sword at chest level, pointed straight at Gimlet's heart.

In an instant, his opponent vanished.

Dan gasped.

Looking in the brush to D's left, at the feet of a statue diagonally behind him, right behind his back—there was now a circle of countless Gimlets fifteen feet from him in any direction.

Gimlet—the man was as streamlined as the tool he was named for. As a result of a mutation, he was capable of superhuman bursts of speed in the vicinity of three hundred miles per hour. His body didn't sport a single hair, and his face was relatively free from sharp features; it was nature's way of reducing wind resistance during his superhuman sprints.

However, moving at super speed wasn't his only talent. He would run a few yards, pause for an instant, and then run some more. By doing this over and over, he could leave afterimages of himself hanging in midair.

The foe right before you would multiply and be to your left one second, to your right the next—what warrior wouldn't be distracted by that? Show him an opening for even an instant, and all the Gimlets to the front and to the rear, to the left and to the right, would brandish their bowie knives and move in for the kill.

Taking on Gimlet was the same as engaging dozens of opponents at the same time.

It came then as little surprise that quick-draw master O'Reilly hadn't even freed his precious pistol before he was dropped from behind.

D's gonna get himself killed! Tears glistened in Dan's eyes. Not so much tears of fear as of parting.

As he raced around doing his special technique, it was actually Gimlet who was horrified. *It's not that this bastard can't move, it's just that he won't let himself be moved!*

That's right. Eyes half closed, D stood without making the slightest movement. Gimlet knew better than anyone that D's tactic was the only way to negate his disorienting movement.

His powers could be used to their best advantage when his countless other selves made his enemy change their stance, forcing them to leave themselves open. Nevertheless, the gorgeous young man before him didn't look at him or change his stance. Gimlet was little more than a clown prancing around in circles.

"What, aren't you coming for me? Only three seconds left."

When that icy voice pushed him over the brink, was it despair or impatience that launched Gimlet at D's back? His murderous dash at three hundred miles per hour was met by the blade of Vampire Hunter D—who'd taken down a werewolf running at half the speed of sound. A flash of steel shot out, cutting Gimlet from the collarbone on his left side to the thoracic vertebrae on the right. Sending bloody blossoms of crimson into the air, the streamlined body of the runner hit the ground with incredible force.

The next battle was truly decided in a heartbeat.

"Look out behind you!"

D turned even faster than Dan could shout the words, and found a black cloud eclipsing his field of view. A massive swarm of minute poisonous spiders was pouring out of Chullah's back, riding the wind to attack him. No matter how ungodly his skill, D's sword couldn't possibly stop this.

However, Dan saw something as the wind roared.

D's left hand rose high above his head, and the black cloud that covered half the depression became a single line that was sucked into the palm of his hand. The roar was not the sound of a wind blowing out, but rather of air being sucked back in.

The cloud was gone like *that*.

D raced like a gale-force wind.

His head split by a silvery flash of light, Chullah fell backwards—but from the moment his beloved spiders had been lost, he'd been nothing more than an empty husk with the shape of a man.

"Forty-three seconds all told—nicely done." Rei-Ginsei watched D with fascination as the Hunter walked toward him, holding his bloody sword and not even breathing hard. Taking a shrike-blade from his belt, for some reason Rei-Ginsei slashed through the bonds that held Dan.

"D!"

Dan ran over to D without even bothering to rub his bruised arms and legs, and the Hunter gently put the boy behind a statue for safety's sake before squaring off against the last of his foes.

"I'm in a hurry. Let's do this!" Moving faster than his words, D's longsword made a horizontal slash that reflected the red sunset.

Barely leaping out of the way, Rei-Ginsei stood at the bottom of the depression that until now had served as an arena.

"Please, wait—" he said, unable to conceal the quavering of his voice. His shirt had a straight cut running from the right side of his chest to the left, the result of D's attack. D was ready to pounce on him.

"Wait—Miss Lang's life hangs in the balance!"

Those words left Dan paler than D. Satisfied at the hint of unrest showing in D's eyes, Rei-Ginsei felt his cheeks rise at last with his trademark angelic smile.

"What are you talking about?" Surprisingly, D's tone was as calm as ever.

"Miss Lang is with Dr. Ferringo, is she not?"

"So what if she is?" D said.

"Right about now, the girl is being delivered to the Count. The poor thing had no way of knowing the good doctor she trusts more than anyone became a servant of the Count last night."

"What?!"

Rei-Ginsei was shocked to see the look of naked surprise and remorse that came over D. He didn't know that D had personally escorted Doris to the doctor's house. "Come now. Relax, relax. I shall tell you exactly where they're to meet the Count. That is, if you agree to what I propose."

"And what proposition would that be?"

"That the two of us replace the Nobles," Rei-Ginsei said, his voice brimming with confidence. "I have an arrangement with Count Lee. If he can take possession of the girl as a result of me slaying you, I shall be made one of the Nobility. To be perfectly honest, if I decided to kill you, there's still a very good chance I would succeed. However, having seen you in action for myself, I've had a change of heart. Even if I were to be made a Noble, as the good doctor was, I'm certain that, as a former human, I would be treated as a servant. I would prefer to become the Count instead." Having rattled all that off in a single breath, Rei-Ginsei paused. Tinged with a hint of blue, the glow of sunset left delicate shadows on his beautiful profile. The shadows made his visage so indescribably weird that Dan trembled in the safety of the statue.

"In the world today, what keeps the Count in that position, aside from his immortality as a vampire? It's his castle, and the fear that's been fostered in the hearts and minds of the populace since ancient times. It's that and that alone. They had their time once. But now they lie shrouded in the afterglow of destruction, vanishing into the depths of legend. If you and I should join forces, we could do so much—kill the Count and all his followers, claim their fortune and their throne as the new Nobility. We might even bring the majesty of true Nobles into the world with no destruction."

D watched Rei-Ginsei's face. Rei-Ginsei watched D's.

"You are already a dhampir—half Nobility. Let me pretend I have killed you and have the Count drink my blood. And then ..." Rei-Ginsei laughed, "Surely there has never been such an exquisite couple in the entire history of the Nobility."

Rei-Ginsei's laughter was cut short by what D said next. "You like to kill, don't you?"

"Huh?"

"It's only fitting the Nobility be destroyed."

In a flash, Rei-Ginsei was leaping away for the second time. In midair he shouted, "You fool!"

Count Lee's daughter had called D exactly the same thing once.

Three flashes of black shot from his right hip. One flew over D's head, arced, and came at him from the rear. One zipped right along the ground, clipping every blade of grass it touched until it turned up at his feet and shot toward his armpit. And one came straight at the Hunter as a distraction. Each was a shrike-blade unleashed on a different course with breathtaking speed.

However ...

All of Rei-Ginsei's murderous implements were knocked out of the air with a beautiful sound.

A pained cry of "Ah" could be heard from the bushes, as Rei-Ginsei's left hand was severed at the elbow. It flew through the air, a candle still held tight in its fist. D, who'd rushed to where Rei-Ginsei had landed the moment he'd fended off the three attacks, had chopped it off.

As blood spilled from Rei-Ginsei—just as it had from his three companions—his expression said less about his pain than it did of his disbelief. At the same time he was hurling his shrike-blades, he shook the Time-Bewitching Incense, but it hadn't given off its beguiling scent. In fact, the candle hadn't even lit. It's a fake! *But when was it switched, and who could've done it?!*

As agony and suspicion churned together in his gorgeous face, a naked blade was thrust under his nose.

"Where is Miss Lang?"

"How foolish," Rei-Ginsei groaned as he pressed down on his bloody, dripping wound. "Out of some duty you feel for no more than a human girl, you would cut me down—me, a human who told you of my contempt for the Noble, and that I would take his life. Accursed one, thy name is dhampir ... You share the Noble's world by night and the mortal's by day, but are accepted by neither. You shall spend all the days of your life a resident of the land of twilight."

"I'm a Vampire Hunter," D said softly. "Where is Miss Lang? That face you're so fond of will be the next thing I carve."

There was something about his words that wasn't a mere threat. The ghastly aura that had stopped Rei-Ginsei in his tracks that time in the fog now hit him with several times its previous power. Rei-Ginsei heard his words come out of his mouth of their own volition, due to a terror beyond human ken. "The forest ... Go straight in at the entrance to the north woods ... "

"Fine." D's ghastly aura died down instantly.

Rei-Ginsei's body shot up like a spring, and was pierced by a flash of silver.

And yet it was D that fell to one knee with a low moan.

"What?! That's impossible ... " It was only right that Dan exclaimed this as he peeked around the statue.

As Rei-Ginsei was leaping into the air, D's sword slid into his belly in the blink of an eye. Half the blade's length had clearly gone into his opponent. And yet the tip of the blade had emerged from D's own abdomen!

"Damn!" Rei-Ginsei spat, leaping away. And as he did, something even stranger happened—naturally the sword in D's hand came out of Rei-Ginsei's belly, but at exactly the same rate the blade jutting from D's stomach pulled back *into the Hunter's body!*

Dan watched in astonishment.

"I see now. I'd heard there were mutants like you," D muttered. Not surprisingly, he was still down on one knee, and wincing ever so slightly. A deep red stain was spreading across the bottom of his shirt. "You're a dimension-twister, aren't you, you son of a bitch? That was close."

Having leapt ten feet away, Rei-Ginsei's eyes sparkled, and a loathsome groan escaped his throat. "I can't believe you changed your target at the last second ... "

Here's what they meant by "that was close" and "you changed your target."

Rei-Ginsei hadn't beat back the pain of his severed arm and leapt up to launch an attack of his own. He expected to have his own heart pierced by D's sword. At that instant, the sword was indeed headed straight for his chest, but at the last second it pulled back and pierced his stomach.

That was why he shouted, "Damn"—Rei-Ginsei realized D had noticed the way he'd adjusted the speed of his leap so his chest would be right where the Hunter could stab it. After all, a single thrust through the same vital spot as vampires could kill dhampirs too. Still, why had he resorted to such an outrageous tactic—allowing himself to be stabbed to kill his opponent?

Rei-Ginsei was a dimension-twister; through his own willpower, he could make a four-dimensional passageway in any part of his body but his arms and legs and link it with the body of his foe. In other words, when his foe attacked him, the bullets and blades that broke his skin would all travel through extra-dimensional space into the body of his assailant, where they would become real again. A bullet that was supposed to go through his heart would explode from the chest of the person that fired it;

bringing a vicious blade down on his shoulder would only split your own. What attack could be more efficient than that?

After all, he simply had to stand there, let his attackers do as they pleased, and his foes would die by their own hands.

But Rei-Ginsei leapt away. A belly wound wasn't life threatening for a dhampir, and he was badly wounded himself.

"I'll see to it you pay for my left hand another time!" he could be heard to say from somewhere in the bushes, and then he was gone without a trace.

"D, it's all right now—oh, you're bleeding!"

Ignoring Dan's cries as the boy ran over to him, D used his sword like a cane and got right up.

"I don't have time to chase after him. Dan, where's the north woods?"

"I'll show you the way. But it'll take three hours to ride there from here." The boy's voice was filled with boundless respect and concern. The sun was already poised to dip beneath the edge of the prairie. The world would be embraced by darkness in less than thirty minutes.

"Any shortcuts?"

"Yep. There is one, but it cuts right through some mighty tough country. There are fissures, and a huge swamp…"

D gazed steadily at the boy's face. "What do you say we give it a shot?"

"Sure!"

Death of a Vampire Hunter

I t was Greco who'd used the Time-Bewitching Incense to save Doris. The morning after he eavesdropped on the conversation between Rei-Ginsei and the Count, Greco had one of the thugs who usually watched out for him pose as a visitor and call Rei-Ginsei down from his hotel room to the lobby. The thug was gone before Rei-Ginsei got there, however, and by the time Rei-Ginsei returned to his room, the Time-Bewitching Incense had been replaced with an ordinary candle that looked just like it. With the incense in his possession, Greco had kept watch on Dr. Ferringo's house, and when the vampire-physician left with Doris, he'd followed after them but kept far enough back so they wouldn't notice.

He intended to rescue Doris and bind her fast with the shackles known as obligation. And, if the fates were kind, he would also slay their feudal lord, the Count. In one fell swoop, he would become a big man in town, and he had ambitions of heading to the Capital. The fact that he had single-handedly dispatched a Noble would clearly be his greatest selling point to the Revolutionary Government, and his best chance to win advancement into their leadership.

However, the situation had changed somewhat. The buggy was supposed to go straight to the Count, but it had stopped when a girl in white suddenly appeared, and on top of that, the very same girl staked Dr. Ferringo. No longer sure exactly what was going on, Greco was convinced that something had gone wrong. He got closer to the wagon. Seeing the vampiress and her lurid expression as she prepared to sink her claws into Doris' throat, he'd given the Time-Bewitching Incense a desperate shake.

Timid at first, when he saw Larmica writhing in agony and he approached the buggy with his head held high. The incense was in his left hand. In his right hand, he was gripping a foot-long stake of rough wood so fiercely that it pressed into his fingers. Stakes were everyday items on the Frontier. The ten-banger pistol holstered at his waist with the safety off, and the large-bore heat-rifle stuck through the saddle of the horse he'd tethered in the trees, were for dealing with the Nobility's underlings. His beloved combat suit was in the shop for repairs, just like most of his flunkies' gear.

"Oh," Doris groaned as she got up. In her writhing, Larmica must've struck some part of Doris' body and brought her around. Her eyes were torpid for a brief moment, but they opened wide as soon as she noticed Larmica. Then she looked at Dr. Ferringo's body, lying on the ground not far from the buggy, and at Greco and said, "Doc ... why in the world?...What are you doing way out here?"

"So that's the thanks I get," Greco said, clambering up into the backseat of the buggy. You know, I kept that bitch from making chunky splatter out of you. I followed you out here from town in the dark of night. You'd think that'd win a little favor from you."

"Did you kill Doc, too?"

Doris' voice shook with sorrow and rage.

"What, are you kidding? The bitch did it. Although, it did making rescuing your ass a little easier."

Being careful not to let the tiny flame go out, Greco moved Larmica into the backseat with his other hand. The young lady in white curled up under the seat without offering the slightest resistance. Not only was she deathly still, but she also seemed to have stopped breathing.

"That's the Count's daughter. Was she responsible for turning Doc into a vampire, too?"

"No, that was the Count. See, he attacked him last night so he could use him to lure you out here." Greco quickly shut his mouth, but it was too late.

Doris stared at him with fire in her eyes. "And just how the hell do you know all this? You knew he was gonna be attacked and you didn't even tell him, did you? You dirty bastard! What do you mean you saved me? You're only looking out for yourself!"

"Shut your damn mouth, you!" Turning away from her burning gaze, Greco reasserted himself. "How dare you go talkin' to me that way after I saved your life. We can hash that out later. Right now, we've got to decide what to do about her."

"Do about her?" Doris knit her brow.

"Sure. As in, do we kill her or use her as a bargaining chip to negotiate with the Count."

"What!? Are you serious?"

"Dead serious. And don't act like this don't concern you. I'm doing all this for you."

Doris was in a daze as she watched the young tough make one preposterous statement after another. Then her nose twitched ever so slightly. She'd caught the scent of the Time-Bewitching Incense.

Come to think of it, the moonlit night felt strangely like a brilliant, sunny day. Greco said with pride, "The perfume in this candle is to thank. The Nobility has them, and apparently they can change day into night and vice versa. As long as it's lit, the bitch can't move a muscle and the Nobility can't come near us—which is what got me thinking. It'd be so easy to kill her, but considering how she's the Count's daughter, there'd be hell to pay later. So, we take her hostage to set up a trade, then take the Count's life, too, if all goes well."

"Could you ... could you really do that?" Her plaintive voice made Greco's lips twist lewdly, and when Doris averted her gaze she saw the pale face of Larmica as she lay beneath the backseat breathing feebly.

Larmica was lovely, and didn't look very far in age from herself. Doris felt ashamed for having considered for even a moment using the young lady as a bargaining chip.

"Noble or not, there ain't a parent out there who don't love their own daughter. That's how we can trip him up good. We'll say we want to trade her for some treasure. Then when he comes out all confident, bang, we use the incense to nab him and drive this here stake through his heart. Rumor has it their bodies turn into dust and disappear, but if someone like my father or the sheriff is there to see it, they'd make a first-class witness when I give the government in the Capital my account."

"The Capital?"

"Er, forget I mentioned it." In his heart, Greco thumbed his nose at her. "At any rate, if we kill 'em, the two of us will get the Noble's stuff—their fortune, weapons, ammo, everything! All for the huge service to humanity we'll be doing."

"But this woman ... she hasn't done anything to anyone in the village," Doris said vehemently, sifting through everything she could remember hearing since childhood.

"Open your eyes. A Noble's a Noble. They're all bloodsucking freaks preying on the human race."

Doris was dumbstruck. This coarse thug had just hurled the same curse on them that she had once said to D! *I was just like him then. That's not right. Even if they are Nobles, I can't use someone's helpless daughter to lure them to their death.* Just as Doris was about to voice her objections, a voice dark as the shadows held her tongue.

"Kill me ... here ... and now ..."

Larmica.

"What's that?" Greco sneered down at her in his overbearing manner, but her expression was so utterly ghastly it took his breath away. Even as she was subjected to the agony of her body burning in the midday sun, she showed incredible willpower.

"Father ... is not so foolish he would exchange his life for my own. And I will not be a pawn in your trade ... Kill me ... If you don't ... I shall kill you both someday ..."

"You bitch!" Greco's face seemed to boil with anger and fear, and then he raised his stake. As a rule, he hadn't had much self-restraint to start with.

"Stop it! You can't do that to a defenseless person!" As she spoke, Doris grabbed his arm.

The two of them struggled in the buggy. Strength was in Greco's favor, but Doris had fighting skills imparted to her by her father. Suddenly letting go of his arm, she planted her left foot firmly and put the full force of her body behind a roundhouse kick that exploded against Greco's breastbone.

"Oof!"

The cramped buggy, with its unsteady footing, was too much for him. Greco reeled back, caught his leg on the door, and fell out of the vehicle.

Not even looking at where the dull thud came from, Doris got out of her seat and tried to talk to Larmica. "Don't worry. I'm not gonna let that jerk do anything to you. But I can't very well just send you on your merry way, either. You know who I am, right? You'll have to come back to my house with me. We'll figure out what to do about you there."

A low chuckle that seemed to rise from the bowels of the earth cut off all further comment from Doris. "You are free to try what you will, but I won't be going anywhere." Doris thought her spine had turned to ice when she saw the beautiful visage look up at her, paler than moonlight and filled now by an evil grin of confidence. She didn't know what had just happened. When Greco had fallen from the buggy, the Time-Bewitching Incense had gone out!

Larmica caught hold of Doris' hand with a grip as cold as ice. In the darkness, Doris' eyes made out pearly fangs poking over the lips of the child of night as she got to her feet.

Doris was pulled closer with such brute strength Greco couldn't even begin to compare. She couldn't move at all. Larmica's breath had the scent of flowers. Flowers nourished with blood. Two silhouettes, two faces overlapped into one.

"Aaaagh!" A scream stirred the darkness, and then was gone. Trembling, Larmica shielded her face.

There in the dark she'd seen it. No, she'd felt it. Felt the pain of the same holy mark of the cross her father had seen on the girl's neck two days earlier! It would make its sudden appearance only when the breath of a vampire fell on it.

The vampires themselves didn't know why they feared it. All that was certain was that even without seeing it their skin could feel its presence. In that instant some nameless force bound them. This was the mark they couldn't allow humans to know about, something that had supposedly sunk into the watery depths of forgetfulness thanks to ages of ingenious psychological manipulation—so how could this girl have the holy mark on her neck?

Though Doris didn't understand why Larmica—who'd enjoyed an overwhelming advantage until a second earlier—had suddenly lost her mind, she surmised that she'd been saved. Now she had to run!

"Greco, you all right?"

"Oooh, kind of." The dubious response that came from the ground beside her suggested he might have hit his head.

"Hurry up and get in! If you don't get your ass in gear I'll leave you out here!"

And with that threat she took the reins in hand and gave them a crack. She intended to throw Larmica off with a sudden jolt forward. But the horses didn't move.

Doris finally noticed a man wearing an inverness standing in front of the horses and holding them by their bridles. For some time now, a number of figures had been standing at the edge of the woods.

"As the doctor was late, I thought something might be amiss, and my suspicions proved correct," one of the silhouettes said in a voice of barely suppressed rage. It was the Count. Though her heart was sinking into hopelessness, Doris was still the same warrior woman who'd bitterly resisted the Count all along. Seeing that the whip Doc had taken from her earlier was lying on the seat beside her, Doris snatched it up and swung it at the man in the inverness.

"Huh?" Doris cried, and the man—Garou—grinned broadly. She was sure she'd split the side of his face open, but he bobbed his head out of the way and caught the end of the whip between his teeth. Grrrrr! With a bestial growl he—it—started chewing up Doris' whip, a weapon that had stood up to swords without a problem.

"You're a werewolf," Doris shouted in surprise.

"That's correct," the Count responded. "He serves me, but unlike me he is rather hot-blooded. Another thing you may wish to consider—I told him that, should you give us any trouble, he had my permission to hurt you. It might be amusing to see a bride missing some fingers and toes."

Suddenly a boom rang out. Still flat on his ass on the ground, Greco had fired off his ten-banger. High-power powder—the type that could easily punch a hole through the armor of larger creatures—enveloped the Count and those near him in flames. The Count didn't even glance at Greco, and the flames were promptly swallowed by the darkness. Such was the power of the Count's force field.

"Raaarrrrr!" The werewolf snarled at Greco. Halfway through its transformation, it glared at Greco with blood-red eyes. Greco gave a squeal and froze. White steam rose from the crotch of his pants. Fear had gotten the better of his bladder, but who could blame him?

Doris' shoulders sank. The last bit of will she possessed was thoroughly uprooted.

"Father ... "

Larmica drifted down to the ground like a breeze. With glittering eyes, the Count gave her a hard look and said, "I have an excellent idea of what you were trying to do. Daughter or not, this time I'll not let you get away with it. You shall be punished on our return to the castle. Now stand back!" Ignoring Larmica as she headed silently to the rear, the Count extended a hand to Doris.

"Well, now, you had best come with me."

Doris bit her lip. "Don't be so pleased with yourself! No matter what happens to me, D is gonna send you all to the hereafter."

"Is he really?" The Count forced a smile. "Right about now the stripling and your younger brother are both being taken care of by our mutual acquaintances. In a fair fight, he might have prevailed, but I gave his foes a secret weapon."

"Father ... " From the tree line to the Count's rear, Larmica pointed to where Greco crouched on the ground. "That man had Time-Bewitching Incense."

"What!" Even through the darkness the sudden contortion of the Count's face was clear. "That cannot be. I gave it to Rei-Ginsei." Here he paused for a beat, and after closely scrutinizing his daughter's face said, "I can see that you speak the truth—which means the stripling is—"

"Correct."

A low voice made all who stood there shrink in fear. The Count looked over his shoulder again, and Doris' eyes darted in the same direction—toward Larmica. Or rather, toward something looming from the trees to her back. A figure of unearthly beauty.

"I'm right here."

A groan that fell short of speech spilled from the Count's throat.

Never did I imagine this rogue might come back alive …

If Time-Bewitching Incense hadn't played its pivotal role in the duel, the Hunter's survival was far from impossible. But unless he had an aircraft of some sort, it should've taken D another hour by horse to cover the distance from the site of his duel with Rei-Ginsei.

And yet D was here. He had been one with the darkness, and neither the Count's night-piercing gaze nor the three-dimensional radar of the robot sentries had detected him.

The robot sentries turned in D's direction, but an attack was impossible, of course.

"Don't try anything funny—I'll show her no mercy." Garou was just about to pounce on Doris when a low but not particularly rough voice stopped him in his tracks.

"Doris, you and what's-your-name—bring the wagon over here. Be quick about it!"

"Ye—yessir!" Doris answered dreamily, not just because of the relief she felt in being rescued, but because D had called her by name for the first time ever.

"Garou, grab the girl," the Count commanded sharply.

As the black figure prepared once again to leap up into the buggy, it was buffeted with another castrating voice—Doris'. "You come near me and I'll bite my tongue off!"

The werewolf snarled loudly and stopped. So many irritations. Greco flopped into the buggy.

"I'm prepared to die before I'd ever become one of your kind. If it's gotta be here and now, that won't bother me." The threats of an insignificant human—a mere girl of seventeen—silenced the Count. To all appearances, D and Doris had won this *outré* encounter. The Count was obsessed with Doris, and would have her at any price. Conversely, if Doris were to die, that would be the end of everything.

"We shall settle this another time."

The buggy stirred the night air as it sped to D's side, and the Count put his arm around Larmica's shoulder for the first time. The next instant, the two figures nimbly made their way up into the buggy.

What was astonishing about this whole encounter was that D never even touched the sword on his back. Even when he'd taken Larmica hostage, he hadn't threatened her with his blade. Larmica had moved to the back as her father ordered, and the second she sensed D's presence behind her, she found she couldn't move a muscle. She was paralyzed by the overwhelming aura that radiated from him—one that the superhuman senses of vampires alone could fully appreciate. The same aura had prevented the Count and Garou from raising a hand against him.

"What do you intend to do with my daughter?" the Count called out to D, who kept a steady gaze trained on him and his party from the backseat of the buggy.

There was no reply

"The little imbecile has crossed me at every turn and cost me the chance of a lifetime—I no longer consider her my daughter. Let her lie in the sun till decay takes her to the marrow of her bones!"

His words were unthinkably harsh for a father, but then, on the whole, the vampire race had extremely dilute notions of love and consideration, compared to human beings. Quite possibly it was this trait that had both led them to the heights of prosperity and guided them to their eventual downfall. When her father's words reached her ears, Larmica didn't even raise an eyebrow.

"Doc, we'll come back for you later!" Following Doris' sorrowful cry, the buggy took off.

After they'd gone a short way across the plains, they could hear a horse whinnying up ahead. Apparently, whoever was out there had noticed them.

"Who's that? Is that you, Sis?!"

"Dan! You're all right, are you?!" Doris asked, her voice nearly weeping as she drove the buggy over to her brother. He was on horseback. And he held the reins to a second horse. That one had been Rei-Ginsei's, and they'd brought it for Doris. They'd planned on having her ride home with them, but unfortunately they'd picked up some unwanted baggage. The whole reason D had taken Doris and Greco out in the buggy was to solve their transportation problems.

"I'm going to lighten our load. You two get on the horse. Dan, you come over here with me."

By "you two" he meant Doris and Greco. Because so many of the things that'd been happening were beyond his comprehension, Greco felt like his brains were half scrambled, so he followed orders without the slightest protest. The transfers were effected in a matter of seconds.

"Are you sure you can still handle the buggy if you've got her riding with you?" Doris asked from her seat in the saddle. The real question was: how many present noticed the jealousy in her voice? D made no answer, but silently lashed the horses with Doris' whip.

The wind howled in the girl's ears as the forest and fiends were left further and further behind.

"Dan, you weren't hurt, were you?"

Doris barely squeezed the question out as she rode alongside them. They were going full speed to keep the Count from catching up, and the wheels of the buggy spun wildly.

"Not a bit. I was gonna ask you the same thing—hey, of course you're fine. D's on the job. He wouldn't let anyone harm a hair on your head."

"No, I suppose he wouldn't," Doris concurred, her eyes full of joy.

"I wish you could've seen it," Dan said loudly. "It took him less than fifteen seconds each to get rid of them freaks. It's too bad the last one got away, but that couldn't be helped with D being hurt and all."

"Huh? Was he really?"

It was understandable that Doris grew pale, but why Larmica suddenly looked over at D from her seat was unclear.

"Hunters are really great, though. He got stabbed through the gut and it didn't even bother him—good ol' D rode through the roughest country with me on the back and pulling another horse behind us. You should've seen it. When D had the reins, them darned horses would jump right over the biggest crevice or a swamp full of giant leeches without batting an eye. Oh yeah, and they wouldn't stop no matter how steep the grade got—I'm gonna have him teach me all that horse and sword stuff later!"

"Oh, that's great. You pay good attention when he does now…" Doris' words were exuberant, but the power petered out of them and they were shredded by the wind. Perhaps her maiden instincts had given her some hint of how their story was going to end.

Deathly still and watching the darkness ahead, Larmica suddenly muttered, "Traitor."

"What did you say?!" Doris was the picture of rage. She realized the vampiress was referring to D. Larmica didn't even look at the girl, but bloody flames fairly shot from her eyes as she stared at D's frigid profile.

"You have skill and power enough to intimidate Father and myself, but you have forgotten your proud Noble blood. You feel some duty to the humans—worse yet, you are foolish enough to serve them by hunting us. I feel polluted simply speaking to you. Father wouldn't bother to follow you this far. Slay me here!"

"Shut up! We don't take orders from prisoners," Doris roared. "What have you high-ranking Noble types done to us? Just because you wanna feed, because you want hot human blood, you bite into the throats of folks who never did you any harm and make them vampires. They just turn around and attack the family that loved them—in the end, their family has to drive a stake through their heart. Demons is what you are. You're the Devil. Do you have any idea how many people die every year, parents and children crying out to their loved ones as they're killed in tidal waves and earthquakes caused by the weather controllers your kind runs?" Doris spat the accusations at her like a gob of blood, but Larmica just smiled coolly.

"We are the Nobility—the ruling class. The rulers are entitled to take such measures to ensure the rebellious feelings of the lower class are kept in check. You should consider yourself lucky we even allowed your race to continue." And then, with a long gaze at Greco as he brooded and raced along on his horse, she said, "Indeed, we will attack your kind to drink but a single drop of sweet blood. But what has that man done? I heard. For wanting you, he did nothing to warn that decrepit old man, even when he knew he was to be attacked, did he not?"

Doris couldn't find a thing to say.

Larmica's voice continued to dominate the night. "But I do not condemn him for that," she laughed. "To the contrary, the man is to be lauded. Is it not appropriate to sacrifice others to satisfy our own desires? The strong rule the weak, and the superior leave the inferior in the dust—that is the great principle that governs the cosmos. There are many among you who seem to share our point of view."

"Ha ha ha," Doris suddenly laughed back mockingly. "Don't make me laugh. If you're such great rulers then what do you want with me?" Now it was Larmica's turn to be silenced. "I heard something, too. It made me sick to hear it, but it seems your father wants to make me his bride. Every night he comes sniffing around my place like a dog in heat, and I turn him down—you'd think he'd be tired of it by now. The Nobility must be hard-pressed for women. Or is it something else? Could it be your father's just weirder than the rest?"

The killing lust in Larmica's eyes was like a heat ray that flew at Doris' face. Not to be outdone, Doris met it with a shower of sparks from her own hatred. It was as if there was a titanic spray of invisible embers between the galloping horse and racing buggy when their eyes locked.

Suddenly, D pulled back on the reins.

"Oh!" Doris gasped as she hastened to stop her horse as well. Greco alone was at a loss as to what to do, but then he decided staying with them any longer would only make matters worse, and he rushed away into the darkness.

Though no one was quite sure what he was doing, all of them followed D's lead, dismounting when he climbed down from the buggy. Larmica quickly turned to face the other three.

"What do you intend to do?" Larmica asked.

"As you yourself said, we've gone far enough the Count won't give chase. Now all we have to do is deal with you," D said softly. A tense hue raced into Larmica's face, and then into those of Doris and Dan. "I've been hired to keep her safe. Therefore, I'll have to slay your father. But anything else is another matter— meaning I now need my employer to decide what to do about you. Well?"

His final "Well?" had been directed at Doris. She was perplexed. They'd just been arguing a few seconds earlier. She'd thought she hated the vampiress enough to kill her, but the girl she saw looked like a beautiful, defenseless young lady about her own age.

This daughter of the detestable Nobility. *If not for her family, me and Dan would be living in peace now—I wanna kill her. I've got it. I can give her my whip and have her fight D. That'd be fair. If we gave her a chance like that, there'd be nothing to be ashamed about.*

"What do you want to do?" D asked.

"Slay me," Larmica said with eyes ablaze.

And then Doris shook her head.

"Let her go. I don't have it in me to murder. I couldn't do that to her, even if she's a Noble ..."

D turned to Dan. "What about you?"

"It's plain as day, ain't it? I couldn't do nothing as low as cutting down a woman in cold blood—and you couldn't either, could you?"

Then the Langs saw a smile spread across D's face. For years after, even for decades after, the two of them would remember D's expression, and take pride in the fact they were responsible for it. It was just such a smile.

"Well, there you have it. You'd best go now."

And with that D turned his back to Larmica, but she flung abuse at him anyway.

"The stupidity of the lot of you amazes me. Do not delude yourselves that I am in any way grateful. I will make you rue your decision to set me free! Had I been in your position, I would have had you slaughtered like a sow. And your brother as well."

The other three didn't turn to look at her again, but went back to the buggy.

"Take this horse."

Doris dropped the reins in front of Larmica.

"Even children know the cosmic principle, it seems," D said calmly from the driver's seat.

"What?"

"Survival of the fittest, might makes right—that's not what your Sacred Ancestor used to say."

Larmica's eyes bulged, but a moment later she laughed out loud. "Not only are you sickeningly soft-hearted, but it appears you're given to delusions as well. Did you mention the Sacred Ancestor? There's no chance a lowly creature like you would know someone of his greatness. He who made our civilization, our whole world, and the laws by which we ruled. Every one of us faithfully followed his words."

"Every one of you? Then why was the poor old bastard always so troubled ..."

"The poor old bastard? You mean ... No, you couldn't ..." Larmica's voice carried a hint of fear. She recalled a certain plausible rumor that had been whispered at a grand ball at the castle when she was just a child.

"Such skill, and such power ... Might it be that you are ... " The whip cracked.

When the buggy had dashed off leaving only the tortured squeal of its tires in its wake, the daughter of the Nobility forgot all about gathering the reins of the horse before her as she stood stock still in the moonlight.

"Milord, might it be ..."

The next day, Dan and D accompanied Doris when she went out to claim Dr. Ferringo's body. They then paid a call on the sheriff and entrusted him with the remains before bringing all of Rei-Ginsei and Greco's misdeeds to light.

Having received a communiqué from the village of Pedros about the Frontier Defense Force, the sheriff had been out to the ruins himself and discovered the trio of lurid corpses there. Based on Doris' testimony, he concluded Rei-Ginsei's gang was connected to the disappearance of the FDF patrol. In an attempt to ascertain the whereabouts of that patrol, special deputies rushed off to the neighboring villages.

"Well, Rei-Ginsei won't be at large for long now. Of course, there's also a good chance he made like the wind last night right after you lopped off his cabbage-collector."

On the way back to the farm, Doris' expression was sunny— she had at least one of her problems taken care of. But D told her simply, "If he becomes a Noble, he could lose all his limbs and still be a threat."

Rei-Ginsei had ambitions of joining the Nobility. Given his skill and scheming nature, to say nothing of a vindictiveness that put a serpent to shame, it was unthinkable that he would run off with his tail between his legs, or quit before he'd achieved his ends. He may have fled, but it was clear he'd hidden himself somewhere and would be vigilantly watching what they did. He might still carry out the Count's orders.

A daylight foe—because of him, D's movements were greatly restricted. Up until now, he'd only had to worry about taking up his blade by night. But now, it would be patently impossible to go attack the Count in his castle and leave Doris and Dan under the scrutiny of an appreciable foe who possessed both weird weapons and even stranger skill.

"Still, it's too bad they didn't lock that bastard Greco up," Dan muttered.

The sheriff was wrapped up in the Rei-Ginsei case, but couldn't get to the bottom of Greco's activities. The three of them had accompanied the lawman to the mayor's house to question him, but the thoroughly disgusted mayor appeared and informed them that Greco had returned quite agitated the previous night, grabbed all the money in the house as well as the combat suit that'd just come back from the repair shop, and took off on his horse. The sheriff had Doris and the others wait in his office while he checked with some of Greco's partners-in-crime, but they all said they didn't know where he was.

Rei-Ginsei and Greco—with the whereabouts of both of them unknown there was little the sheriff could do. He informally sent Greco's description to the other villages and requested that if the man was found, he was to be detained for having important information about the murder of Dr. Ferringo.

"But we can't charge him in this case," the sheriff told a visibly dissatisfied Doris. "From what you tell me, it seems Doc was killed by this Noble girl. And as for the matter of being turned into a vampire in the first place—well, even now it's not clear if a person suffers any harm when that happens. I wish to hell the Capital would give us a clear ruling on that ..."

Doris nodded reluctantly.

It was unclear whether or not turning someone into a vampire could be considered murder. From one perspective, the change merely caused a shift in personality, not an absolute loss of life. The question dogged mankind throughout history, remaining undecided to this very day. Consequently, Greco couldn't be charged with a crime, even though he didn't inform the sheriff when he knew the Count was going to "kill" Dr. Ferringo.

"Quite the contrary, in the eyes of the law Greco might be considered a hero for rescuing you." Seeing Doris' slender eyebrows rise in wrath, the sheriff hurriedly added, "And while I don't have any authority to get caught up in personal squabbles ..." The rest was implied—*when I find the weasel, I'm gonna belt him good.* Doris and Dan looked at each other and grinned.

Doris found herself in the first peaceful lull since the Count had attacked her.

There was a mountain of work to be done. Synthesized protein harvested by the robots had to be put into packages, stacked at the edge of the garden, and covered with a water-repellent tent until the traveling merchant made his monthly call. The Langs didn't sell it, but rather traded it for daily necessities. The protein Doris and Dan grew was well known for its density, and the merchant always gave them an exceptional rate in trade for it.

The milking and general care of the cows had been neglected as well. Of course, the village of Ransylva was where most of that was traded; even though she'd been shut out of all the shops, she couldn't let the cows go any longer. Doris' battle with the Count didn't put food on the table.

With Dan and a battered robot to help her, the job would've taken three whole days, but D did it in half a day. He skillfully poured huge bowls of milky protein extract into plastic packages, and then carried them from the processing area to the garden when he had a pile of a certain size. The boxes weighed a good seventy pounds each, and he carried three of them at a time. When he first saw it, Dan bugged out his eyes and exclaimed, "Wow!" but after three straight hours of this superhuman toting, his jaw dropped and he was left speechless.

The speed with which D milked the cows was almost miraculous. In the time it took Doris to do one cow, he did three. And that was only using his left hand. His right hand was left empty to go for the sword by his side at any time. That was the way Hunters were.

I wonder what kind of family he comes from?

It wasn't the first time this question had occurred to her, but it hadn't been answered in the days they'd been fighting, and even then Doris hadn't had the time ask anyway. Actually, it was the code of the Frontier that you didn't go poking into the background of travelers, and D's bearing in particular didn't invite questions.

Doris watched D's profile with a distant look in her eyes as he silently worked one hand on the cow, the white fluid collecting in an aluminum-plated can.

The scene seemed so familiar; maybe it was the girl's feverish, young heart that made her feel like it would go on this way forever. While it wasn't that long ago that Doris had lost her father—and her battle to protect her brother and the farm began—she suddenly realized how exhausted she was.

"Done. Aren't you finished yet?"

At D's query, Doris returned from her fantasies. "Er, no, I'm done here."

As she stood up and pulled the can out from under the cow, she felt as if she was naked before him.

"Your face is flushed. You coming down with a cold or something?"

"No, it's not. It must just be the sunset."

The interior of the barn was stained red.

"I see. The Count will probably come here again. You'd best eat early and get Dan to bed."

"I suppose you're right."

Doris grabbed the handle of the can with both hands and carried it to one side of barn. For some reason she had no strength.

"Leave it. I'll carry it," D said, having seen how wobbly her legs were.

"I'll be fine!"

Her tone was so rough she surprised herself. Tears rolled out with the words. Dropping the can to the ground, she ran out sobbing.

As D went after her—though his casual pace hardly made it seem like pursuit—Dan trained an apprehensive gaze on him from the porch.

"Sis ran around back crying. You two have a fight or something?"

D shook his head. "No. Your sister's just worried about you."

"You know, someone told me a man shouldn't make women cry."

D smiled wryly. "You're right. I'll go apologize."

Taking a few steps, D then turned to Dan again.

"You still remember that promise you made, do you?"

"Yep."

"You're eight now. In another five years, you'll be stronger than your sister. Don't forget."

Dan nodded. When he raised his face, it was shining with tears.

"Are you gonna go away, D? Once you've killed the Count, I mean."

D disappeared around back without giving an answer.

Doris was leaning against the fence. Her shoulders were quaking.

D's footsteps didn't make a sound as he went and stood behind her.

A cool breeze played through the grassy sea beyond the fence and through Doris' black tresses.

"You should go back to the house."

Doris didn't reply, but after a bit she mumbled, "I should've looked for someone else. Once you're gone, I won't be able to live like I did before. That milking can just now—I used to be able to carry two at a time. I won't be able set Dan straight when he needs it, or have the strength to fend off any fellahs who come out here courting me. But you're gonna go just the same."

"That was the deal. That will end your sorrow. That or my death."

"No!" Doris suddenly buried her face in his muscular chest. "No, no, no."

She didn't know what she was protesting. Nor did she know why she cried. Neither the young woman weeping—as if weeping could keep a phantom from vanishing—nor the young man with the melancholy air supporting her moved for the longest time. And then, after a little while …

Doris lifted her face suddenly. Just above her head, D had started to growl softly. Doris was about to ask, "What is it?" when her head was forced back against his chest by his formidable strength. A few seconds more passed.

The two silhouettes were fused in the red glow, but from between the two of them came the words, "I'm okay now," in a feverish voice.

Nothing else was said, and soon D gently pushed Doris away and quickly walked back toward the house.

As he rounded the corner of the barn, a voice said teasingly, "Why didn't you drink her blood?" It originated around his waist.

"Shut up." For once D's voice bore undisguised emotion.

"The girl knew. She knew what you wanted. Oh, now don't you make that face with me. You can fight it all you like, but you've got the blood of the Nobility in the marrow of your bones. The fact that when you fancy a woman you're more interested in latching onto her pale neck instead of getting her in the sack is proof of that."

It was true. When Doris had bared her soul to him, and he felt her warm body sobbing against his chest, D's expression became the same lurid vampire visage he'd worn when he drank the blood of the Midwich Medusas in the darkness of the subterranean aqueduct. But somehow, with his truly impressive willpower, he'd managed to fight the urge this time.

As D kept walking, the voice said to him, "The girl saw your other face. Not just that, but I bet she smelled your breath as it brushed her neck. Smelled the scent of your cursed blood. And still she said she didn't mind. Go easy on the nice guy routine. You fight your own desire and deny the wishes of the girl—is that any way for a grown dhampir to act? You're always on the run— from your blood, and from the people who want you. When you tell them you were fated to part, that's just dressing it up in a pretty excuse. Listen to me. Your father—"

"Shut up." The words D said were the same as a moment earlier, but the eerie aura behind them made it plain this was far more than just a threat. The voice fell silent. Climbing the stairs to the porch, D turned a thoughtful gaze to the prairie and muttered, "Still, I've got to go—go and find *him*."

"**O**h, shit!"
As D's hard gaze filled the lenses' field of view, a shadowy figure hurriedly ducked, afraid that D would see him. But he forgot he was now on a hill a good thousand feet away. It was none other than the mayor's hell-raising son Greco, who most believed to have long since fled the village. He was wearing his combat suit.

"That son of a bitch gets to have all the fun," Greco said, slamming his electronic binoculars against the ground. The previous night, after deciding discretion was the better part of valor, he'd come up to the top of this hill and kept an eye on the farm. Lying flat on his belly, he reached over to his saddlebags and pulled the Time-Bewitching Incense out from among the food and provisions packed in there.

"Heh, you'll get yours once the sun's down. I'll use this baby to get you down crawling on the ground, then nail you with a stake. Then yours truly will take Doris by the hand and kiss this godforsaken shithole goodbye," he said spitefully, turning his eyes toward the farm again. The previous night he'd been so scared by the Count and his werewolf that he'd abandoned all thought of killing them and decided to abduct Doris instead. And clearly, the person he talked about dispatching with a stake was D.

"I wonder if it'll go as smoothly as all that?" The words rained down on Greco in a cool voice.

"What the—?!"

Looking up, Greco saw a handsome young man sitting on a branch directly overhead. He wore an innocent smile, but his left arm was missing below the elbow, and its stump was wrapped in a bloody white cloth. He needed no introduction. And yet, less than twenty-four hours after losing one arm he'd climbed up into a tree and scared the daylights out of Greco while looking no worse for wear, aside from a little darkness around his eyes. What strength he had, both physically and mentally!

Rei-Ginsei got back down to the ground without making a sound.

"Wh … what the hell do you want?"

"Don't play the innocent. I'm the rightful owner of that candle. Thanks to you, I lost my arm. I came out to the farm in the hopes of encountering the Count, but lo and behold, I've run across someone else of interest to me. So, are the three of them still hale and hearty?"

His speech was refined, but Greco felt a crushing coercion in it that left him bobbing his head in agreement.

"I suspected as much. In which case, I shall have to score some quick points here if I'm to be made one of them." After that enigmatic statement, the handsome young man addressed Greco with familiarity. "What do you say to joining forces with me?"

"Work with you?"

"From what I observed up in the tree, you seem obsessed with the young lady on the farm. Yet her bodyguard remains an obstacle. I have another reason for wanting him out of the way. What say you?"

Greco hesitated.

Rei-Ginsei chided him. "Are you certain you can finish him, even with the candle and your combat suit? With your skill?"

Greco was at a loss for an answer. That was exactly why he hadn't gone down and abducted Doris yet. Thanks to the effect it had on the Count's daughter, he'd been able to verify that Time-Bewitching Incense was highly effective against pure vampires, but when it came to a half-human dhampir, he didn't have much confidence. He'd donned the combat suit, but since it was just back from the repair shop he wasn't used to wearing it or using it, and if he had to call upon its power, it was doubtful he could use it to its full potential. "You mean to say, if I hook up with you, we might be able to do this?" His words were proof enough he'd fallen under Rei-Ginsei's spell.

Killing his smile, the handsome young man nodded. "Indeed. Once the sun has set I shall fight him, so watch for the right moment to light the candle, if you please. Should he leave himself open for even an instant, well, that's where my blades come in," he said, pointing to the shrike-blades on his hip.

Greco made up his mind. "Sure ... but what happens after that?"

"After that?"

"I know you're planning on handing the girl over to the Count, but that's exactly what I've been busting my hump to keep from happening."

"In that case, take her and flee," Rei-Ginsei said casually. Seeing the now-stupefied Greco, he added, "I merely promised him I would slay the dhampir. I don't care a whit whose property the girl becomes. That matter is between yourself and the Count, is it not? But you being a fellow human and all, if you like I shall tell my compatriots scattered across the Frontier to aid you in your flight from the Count."

"Would you really?" Greco's tone had become an appeal. The question of how he could shake the pursuing Noble if he managed to make good his escape with Doris was a point of concern for him. But why on earth would Rei-Ginsei say such a thing to him? Because he wasn't sure that just getting the Time-Bewitching Incense would be enough to beat D.

The indescribable swordplay the Hunter displayed as he made good his promise to dispatch three of the superhuman gang leader's valued henchmen in less than fifteen seconds each, and the invincibility he demonstrated in getting to his feet again despite the sword sticking out of his belly—the mere thought of these things was enough to give Rei-Ginsei gooseflesh. Just to be prepared for any eventuality, he decided to use the stupid little hood he'd found. Once D had been slain, Greco would have outlived his usefulness, and he would be crushed like an insect. "Well, I believe we have a bargain then." Rei-Ginsei flashed a smile so beautiful it would put a flower to shame, and held out his remaining hand.

"Um, okay." Greco hesitated to take his hand. "But I don't completely trust you yet. Just so we're clear, if you try anything funny I'll wreck the candle on the spot."

"Fair enough."

"Then that's just great."

They shared a firm handshake.

The round moon rose. Strangely large and white, the unsettling lunar disc sent wild waves of anxiety across the hearts of all who looked up at it. An old farmer named Morris snapped awake when he felt a chill. Sitting up in bed, the old man looked to the bedroom window and felt his hair rising on end. The window he was certain he'd locked was open now.

But that wasn't what terrified the old man.

His granddaughter Lucy, whom he'd looked after since she'd lost her parents in an accident, stood by the window in her little nightgown, staring at her grandfather with vacant eyes. Her face was paler than the moonlight spilling in through the window.

"Lucy, what's the matter?"

When he noticed the twin streaks of red coursing down his granddaughter's throat, the old man froze in his bed.

"I am ... Count Lee," Lucy mumbled. In a man's voice! "Give me Doris Lang ... If you do not ... tonight, tomorrow night ... every night the ranks of the living-dead shall swell ... "

And then his granddaughter collapsed on the floor.

After dinner, Dan had been inseparable from D, but even he couldn't resist the sandman indefinitely, and he had to retire to his room. Doris disappeared into her own bedroom, leaving D alone in the living room, which was lit only by stark moonlight. He'd been sleeping there since the first night, since he said the room to the back of the house was too cramped. He lay on the sofa, his eyes cold and clear as ice. The hour was nearing eleven Night.

A white light flickered.

The bedroom door opened, and Doris stepped out. A threadbare bath towel covered her from her breasts to her thighs. Crossing the living room without a sound, she stood before the sofa. Her ample bosom was heaving. Taking two deep breaths, Doris let the towel fall.

Unmoving, unblinking, D fixed his eyes on the girl's naked form. Her well-proportioned and slightly muscled body wasn't yet endowed with all a woman's sensuality, but it had more than enough of the pale virgin charm that always took men's breath away.

"D ..." Doris' voice caught in her throat.

"I haven't finished my work here."

"I'll pay you in advance. Take it ..."

Before he could even speak, her warm flesh was on top of him and her sweet breath was tickling his nose.

"Hey, I'm ..."

"The Count's gonna come again," Doris panted. "And this time it's gonna get settled—at least, that's the feeling I get. I probably won't get a chance to give you your reward—so take me, suck my blood, do whatever you like to me."

D's hand brushed the girl's lengthy tresses aside, exposing the face they'd hidden to the night air. Their lips met.

For a few seconds they remained together—and then D sat up quickly. His eyes raced to the window. That way lay the main gate.

"What is it? The Count?" Doris' voice was taut.

"No. I sense two groups. The first is a pair, and the second—there's a lot of them. Fifty, no, close to a hundred strong."

"A hundred people?!"

"Go wake up Dan."

Doris disappeared into her bedroom.

Near the gate to the farm, a pair of silhouettes suddenly halted their horses and looked back across the prairie. Countless points of light swayed closer, coming from the direction of town. As the pair strained their ears, they could hear a rumble of voices that bordered on rage, mixed with the beating of numberless hooves.

"What could that be?" mumbled Rei-Ginsei.

"Folks from town. Something must've happened," Greco said, watching the points of light nervously. Those were flaming torches.

"At any rate, we'd do well to conceal ourselves and see what transpires."

The two of them quickly melted into the shadows of the farm's fence.

They didn't have long to wait; the procession of villagers assembled before the entrance to the farm shortly after they'd hidden themselves. Greco's brow furrowed. Leading the pack was his father, Mayor Rohman. Steam was rising from his bald pate. Around him were his family's hired hands, all armed to the teeth with crossbows and laser rifles; the villagers carried spears and rifles as well.

More than half of them looked like they'd just been dragged out of bed, dressed in pajamas and slippers. Humorous as it appeared, it testified to exactly how serious the situation had become. The shadows of hatred and fear fell heavily on every face.

This was a mob. There was no sign of the sheriff.

"Doris! Doris Lang! Turn this barrier off," the mayor roared in front of the gate.

A light went on in one window of the house.

Soon after, a pair of figures loomed on the front porch.

"What in the blazes is your business at this hour of the night! You bring the whole damn town out here to rob the place or something?" That was Doris' voice.

"Just turn the barrier off already! Then we'll discuss it," the mayor bellowed back.

"It's already off, you moron. You gonna stay out there all night?"

A number of fiery streaks shot out from around the mayor, melting the chain off the gate.

The crowd spilled into her front yard.

"Hold it right there! Come any closer and I'll shoot you dead!" More than Doris' threat, more than the laser rifle propped against her shoulder, it was the sight of D standing there behind her that checked the crazed mob and stopped them ten feet shy of the porch.

To cow a group, you had to take aim at a person at the center of their rampage and carefully cut them off from the others. Just as her father had taught her, Doris aligned the barrel of her laser rifle perfectly with the mayor's breastbone, letting the promise that she wouldn't give an inch flood through her entire being.

"Okay, I want some answers. What's your business? And where the heck's the sheriff? I'm warning you right now, if he's not here I don't owe you a good answer no matter what kind of complaint you got. Dan and I both pay our taxes."

"That pain in the ass got slapped around a little and thrown in his own jail. We'll let him out again once we've taken care of the lot of you," the mayor said with disgust. And then, still glaring at Doris, he gave a wave of one hand. "Come on, show her."

The crowd parted and a hoary-headed old man stepped to the fore. In his arms he held a little girl with braids in her hair.

"Mr. Morris, is Lucy…" Doris began, but swallowed the rest of her words. Two repugnant streaks of blood marked the girl's paraffin-pale throat.

"There are more."

With the mayor's words as their cue, two pathetic couples came forward.

The miller Fu Lanchu and his wife Kim, the huntsman Machen and his spouse—both couples were in their thirties, though the wives of both men were still renowned in the village for their beauty. The sight of the women—now held up by their husbands as their vacant eyes pointed to the heavens and fresh blood dripped down their throats—told Doris everything.

"The Count did this, the ruthless bastard …"

"That's right," Machen said with a nod. "The wife and I were tuckered out from a hard day's work, and headed off to bed early. Not long after that, I woke up feeling chilled and found my wife not by my side where she should be but standing over next to a wide-open window, glaring at me with these burning eyes. And when I jumped out of bed to see what the hell was going on—"

The miller Lanchu picked up where Machen left off. "All of a sudden my wife said in a man's voice, 'Give me Doris Lang. If you don't, your wife will remain like this forever, neither alive nor dead.' He said those exact words."

"The moment she stopped speaking, she just keeled over, and she hasn't moved or spoken since!" Machen's voice was a veritable scream. "I rushed to take her pulse, but there wasn't a trace of one. She's not breathing either. And yet, her heart's still beating."

"Now, I didn't believe any of what Greco was saying," said Mr. Morris. "Knowing you, I figured if some vampire had bit you, you'd have done away with yourself. Why, if it was true, I thought I'd lend what aid an old fool could and help you destroy our lord. But why did my granddaughter Lucy have to suffer in your place ... She's only five!"

The old man's teary, grief-stricken appeal gradually brought down the barrel of Doris' weapon. Her voice now stripped of its willfulness, Doris asked, "So what are you saying we should do?"

The mayor turned his dagger-filled gaze at D. Stroking his bald head, he said, "First, chase the punk behind you off your farm. Next, you're going into the asylum. I'm not saying we're going to grab you and give you to the Count as tribute or anything as heartless as all that. But you've got to follow the law of the village. In the meantime, we'll take care of the Count."

Doris vacillated. What the mayor proposed had its merits. Since she'd been bitten by a vampire, the only thing that kept her out of the asylum was the aid of Dr. Ferringo and the sheriff. Now the elderly physician was dead, and the sheriff wasn't here. But there were three people here who'd been made living-dead in her stead, and lots of villagers with hate-filled eyes. Her rifle drooped limply to the floor.

"Take her away," the mayor commanded triumphantly.

And at that moment, D said, "How will you take care of *him?*"

The buzz of the mob, which had gone on incessantly during Doris' discussion with the mayor, came to an immediate halt. Hatred, horror, menace—as they gazed upon him with every emotion they felt toward the unknown, Vampire Hunter D slowly made his way down the porch stairs with his sword over his shoulder. The mob shrank back without a word. All except for the mayor. The instant D's eyes caught him, he became utterly paralyzed. "How will you take care of him?" D asked again, stopping a few paces away from the mayor.

"Well, um ... actually ..."

D reached out his *left hand* and stuck the *palm* of it against the mayor's octopus-like face. For a moment the man's voice broke off, and then he went on again.

"Throw her ... in the freaking asylum ... and then negotiate. Tell him ... he's not to harm anyone in town any more ... If he does, we'll kill the love of his life ..."

The mayor's face twisted and beads of sweat formed chains across his brow, almost as if he was battling some titanic force within himself.

"After we talked to him ... we'd tell Doris we'd destroyed the Count or something ... let her out ... After that, he could do what he liked—make her one of his kind, bleed her to death, whatever ... You're the devil ... you little punk. If you give Doris any more help ... "

"Aren't you the cooperative one?"

D took his hand away. The mayor took a few steps back, his face looking like whatever demon had possessed him had just left. Beads of sweat streamed down his face.

"This young lady hired me," D said darkly. "And as I haven't finished what I was hired to do, I can't very well leave now. Especially not after hearing your detailed confession."

Suddenly, his tone became commanding. "The Nobility won't die out if you stand around and do nothing. How many times will you give in, and how many people are you willing to sacrifice to those who have nothing but extinction ahead of them? If that's the human mentality, then there's absolutely no chance I'll let you have the girl. An old man who can only weep for the child taken from him, and husbands who would have another girl take the place of their own defiled wives—the flames of hell can take you, and everyone else in this village as well. I'll take on humans and Nobles alike. I will defend this family even if I have to leave a mountain of corpses and a river of blood the likes of which you can't begin to imagine—any objections?"

The people saw the crimson gleam of his eyes through the darkness—the eyes of a vampire! D took a step forward, and the silenced mob was pushed back by a wave of primal fear.

"I object."

Everyone stopped at what was a beautiful voice for such a loud shout.

"Who's that?"

"Let him through!"

One voice after another arose from the back of the pack, and as the crowd split down the middle, a young man who was almost blindingly handsome stepped forward. While the beauty of his countenance was great, it was the unusual state of both his left and right arms that drew the people's attention. His right arm was sheathed all the way to the shoulder in what looked like the metallic sleeve of a combat suit, and his left arm was missing from the elbow down. Proffering the stump of his arm, Rei-Ginsei said, "I came to thank you for doing this yesterday." His tone made it seemed like an amiable greeting.

"You? Everyone, this is the bastard who attacked the FDF patrol!" The mayor and the rest of the mob started murmuring when they heard Doris shout that.

Rei-Ginsei calmly replied, "And I suppose you have some proof of that, do you? Did you find some trace of the patrol—

their horses' corpses, anything? True, there has been some unpleasantness between us in the past, but I can't have you heaping any further aspersions on my good name."

Doris ground her teeth. Rei-Ginsei definitely had her at a disadvantage where the FDF case was concerned. Without victims, he couldn't be charged with a crime. Though if the sheriff was there, there's little doubt he'd have promptly taken Rei-Ginsei into custody as a material witness.

"Mister Mayor, may I be so bold as to make a suggestion?"

Greeted by a flash of pearly teeth, the mayor smiled back nervously. Like all who'd been enslaved by Rei-Ginsei's grin, he did not notice the devil that hid behind it. "And what would that be?" the mayor asked.

"Please allow me to do battle with our friend, here and now. Should he win, you will leave this family alone, and should I win, the girl shall go to the asylum. How does that suit you?"

"Well, I don't know ..." The mayor vacillated. His position really wouldn't allow him to entrust a matter of this magnitude to a man he didn't know in the least—particularly someone as shrouded in suspicion as Rei-Ginsei was.

"Can the lot of you do something then? Come tomorrow evening, there shall be more victims."

The mayor made up his mind. All the villagers were held at bay by D's energy. He had to see what the man could do. "Very well."

"One more thing," Rei-Ginsei said, extending a single finger of the combat suit. Of course it was Greco's. To keep Doris from realizing as much, he'd only donned the one sleeve. If his connection to Greco came to light, they would realize where the Time-Bewitching Incense was now. "Dispatch someone to the neighboring villages and have the warrants out on me withdrawn."

"Okay—understood," the mayor said, the words coming out like a moan. With no one but this dashing young man to rely on, he had no resort but to concede to his every demand.

Rei-Ginsei turned to Doris and asked, "And is that fine with you, too?"

"Sure. You'll just wind up getting your other hand lopped off," Doris replied.

D asked, "Where do you want to do this?" He made no mention of the fact that his opponent was trying to curry favor with the Nobility, or that he'd attempted to strangle a helpless young boy.

"Right here. Our duel will soon be over."

Only the moon watched the moving people.

In front of the porch the two of them squared off, ten feet apart.

The villagers filling the front yard, and Doris and Dan up on the porch, were on pins and needles. When they all let out a deep breath seemingly on cue, three shrike-blades flew from Rei-Ginsei's right hip. The combat suit's muscular enhancement system made them all faster than ever, faster than the human eye could follow, and yet all of them were knocked from the sky just in front of D by a silvery flash.

In the blink of an eye, D was in the air over Rei-Ginsei's head. Sword raised for the kill, the moment the crowd gasped at their premonition of the blade cleaving Rei-Ginsei's head, the victorious Hunter wobbled in midair.

Who could miss that chance? Once again Rei-Ginsei's right hand went into action, sending out a stream of white light. That was Greco's wooden stake, which he'd kept tucked through the back of his belt. With Rei-Ginsei's normal skill, D most likely would have dodged it despite his throes of agony, but now it had the added speed of the combat suit. Longsword still raised above his head, with the stake stuck through his heart and sticking out his back, D sent out a faint mist of blood as he thudded to the ground.

"Nailed him!"

The jubilant cry came from neither Rei-Ginsei nor the villagers. The crowd was more confused by the strange feeling that night had become day than they were by the duel's gruesome finale.

"Greco! Oh, so you were in cahoots with this jerk!"

With that shout, Doris took aim with her rifle at the figure who'd popped up in front of the fence holding a candle in one hand, but a sudden massive blow to the barrel of the weapon knocked it back, striking its owner in the forehead.

"Now's our chance! Grab her!"

Giving a faint smile to the villagers as they charged Dan and the unconscious sister Dan clung to, Rei-Ginsei fastened the last returning shrike-blade to his belt and stripped off the combat suit sleeve.

The limp Doris was thrown on a horse, as was her bellowing and far-from-cooperative brother, and the villagers went back out through the gate.

"What are you up to?" Greco grimaced, about to go get the horse he'd hidden at the rear of the farm.

Rei-Ginsei was stooping down over the body of the already deceased D. Raising the left hand, he eyed the palm and back of it suspiciously. "I simply don't understand," he groaned. "This is the same hand that swallowed Chullah's spiders and made the mayor spill his secrets …There must be some secret to it." As he said that, he took a shrike-blade from his hip and slashed the left hand off at the elbow, which made Greco's eyes bug in his head. He then discarded the hand in the nearby bushes. "I couldn't rest easy if I didn't do that. Also, I believe that makes us even," he said coolly.

Rei-Ginsei walked toward the gate without so much as a glancing back, but Greco called out in an overly familiar tone, "Hey, wait up. Why don't we have a drink in town or something? Together, me and you could do big things."

Stopping dead in his tracks, Rei-Ginsei turned around. The look in his eyes riveted Greco. "The next time we meet, consider your life over."

And then he left.

"Sheesh, you're pretty damn full of yourself," Greco muttered with all the venom he could muster, and then he too headed for the exit. His legs froze. He turned around, looking scared out of his wits. "I must be imagining things," he mumbled, and then he wasted little time getting back out through the gate.

He thought he'd heard what sounded like chuckling. And it hadn't come from D's corpse, but from the dark bushes where his severed left hand had been discarded ...

"Ha ha ha ... Everything has gone exactly as planned. It's unfortunate I had to wait an additional day, but I suppose that has only increased my ardor all the more."

Standing on the same hilltop where Greco had encountered Rei-Ginsei by day, the figure took the electronic binoculars from his eyes and laughed softly. With white fangs spilling over his red lips, it was none other than Count Magnus Lee.

A carriage was parked by a tree, and the moonlight illuminated the werewolf Garou standing beside it in his inverness. Naturally, he had his human face and form at the moment.

He asked, "So, what shall we do next?"

"That should go without saying. We force our way into that miserable little hamlet and take the girl. That damned mayor of theirs undoubtedly plans on locking her in the asylum while he negotiates with me, but I shall have none of that. For all the inconveniences they've caused me thus fur, I shall create more living-dead in their village tomorrow night, and still more the night after that. Their children and their children's children shall have a tale to tell of the horror of the Nobility. Consider it a gift to commemorate my nuptials. Upon our return, order the robots to commence preparations for the ceremony immediately."

"Yessir."

Giving a magnanimous nod to his deeply bowing servitor, the Count was about to get into his carriage when he turned and asked, "How is Larmica?"

"As you instructed, sire, she was punished with Time-Bewitching Incense, and she appeared to be in severe pain as she was still lying on the floor of her room when I took my leave."

"Is that so? Very well then. If this serves to keep her from harboring any further thoughts of disobeying her father then everything will once again be as it should. I merely wanted to take the human girl as my wife. To live forever, sucking the blood as it gushes from her pale-as-wax throat night after night. Transient guest? The words of our Sacred Ancestor do not apply to me, I dare say. The rest of my kind may face extinction, but the girl and I shall stay here forever and hold the humans down with power and fear. Just you watch!"

Once again Garou gave a deep nod.

The Count shut the carriage door firmly from the inside.

"Go! The dawn is nigh. Of course, I don't believe there shall be any need to burn it, but I have Time-Bewitching Incense ready just in case."

Neither the Count nor Garou had noticed that, soon after D had been felled by Rei-Ginsei's stake, a carriage had come from the woods on the opposite side of the farm and headed toward town.

For some time after Greco left, only a refreshing breeze and the light of the moon held sway at the farm. The cattle were sleeping peacefully, but an unsettling chuckle suddenly arose in the otherwise silent, solemn darkness.

"Heh heh heh ... It's been a while since I got to take center stage. Eating spiders and making baldy spill his guts is all well and good, but I want a little more time in the limelight—of course, he and I might both be happier if I left things the way they stand now, but there's still things that need doing in this life. And I kinda like that firecracker and her squirt of a brother. I'm loathe to do this, but I guess I can bail him out once again."

By "him" it meant D.

The voice came from within the bushes. At the same time, something seemed to be moving around in there. Oh, it was the hand. The fingers. As if it possessed a mind of its own, the left hand Rei-Ginsei had hacked from D and thrown away was now moving all five of its fingers.

The hand had its back to the ground and its palm pointed to the sky. The surface of the palm rippled, like a lump of muscle was being pushed to the surface from the inside. But the truly startling part was still to come. A few creases shot across the surface of the lump, depressions formed in the flesh in some places while other parts swelled up—forming at last a human face!

Two tiny nostrils opened on the slightly crooked, aquiline nose, and when the lips twisted in a sarcastic smile they exposed teeth like tiny grains of rice. The disturbing tumor with a face took a breath, and then its hitherto closed eyelids snapped open.

"Well, time to get started I suppose."

With those words as a cue, the arm started to move. Though the nerves and tendons had been severed, the weird countenanced carbuncle had the ability to reanimate the arm portion and make it do its bidding. The fingers of the prone hand swam in the air and grabbed hold of a branch of the shrubbery directly overhead. Clinging to the branch and pulling itself up, the hand flopped back to the ground palm down. "Okay, time to take a little trip." The five fingers curled like spider legs and the wrist arched into the air. Dragging the heavy forearm behind it, it cleverly wound its way through the bushes and inched toward D. When it came to the stump of his left arm, the fingers once again scurried around busily, turning to the right and matching both sides of the cut together perfectly.

D had fallen on his back, so the palm of his hand naturally faced the sky. The countenanced carbuncle's bizarre visage was left naked in the moonlight. And this is when it—the hand—began to act truly strange. It inhaled for a long time, like it was taking a deep breath. Given the relatively small size of D's palm, it seemed to have an incredible lung capacity. The wind whistled and howled as it coursed into the tiny mouth. After this amazing display of suctioning skill had gone on for a good ten seconds, it paused for a breath and repeated the same behavior three more times. And then the countenanced carbuncle did something even more wondrous.

Cleverly flipping over from the elbow so that the palm faced down, the fingers sank into the ground and began tearing up the soil.

Thanks most likely to D's steely fingertips, they scooped up the hard ground like it was mud, and before long there was a sizable mound of dirt into which the palm proceeded to shove its own face. In the hush, an eerie munching sound could be heard. The tumor was eating the dirt! By the light of the moon this unearthly repast continued, and several minutes later the mound of dirt had vanished completely. Where had it gone? Right into the countenanced carbuncle's maw. But where in the world could it put all that dirt? The shape of the arm hadn't changed in the least. And yet, the severed hand had consumed both the air and the earth. But toward what end?

The down-turned palm let out a small burp.

"Without water and fire this may take a while, but there's not much we can do about that," it said to itself, and then the whole arm abruptly reached for D's chest.

It couldn't be! The two sides of the slice along D's arm were together again, even though reattaching the arm after both sides had bled dry should've been impossible. But the arm rose nonetheless.

Then the countenanced carbuncle said simply, "This should be a lot faster than using my fingers."

With that it opened its mouth wide and bit down on the end of the stake jutting from D's chest.

"Oof!"

With a weird grunt it pulled the stake right out.

Disposing of the wooden implement with a flick of the wrist, the palm once again turned to the sky.

The air howled. Once more it was being savagely sucked in, though it was now clear it was being consumed just as the earth had been. Pale blue flames could be seen flickering deep in the cheeks of the countenanced carbuncle every time it inhaled. With its third such breath, flames spouted from its mouth and nose. Earth, wind, fire, and water were commonly known as the four elements. Having consumed only two of them—earth and wind—the countenanced carbuncle had turned them into heat within itself, and then into life force, and now it was pumping life itself back into D's body.

This gorgeous youth—the great Vampire Hunter D—had a life-force generator living in the palm of his hand!

At some point the wind died down, and the tranquil farm was made all the more serene by the moon, but in one part of the farm the disturbing miracle continued. And the wound the stake had left in D's heart—a wound that was certain death for all descendants of vampires—gradually closed.

Flashing Steel Cuts the Ceremony Short

CHAPTER 8

"**L**et us out of here, damn you! Let us out!"

"If you don't let my brother out, I swear I'm gonna come looking for you every night once the Nobility make me one of their own!"

Wham!

Slamming the door shut with all his might and cutting off further bluster from the Langs, the man returned to his cramped office. Moments earlier, the mayor and other important members of the community had headed home. Here in the asylum, with no furniture save a battered desk and chair, their buzz still seemed to hang in the air.

"Those freaking kids. I figured at least one of 'em would be crying and pleading, but both of 'em go and threaten a grown man."

As he grumbled to himself, the man pulled out the wooden chair and took his post in front of the steel door that separated the office from the lock-up area otherwise known as the cages. There were ten individual cells in the cages, each surrounded by bars of super-high-density steel. They'd been built to be a comfortable size, and Doris and Dan had been locked up together. Originally, a family had kindly volunteered to look after

Dan while Doris was confined, since the boy wasn't involved in this, but Dan had fought like a tiger and said he'd die without his sister. There was also a very good chance that, if left to his own devices, he'd have tried to spring Doris, which is how the current arrangement had been reached.

Victims of the Nobility were confined here regardless of the degree of their affliction; if the Noble responsible was destroyed then the curse on them would be lifted and all would be well. If not, the standard operating procedure was to release the victim after a given period and chase them out of town.

That "given period" was the number of days until the frustrated Noble attacked someone else, but this varied from village to village. In Ransylva it was approximately three weeks. The reason it was so long was because, based on past experience, it took an average of three attacks before the Count was done draining his victim, and there was usually an interval of three to five days between attacks.

Of course, because every village could expect their asylum to be stormed by the Nobility during the victim's confinement, for the most part the asylums were guarded by well-armed men confident in their fighting abilities. Because they'd have the Nobility to contend with, no village ever skimped on buying armaments for the asylum. In fact, in addition to the five fully automated, steel-spear launchers and the ten remote-controlled catapults surrounding this thirty-foot-long, half-cylinder building, there were also three laser cannons to neutralize the vehicles of the Nobility, and a pair of flame-throwers from the Capital. The villagers wanted an electromagnetic barrier as well, but the Capital's stores were running low, and they were hard to come by even for those willing to pay black-market prices.

The man guarding the cages was a member of the mob that stormed Doris' farm. The reason the mayor left only one man on watch was because he'd decided that, after sucking the blood from three people tonight already, the Count wouldn't be in quite such a hurry to attack Doris. But if it came to that, the guard could wake up the whole village with a single siren, and the weapons outside could be operated from the control panel on his desk. Most importantly, in four more hours the eastern sky would be growing light. The man wasn't concerned.

Just as he was starting to doze off, there was a rap at the door. The man raced over to the video panel and struck a single key. Greco's face showed on a small video monitor inside the asylum. "What do you want?" the man said to the intercom operating through the wall.

"Be a pal and open up. I came to see Doris."

"No way. Your father told me specifically not to let you in."

"Come on, don't be a jerk. You must know how crazy I am about Doris, right? This is just between you and me, but when day breaks they're gonna bring her up to old fang-face's place on orders from my father. Meaning tonight's my last chance to see the woman I love. And, as you can see, you stand to get a little something for your trouble." Greco pulled a few gold coins out of his pocket and waved them in front of the camera. They weren't the new dalas currency the revolutionary government started issuing five years ago. These were the "aristocrat coins" the Nobility had used. When the revolutionaries finally managed to take power, they destroyed vast quantities of these coins in order to get their new government's economic policies off to a good start. One of them was worth at least a thousand dalas on the black market. That was enough to live off for half a year out on the Frontier.

After staring at the shiny gold for quite some time, the man hit a button without a word. The electronic lock on the door was disengaged, the handle spun around, and in sauntered Greco.

"Thanks, buddy. Here you go!"

Three gold coins clattered down on the desk. Forgetting to shut the door, the man snatched up one of the coins and busily bounced his gaze back and forth between it and Greco's face before eventually nodding with satisfaction. As he dropped all three into his shirt pocket he said, "I suppose it'll be all right— but you've only got three minutes to see her."

"C'mon, make it five."

"Four."

"Okay—you drive a hard bargain."

The man shrugged his shoulders, and then turned toward the door to the cages and reached for the key ring on his belt. The keys jingled together as he chose one and fit it into the lock. It wouldn't do to have this door opening automatically.

"Say—" As the man turned around again, his eye caught Greco's strangely bloodless countenance, and a flash of white light headed right for his own chest.

Killed instantly by a stab to the heart, the man's body was laid out at one side of the room, and then Greco turned the key still jammed in the lock, opened the door, and went into the cages. His knife was already back in the case on his belt.

"Greco!"

There were cages to either side of the narrow corridor, and Doris' cry came from the first one on the left. "You bastard, you come here to get your block knocked off or something?"

"Shut up."

Doris fell silent. She got a bad feeling from Greco's expression, which was more foreboding then she'd ever seen it. *What the hell's he up to?*

"I'll get you right out of there. You're gonna run away with me."

Beyond the iron bars, the Lang children looked at each other. In a low voice, Doris said, "Don't tell me you ... you didn't seriously kill Price ..."

"Oh, I killed him all right. And he's not the only one. My father got his, too. That's what he gets for trying to whip the shit out of me when I came home. The old bastard. I help make his job easier, and that's how the ingrate repays me. But that don't matter now. At any rate, I've got to get out of town tonight. Are you with me?" His eyes had an animalistic gleam to them, but his voice was like molasses.

The propriety of his actions aside, some might even go so far as to say the devotion he showed to the woman he loved was admirable, but Doris said flatly, "Sorry. I'd rather go up to the Count's castle than run off with you."

"What the hell do you mean? ..."

Tears sparkled in the girl's eyes. Tears of hatred. "You teamed up with that butcher and ... and killed him of all people ... Just you wait. I don't care what happens to me, I'm personally gonna see to it you get sent to hell."

She'd always been strong willed, but seeing in those beautiful eyes of hers a fundamentally different and desolate light, Greco abandoned all his schemes and dreams. "So that's how it is? You're saying you'd prefer the Nobility to me?"

When he looked up, all emotion had drained from his face, but the gleam in his eyes was unusually strong.

"If that's the way it's got to be, I guess when you've got to go, you've got to go—and you're about to go join that punk in the hereafter." Taking a step back, he drew the ten-banger from his hip.

Dan shouted, "Sis!" and grabbed onto Doris' neck for dear life while she tried to hide the boy behind her back.

"You're out of your mind, Greco!"

"Say what you like. But I'd rather do this than have any other man take you—vampire or otherwise. You and that smart-mouthed little squirt get to check out of this life together."

"Stop!"

That Doris' cry had been to beg for her own life was the last coherent thought to go through Greco's mind. Someone behind him grabbed the hand with the ten-banger by the wrist. Though whoever it was was just barely touching him, his finger lost the strength to finish pulling the trigger. An unearthly chill spread from his wrist to the rest of his body. Breath with the sweet scent of death tickled his nose, and frosty, dark words struck his earlobe.

"Better you had killed me when you had the chance." Larmica's pale face eclipsed the nape of Greco's swarthy neck. Frozen in horror, Doris and Dan watched as Greco's face grew paler and paler, like he was disappearing into a fog. Seconds later, the young lady in the black dress pulled away from the man and approached their cage. With a thread of blood running from the pale corner of her mouth, this beauty that seemed to sparkle in the darkness could be likened to nothing save a vengeful wraith. Perhaps her thirst wasn't sated yet, for a glance from her bright red eyes shook Doris and Dan to the bottom of their souls.

An expression of unfathomable terror plastered on its face, Greco's body fell to the floor, an empty husk drained of the very last drop of blood.

"What do you—"

The tremble in Doris voice was apparent, but Larmica simply urged, "Go." The hue of madness had left her eyes and, quite to the contrary, her expression now seemed tinged with sorrow.

"Huh?"

"Make good your escape. Father will be coming soon. And when he does, I shan't be able to do any more."

"But ... we can't get out of here. Get us the keys, please," Dan said, grabbing the bars. His flexible, eight-year-old mind had already adjusted to this vampiress being their ally.

She seized the steel bars with dainty hands that looked like they'd break in a strong wind. What strength the vampires possessed! With one good pull, the bars of super-high-density steel tore free of the ceiling and floor, sending screws shooting in all directions.

"Unbelievable ... "

Still trying to keep the wide-eyed Dan behind her, Doris asked Larmica, "You're serious—you really want us to get away, don't you? But why are you helping us?"

A shade of sorrow colored Larmica's moonflower of a face when she turned around.

"*He* died ... but he defended you right to the very end. It would sadden him to see you fall into Father's hands. I have no desire to cause the dead any more sorrow ... "

As Dan took her hand and tugged her out to the corridor, Doris realized this fearsome young woman harbored the same feeling as herself.

"You ... you felt something for him ... "

"Go—make haste."

The three went into the office.

A figure in black stood in the center of the room.

"Father!" Larmica cried out in terror.

"What the hell, still nothing?!" the countenanced carbuncle spat in disgust, its face pressed to D's chest. "A sword or spear wound wouldn't have been so bad, but after taking a wooden stake, his little ticker ain't listening to me. Beat. Just give me one good thump—c'mon and beat already."

Making a fist of the hand it occupied, it rose to strike D's chest as hard as it could, but stopped in midair.

Something was coagulating in the night sky.

A host of white, semi-transparent membranes swirled above the house, then started to come together to form a single mass. Once it had drawn itself together, the glowing cloud swooped down toward the farm, oddly shaped organs becoming visible through its partially transparent body. This was another of the artificial monstrosities spawned by the Nobility—a night cloud. A life-form able to reform itself from single cell organisms, by day the cloud remained in the freezing extremes of the stratosphere, and at night it came back down to earth in scattered form to hunt for prey.

Frighteningly enough, these damned things were dangerous carnivores that would form a single mass when they found a victim, enveloping their prey from all sides to digest and absorb it. They posed a major threat to lost children and inexperienced travelers, and, along with dimension-ripping beasts, they caused a great many people to go inexplicably missing. The electromagnetic barrier had been a godsend in that it alone kept them from wreaking havoc on Doris' farm.

At one point the cloud came down about fifteen feet above D's head, but it seemed to catch wind of something and drifted off to one side, toward the barn where the animals were stabled. Only pausing before the doors for a heartbeat, it spread itself flat as a sheet and easily slipped through a gap between the wall and the doors. The shrill cries of cattle reverberated, the walls shook two or three times, and all too soon it was silent again.

"Those things eat like pigs. It'll be back soon. So get busy beating already, you lousy, good-for-nothing heart!" The complaining fist beat wildly against D's chest and sucked in air. The body didn't move in the slightest. "C'mon, you bastard!"

If there'd been anyone there to see the bizarre but desperate one-man show that went on for a few minutes more, they most likely would've laughed out loud.

And then …

The barn doors bowed out from the inside and splintered, flying everywhere. A second later, an unspeakably grotesque thing appeared in the moonlight. Within the semi-translucent cloud mass was a cow, writhing in agony as it dissolved! Its hide split, red meat melted, and the exposed bone slowly wasted away like popping soap bubbles. As flesh and blood mixed in a narrow tube that seemed to be an esophagus of sorts, the liquid swirled around and the cloud began glowing brighter than ever. It was feeding. For a few seconds the corpulent mass wriggled at the entrance to the barn and then, perhaps sensing other prey, it began to drag itself toward D. Thanks to the weight of the half-devoured cow, it was moving in slow motion.

"Look how close it is already. C'mon and start already!" The fist gave D another smack.

The cloud had closed within ten feet of D. Close enough to hear the tortured cow within it.

Three feet away. The cloud rose into the air and flew straight for D.

A flash of light raced through its translucent mass.

The blade seemed to pass right through it without meeting any resistance, but when the bisected cloud fell to the ground in two chunks, it lost its color before it had a chance to split into smaller pieces. It gave off a whitish steam and soaked into the earth. Only the remains of the cow were left behind.

D got to his feet, scattering moonbeams.

"Nice going. You know, you had me scared out of my wits, as usual."

As if this somewhat inappropriate greeting for someone just risen from the dead hadn't reached his ears, D asked, "Where are the two of them?"

"In the asylum, I'd imagine. Every village seems to put it on the edge of town."

With that, all conversation ceased, and D leapt to his feet and headed for the stables.

The tall trees spread their branches like monsters, fending off the invading moonlight. The only light to speak of was the phosphorescent glow of guidepost mushrooms here and there among the roots of the trees, though that didn't amount to much before the mass and density of the crushing darkness. Even a traveler with some source of light would have a hard time traversing this forest late at night without getting lost in the process.

This was the Ransylva Forest—where night was said to live even at midday. And through it, Dan ran desperately. He wasn't alone. From the darkness less than thirty feet behind him came the growl and footsteps of a carnivore. Its identity was clear. The Count's servant—Garou—pursued him.

Caught by the Count just as they were about to flee the asylum, his sister and Larmica had been put into the carriage, while Dan had been left there alone. Promptly deciding to rescue Doris, he'd headed back to the farm to arm himself. Despite his youth, it was clear to him it would be futile to seek assistance in rescuing his sister from anyone in town. And there wasn't a moment to lose. The shortest possible route would be to cut right through the Ransylva Forest instead of taking the road. With only his sister in mind, he did it without a moment's hesitation. However, less than a minute after he'd entered the forest he heard the snarling of the werewolf behind him.

The deadly marathon had begun.

His father and sister had brought him here before in the relative safety of day, and he could even recall playing in the forest alone. Tapping all the knowledge he had, Dan raced down the most serpentine paths he could find, snuck into hollow trees, and hid in the brush in an attempt to confuse his unsettling pursuer.

But whenever he stopped, it stopped. If he ran again, it took off as well. No matter what he tried, the distance between them neither grew nor shrank.

Dan finally figured out it was toying with him. The moment this occurred to him, his admirable sense collapsed and pure, black terror became the sole occupant of his heart. He ran for all he was worth. And yet, the pursuer to his back remained the same thirty feet behind him as always.

His heart was about to explode and his lungs gasped for more air. He could taste his own salty tears on his tongue. And just when he thought he could take no more, he saw a spot of light in the darkness. The way out!

Hope pumped him full of energy. His feet beat the ground in powerful strides until something suddenly grabbed hold of them.

"Waaugh!" Falling face forward, he tried to get up again but was caught by a pair of hands. "Deadman's hand!"

The scant moonlight barely spilling through the interwoven trees showed him what it was. A pale corpse's hand reached from the ground, its five fingers wriggling in a disgusting way. No, not fingers but rather five flowers. Dan was being held to the ground by a pale blossom that looked just like a corpse's hand. As the various botanical horrors sown by the Nobility went, these were rather bizarre but innocuous plants—and the fact that Dan had known where they grew and had still ended up jumping right into the middle of this patch said volumes about how the terror behind him had wiped everything else from his mind. But who could blame a boy of eight for that?

Using all his might, Dan got to his feet again. The deadman's hand still hung from his wrist, pulled-up roots and all.

Just as he was about to start running again—

"Awoooooooooh!"

A terrific howl assailed him from behind, rooting his feet. Seeing the exit so close at hand, this was the battle cry Garou gave when it decided the time had come to put an end to their horrifying chase. It'd been pursuing Dan because the Count was allowing it to dine on a living person for the first time in ages.

All the strength drained from the boy. Sorry, Sis. Looks like I won't be able to save you. Tears of regret rolled down his cheeks.

And then, the howling abruptly halted. In its place, Dan could sense trembling.

At that same moment, Dan heard something. He caught the echo of hoofbeats out beyond the exit, distant but drawing closer with a vengeance. He couldn't hear a voice or see a shape. But Dan knew in a second who it was. "D!" His hopeful cry speared through the darkness.

Once again a howl rang out behind him, and a black whirlwind raced by his side.

"D, watch out!"

He ran a few steps, kicking the tenacious deadman's hand blossoms out of his way. An incredibly bestial roar rose beyond the exit, and was suddenly silenced.

Fairly tumbling headlong out of the forest, Dan saw a rider on a hillock ahead, bathed in moonlight. At his feet lay the fallen werewolf. D galloped over. Getting down off a horse Dan recognized, he asked, "What are you doing out here? Where's your sister?"

Dan was overcome with emotion. "I just knew you were still alive, D. I ... I knew there was no way you'd die on us ... " He couldn't say anything more. When Dan finally settled down and explained the situation, D picked him up without a word and set him on the horse. He didn't tell the boy to go home or offer to bring him back to the farm.

Looking out across the prairie at the Count's castle with a steely gaze, D asked, "Are you coming with me?" It was the same question he'd asked the boy in the ruins a night earlier.

"Sure!"

There was no reason to expect any other reply from the boy.

There was one particular characteristic of the castles of the Nobility that suited their vampire lords. While there were gorgeous sleeping chambers ready for guests and other visitors, there were none for the lord and his family.

They slumbered in a place most befitting their rank, an exalted place that was the stuff of legend: in coffins beneath the earth.

In vast subterranean chambers filled with tiny organisms, where the stench of dankness mixed with the sweet perfume of ancient soil, here alone the true past slept, free of computer controls. The smell of long-unused torches hung in the air of this special place. A stone wall that looked to be perhaps thirty feet tall was covered by a colossal portrait of the Sacred Ancestor. On the crimson dais before it stood the Count in his black raiment and Doris, garbed in a gown of snow white. The girl's eyes were lifeless. She was hypnotized.

To the left of the dais was Larmica, but her eyes looked just as dazed as they wandered through space, avoiding her father and his bride-to-be. This had less to do with the reprimand she'd been given by her father for trying to help Doris escape and more to do with something the beautiful vampiress' heart had lost.

The dark nuptials were about to begin.

"Look. There you shall make your bed from this night forth."

The Count gestured to a pair of black, lacquered coffins positioned on a stone slab in front of the dais. Below where the falcon-and-flames coat of arms was carved, the coffin on the right had a plate with the name "Lee," while the one on the left had already been inscribed "Doris."

"They contain dirt. The same proud soil the Lee family castle is built upon. I am quite sure it shall give you dreams of sweet blood each and every night. Now, then."

The Count took Doris' chin in hand and tilted her head back, exposing more of her pale throat. "Before we exchange the vows of man and wife, I must rid you of that loathsome mark." He pulled out a small signet from the folds of his cape. Its square face was carved with the same coat of arms that decorated the lids of the coffins.

"First the right." White smoke arose from her pale throat as he pressed the signet down into the flesh, and Doris trembled. Performing the same act again, only a little lower, the Count said, "Now the left." Once finished, he brought his abhorrent mouth closer to his bride's throat. Though white smoke still hung in the air, now there wasn't a mark on her virgin neck, aside from the pair of bite marks the Count left the first time he fed on her. Breath that reeked of blood crept along her throat. The mark of the cross that had kept the girl safe didn't reappear.

"Very well. Now I need fear nothing when I give her my kiss."

Grinning broadly as he returned the signet to his cape, the Count turned to his beloved daughter—in a stupor by his side—and said, "You shall have a new mother. Will you not recite some words of congratulation for us?"

Her vacant gaze focused on her father. Larmica's mouth moved sluggishly. "I ..." she began. "I, Larmica Lee, your three thousand seven hundred and twenty-seven-year-old daughter, congratulate my three thousand seven hundred and fifty-seven-year-old father Magnus Lee and my seventeen-year-old mother Doris Lang on the occasion of their marriage." Her voice was vapid, but the Count nodded and pricked up his ears.

What at first had seemed to be Larmica's voice bouncing off the stone floor and ceiling became a unified chant that reverberated through the dim subterranean chamber, like the cries of the writhing dead rising from the earth. "We give Count Magnus Lee our most heartfelt congratulations on the creation of this new union."

The voices came from the occupants of countless coffins stuck in the walls and beneath the floor. A number of them shook and rattled a bit, causing the Count to narrow his gaze.

"Now it's time—" Saying that, as he brought his lips to Doris' still-upturned throat, the transmitter in his jacket pocket emitted a siren. "Oh, you infernal machine," the Count said irritably and pulled it out. "Whatever is it?"

The metallic voice of what must have been a computer responded. "A pair of humans and a horse have just arrived at the main gate. One of the humans is male, approximately eight years of age, the other is a male estimated to be between the ages of seventeen and eighteen."

"What?" The Count's eyes glowed with blood light.

Larmica turned in amazement.

"They must not be allowed to enter. Do not lower the drawbridge. Open fire on them immediately."

"Actually … " the computer hesitated. "The bridge went down as soon as they drew near. We are unable to fire the weapons. It is my belief that the animal or one of the humans possesses a device that interferes with my commands. At present, all of the castle's electronic armaments are inoperable."

"You wretch … " the Count groaned with hatred. "So the stripling still lives, does he? But, how on earth did he come back? Even I know of no way to return from a wooden stake through the heart."

"For one such as he … " Larmica muttered.

"*One such as he?* Larmica, could it be you have some idea as to his identity?"

Larmica said nothing.

"Very well. That question may wait until later. For the time being, I must first slay him. When something interferes like this in the middle of a ceremony, it is customary to postpone the festivities until the nuisance has been dealt with."

"Understood, Father. But how exactly do you intend to deal with him?"

"I know of someone who would like very much to make amends for a blunder."

As a pale blue finally tinged the eastern sky, in the castle's courtyard D and Dan once again faced Rei-Ginsei.

"I haven't been given any more Time-Bewitching Incense," Rei-Ginsei said with a beautiful, devilish smile. On his way from Doris' farm to the castle, Rei-Ginsei had encountered the Count's carriage as it raced back from town at perilous speed, and had accompanied the carriage the rest of the way. "I can understand why the Count was so upset. However, if I dispatch you to the next life once again, I'm quite certain his anger will be appeased. Kindly dismount."

They were ten feet apart, just as they'd been at the Lang farm. Dan took cover along with the horse behind a stone sculpture and waited for the battle to be decided.

But basically it was an absurd challenge. So long as he had no Time-Bewitching Incense, Rei-Ginsei had no way to overcome D. On the other hand, any critical wounds D might deal would be turned back on the Hunter through the extra-dimensional passageway in Rei-Ginsei's body. And yet, each one apparently thought they stood a good chance of prevailing and both of them went into action at once.

"Ugh ... "

D doubled over, and then fell to his knees. A flame danced atop the stick of Time-Bewitching Incense in Rei-Ginsei's right hand. He'd deceived D. In the blink of an eye, a shrike blade was whizzing through the air.

But the reason he'd defeated D back at the farm was because he had the muscle-amplifying components of the combat suit aiding him. His face twisted with agony, D knocked the shrike-blade out of the air and leapt.

It was like a complete reenactment of their duel at the ruins. What was different was that Rei-Ginsei didn't dodge, but left his head wide open for the silvery flash. He imagined D would be aiming for his limbs. However, the instant he realized that the blade coming down at him was unmistakably aimed at his head, he let the extra-dimensional gateway within his body open and didn't try to run.

D's forehead split, but it was just a thin layer of skin. An instant later, bright red blood gushed from Rei-Ginsei's abdomen. The dashing young man's expression was one of stupefaction as he gazed at the blade protruding from his belly...the same blade that was supposed to split D's head in two. The Vampire Hunter had swung his sword overhead and only cut the outermost layer of skin on Rei-Ginsei's brow, then changed his grip on his sword in midair, and drove it right through his own stomach. Already linked by the extra-dimensional passageway, when the blade went into D's body it materialized in Rei-Ginsei's belly instead. Aside from his ability to twist and link points in space, Rei-Ginsei was otherwise a normal human who couldn't survive that sort of punishment. This was the sort of absurd method of killing only a dhampir like D would be capable of.

"Dan, put that candle out for me."

As he listened to the boy dash into action, Rei-Ginsei thudded to the ground. The incense left his hand, and his bright blood stained the earth.

"Hey, don't you keel over yet. Do at least one good thing before your miserable life ends," Dan said, stomping the incense out. A chill came over him as he watched the blade poking from the abdomen of the fallen Rei-Ginsei slide smoothly back into his body. D was pulling his own sword out of himself.

"And what is that ... one good thing?" asked Rei-Ginsei.

"Tell me where my sister's at."

"I don't know ... Search to your heart's contentment ... By now, the Count has made her his bride ... " A clot of blood spilled from his mouth, and the last spasms of impending death twisted his gorgeous countenance. "If only I had been made one of the Nobility ... " And then his head dropped to one side.

"He bit it, the damn jerk," Dan said with sorrow. "If he'd actually acted good instead of just looking good he might've lived a nice, long time ... "

"That's right," D said, breathing heavily. The effects of the Time-Bewitching Incense were gone the instant it was extinguished. The reason he looked to be in such pain was the wound to his stomach.

"Where do you think they've got my sister? This place is so huge, I don't even know where to begin to look." Dan was on the verge of tears, but D tapped him on the shoulder.

"You're forgetting that I'm a Vampire Hunter. Come with me."

The two of them went straight down to the subterranean chamber. Dan watched in wonder as shut doors flew open as soon as D approached. Nothing could stop them. From time to time, they passed expressionless people who seemed to be servants and ladies-in-waiting, but none of them so much as attempted to look at them before disappearing into the darkness.

"Robots, I guess," Dan said.

"Leaders of a false life—this castle flickers in the light of destruction now. As the Nobility themselves have for a long, long time."

Descending a narrow staircase for two stories, they came to a massive wooden door. Studded with hobnails from top to bottom, it testified to the import of the dark ceremony taking place beyond it.

"This is it, right?" Dan was tense.

D took off his blue pendant and put it around the boy's neck. "This will repel the robots. You stay here."

The door had neither lock nor bolt. It looked to weigh tons, but when D's finger brushed it, the hinges creaked and the doors opened to either side. Wide stone stairs worn low in the center flowed down into the darkness. Somewhere far below there was a barely perceptible light. On descending the staircase, D came to the subterranean chamber. Far off to his right flames danced.

Coffins caked with dust, some with skeletal hands and feet protruding through gaps in the half-decayed boards, others with wedges of wood driven right through their lids—this was what greeted D in the darkness. Weaving his way through the final resting place of rows upon rows of the dead, D arrived at last at the blood-hued dais, where he came face to face with the Count.

"I am impressed by the way you managed to come back to life. And to come here." The Count's tone went beyond awe. D turned his eyes to Doris, standing stock still on the dais. A cool smile nudged his cheeks for an instant.

"It seems I'm just in time."

At some point Larmica had vanished.

"There shall be plenty of time for that when you are dead," the Count replied. "However, as Larmica herself has said, it is truly a shame to slay you. You came back to life after taking a stake through your chest—now there is a secret I myself should very much like to know. What say you? Will you not reconsider this one last time? Have you no wish to take Larmica as your wife and live here in the castle? She has lost her soul to you."

"The Nobility died out long ago," said D. For some reason, his voice seemed to have a sorrowful ring to it. "The Nobility and this castle are no more than phantoms forgotten by time. Return to where you belong."

"Silence, stripling!" the Count moaned, gnashing his teeth in rage. "Born of Noble blood as you are, surely you must know what immortality means. Life given until the end of time—it is our duty to do just that, crushing the human worms underfoot all the while."

As he finished speaking, the Count knit his brow. He had just noticed that D was not looking up at himself, but rather at the portrait behind him.

If it had been that alone, he wouldn't have paid it much heed. What triggered this surprise—which was actually closer to horror—was that he saw that the face of the youth in the flickering torchlight was the same as the visage in the portrait holding his gaze.

At the same time, the Count realized words he'd heard twice before were ringing in the depths of his ears. Unconsciously, he let them slip from his mouth.

"Transient guests ... "

In all the proud, glorious history of the Nobility, this one pronouncement of their godlike Sacred Ancestor alone had met suspicion and denial from all Nobles. The Nobility's Academy of Sciences had developed a method of mathematically analyzing fate, and, after they cross-referenced these figures with the historical import of all known civilizations they canceled all presentations on the findings of their research. When they came under fire for this decision, it was the Sacred Ancestor who came to face the critics, appearing in public for the first time in a millennium to control the situation. And those words were the ones he'd let slip out then.

The great, eternally flowing river that was history had a civilization temporarily resting on its placid surface—the Sacred Ancestor referred to those propping up the civilization as transient guests. The question was, did he refer to the Nobility or humans?

The tangled skein of the Count's thoughts grew more knotted, and then a single thread suddenly pulled free. A bizarre rumor that had circulated briefly among the highest-ranking Nobility whispered into life in his ear once more. *Our Sacred Ancestor, it seems, swore to a human maid—they would make children and he would slay them, but even after slaying them he would still have her bear more. Impossible!* The Count's brain was driven to the limits of panic and confusion. *He couldn't possibly be … Could the Sacred Ancestor have planned the joining of human and Noble blood all along?*

Not knowing what was truth or lies, the Count stepped forward, chilled by his own thoughts. "Stripling, I shall see to it you feel the full might of the Nobility before you die."

As he finished talking, his cape fluttered. The lining was red and glistening. The air howled around the chamber and every flame danced a step shy of being snuffed. Astonishingly, the cape spread like a drop of ink dissolving in water and tried to wrap around D.

D drew his sword and slashed at the edge of it in one fluid motion. His blade stuck to the lining. This was the same blade D had used to destroy the bronze monstrosity Golem and slay a werewolf running at half the speed of sound!

The lining twined around and around his sword, tearing it from D's grasp a second later. But actually, D himself had released it. Had he resisted, his own hand might have been wrapped up and crushed in the process.

"And now you stand naked," the Count laughed snidely, taking D's sword in his right hand. His cape returned to its normal dimensions. Making another grand sweep of it, the Count said, "This was stitched together from the skin of women who'd slaked my thirst, and it was lacquered with their blood. Thanks to secret techniques passed down through my clan, it's five times as strong as the hardest steel and twenty times more flexible than a spider's webbing. And you have just witnessed its adhesive power for yourself."

Several flashes of light scorched through the air. The cape spread. All the wooden needles D had hurled dropped to the floor in front of the Count.

"Enough of your foolish resistance." The cape opened like the wings of a dark, mystic bird and the Count threw it and himself forward.

D leapt out of the way. The sleeve of his coat sported a fresh tear. That was thanks to the trenchant blade the cape had become.

"Oh, whatever is the trouble, my good Hunter? Could it be you're powerless now?" His snide laughter came over the top of the attacking cape. The speed with which he swept it around was incredible. Unable to close the gap between the Count and himself, D moved like the wind to evade the assaults.

At some point the two of them had changed positions, so that D now stood in front of Doris, shielding her.

The Count's eyes glowed. His cape howled through the air.

As D was about to leap away once more, something wrapped around him from behind. Doris' arms!

A heartbeat later D's body was entwined in the cape. In this battle that demanded the utmost concentration, even he'd forgotten for a moment that Doris was in the Count's thrall.

D's bones creaked from the enormous pressure. His gorgeous countenance twisted. And yet, who else would've been skilled enough to push Doris out of harm's way a split second before the cape engulfed him? D's sword glittered in the Count's hands.

"Your destruction will come on your own blade."

The Count intended to lop off his head. D's body was wrapped in a cape his blade hadn't been able to pierce, and the sword mowed through the air with all the Count's might behind it, until it suddenly it stopped.

At the same time the cape crumpled and D leapt clear of the bizarre fabric restraints. The instant the Count's concentration had been broken, the spell over his cape had faltered as well. He landed right before the Count. And what did the Count make of that?

"Ha!"

With a premonition of his firmly skewered foe bringing a smile to his face, the Count thrust the blade. The sword was caught and stopped dead right in front of D's chest. Caught between the palms of the Hunter's hands. Their roles had been completely reversed from their first encounter!

Without letting up in the slightest on the unspeakable pressure he brought to bear four inches from the weapon's tip, D twisted both hands to one side. The Count didn't go sailing through the air, but the end of the blade snapped off. The broken tip still between his hands, D leapt back ten feet.

"Why, that's the very same trick … "

It was truly grand the way the Count sent out his cape even as he shouted this, but the difference between being the one doing the trick and the one on the receiving end in this case became the difference between life and death. The tip of the sword flew from D's folded hands in a silvery flash that neatly knifed through the heart beneath that black raiment.

For a few seconds the Count stood stock still. Then the flesh on his face began to melt away, and his eyes dropped to the floor, trailing optic nerves behind them.

Mere moments after he hit the floor, his rotting tongue and vocal chords forced out his final words.

"I ... I had to beg our Sacred Ancestor to teach me that very same trick ... Could it be ... *Milord, are you truly his ...* "

D quickly made his way over to Doris, who lay on the floor. Something strange was happening to the castle. The faint ringing of the warning bell from the Count's chest was proof of that. The Count's deadly attack had faltered because the bell had caught his ear—turning him from the path of certain victory to a plunge into the abyss of death. The floor shook ever so slightly.

A light tap to her cheek was enough to wake Doris. There was no trace of the fang marks on her neck any longer.

"D—what in the world is going on?! You're alive?"

"My work is done. The wounds on your throat have vanished." D pointed to the far end of chamber and the way he'd come. "If you go up that staircase you'll find Dan. The two of you should go back to the farm."

"But you—you've got to go with us."

"My work is finished, but I still have business here. Hurry up and go. And please be sure to tell Dan not to forget the promise he made his big brother."

Tears sparkled in Doris' eyes.

"Go."

Turning time and again, Doris finally disappeared into the darkness. A salutation rang from D's left hand, though it probably never reached her ears.

"So long, you tough, sweet kids. Godspeed to you."

D turned around. To one side of the chamber stood Larmica. "Was that your doing?"

Larmica nodded and said, "I reversed all the computer's safety circuits. In the next five minutes the castle shall be destroyed—please, flee while you may."

"Why not live here in your castle until the end of time, with the darkness as your companion?"

"There's no longer time for that. And the Lee family died out long ago. It died when my father chose a pointless, eternal life of nothing save drinking human blood."

The trembling grew stronger, and the whole chamber began to groan. The white detritus falling from the ceiling wasn't common dust, but rather finely powdered stone. The molecular bonds of the entire castle were breaking down!

"So, you'll stay here then?"

Larmica didn't answer the question, but said instead, "Kindly allow me to ask one thing—your name. D ... Is that D, as in Dracula?

D's lips moved.

The two of them stood motionless, with white powder raining down. His reply went unheard.

Appropriately enough, the vampire's castle turned to dust like its lord and was gone. Their field of view rendered pure white by the clouds of powdered rubble, Doris and Dan couldn't stop coughing from all the dust.

They were atop a hill less than a hundred yards from the castle.

Wiping at her tearing eyes, when Doris finally raised her face again another sort of tears began to flow.

"It's gone ... everything. And he's not coming back either ... "

Putting a hand on his distracted sister's shoulder, Dan said cheerily, "Let's go home, Sis. We got a heap of work to do."

Doris shook her head.

"It's no use ... I just can't do it anymore ... Can't use a whip like I used to, can't look after you or do my work around the farm ... And all because I found someone I could depend on ... "

"You just leave it to me." The boy of eight threw out his chest. His little hand gripped D's pendant. "We've just gotta hold on for five more years. Then I'll be able to do everything. I'll even find you a husband, Sis. We got a long road ahead of us—so buck up."

He knew that he was no longer just an eight-year-old child.

Doris turned to her brother, looked at him like he was someone she'd never seen before, and nodded. Five years from now, he'd still be a boy. But in ten years, he'd be able to rebuild the house and hunt down fire dragons. It would take a long while, but time had a way of passing.

"Let's go, Dan."

Finally reclaiming her smile, Doris walked toward their horse.

"Sure thing!" Dan shot back, and, though his heart was nearly shattered with sorrow, he smiled to hide it.

With the two of them on its back, the horse galloped off to the east, where blue light filled the sky and their farm awaited them.

D had kept his promise.

Now it was the boy's turn.

Postscript

Or actually, an explanation of the dedication.
Most fans of *outré* cinema should be familiar with the film
Horror of Dracula, produced in Britain by Hammer Films in 1958.
Along with the previous year's *The Curse of Frankenstein*, this
classic helped fire a worldwide boom in horror films, and, in
addition, served as the first inspiration for this humble horror
novelist. I've seen quite a few horror and suspense movies, but no
film before or since accomplished what this one did—to send me
racing out of the theater in the middle of the show. Though most
will find this information superfluous, Terence Fisher directed it,
Jimmy Sangster wrote the script, and Bernard Robinson was the
production designer. Surely the film's stars, Christopher Lee and
Peter Cushing, require no introduction. The whole incredible
showdown between Count Dracula and Professor Van Helsing—
from the fiend's appearance in silhouette at the top of the castle's
staircase, to the finale where sunlight and the cross reduce him to
dust—is something horror movie fans will be talking about until the
end of time. I hope it's made available on video as soon as possible.

At present, Kazuo Umezu could be regarded as the leading
man of horror manga in Japan, but so far as I know, the only
male manga artist in the past with such a distinct horror style

(I don't know about female manga artists) would be Osamu Kishimoto. But rather than aiming to produce more of the same Japanese-style horror that had preceded him, this man created a gothic mood in the Western tradition. Whether it was a weird western-style mansion standing right in the middle of the city, with coffins resting in its stone-walled basement and a horde of creepy inhabitants, or the logic of the conflict that runs through all his stories (such as the cross against vampires or the power of Buddhism against kappas), the way he succeeded in bringing his creatures to life in a field like Japanese horror manga, where they were so sorely lacking, was, in a word, refreshing.

It would be most unfair if someday someone were to write a history of horror manga in Japan and dismiss Osamu Kishimoto as merely one more author of sci-fi and adventure manga. Even now I get goose bumps as I recall the short tale about the kappa that turned itself into a beautiful woman when runoff from a factory polluted its lake, and later took up residence in a brother and sister's house, as well as many other tales. Lately I haven't seen much work by him, but I sincerely hope to see him in better health and producing new stories in the future.

Hideyuki Kikuchi
December 6, 1982, watching *Horror of Dracula*

And now, a preview of the next novel in the
Vampire Hunter D series

Vampire Hunter D

Volume 2

Raiser of Gales

Written by
Hideyuki Kikuchi

Illustrations by
Yoshitaka Amano

English translation by
Kevin Leahy

Coming in August 2005
from DH Press and Digital Manga Publishing

A Village in Winter

Wintry sunlight fell from high in the hollow sky to the valley below. Bright enough to trick a smile out of you and cold enough to empty your lungs in a cloudy white chain of coughs, the rays bound for the narrow and more-or-less straight trail were also quite refreshing. Perhaps that was because spring wasn't so far off.

Not far from there the road through the valley came to a modest plain surrounded by black woods and ushered travelers into a tiny Frontier hamlet.

Including the ranches and solar farms scattered about the area, there were still probably less than two hundred homes. The roofs of wooden and tensile plastic houses were crusted with white remnants of snow, as were alleys that never saw the light of day. And the people here, so bundled in heavy furs they might easily be mistaken for beasts, wore stern expressions. For all the younger folks, even the littlest of children, the single-minded determination to live made a hard mask of their features.

A narrow stream ran through the center of town from east to west. The surface of its clear waters reflected a sturdy bridge, and at this moment a silent procession of people crossed the bridge with a grave gait.

Ten men and two women were in the group. Sobs spilled from one woman's lips as she hid her face with the well-worn sleeve of an insulated overcoat. Graying hair reached her shoulders, and the other woman—also in her forties, by the look of her—stood by her side with an arm around her back for support. No doubt they were neighbors. Although this pair set the tone for the whole party, their grief hadn't yet elicited a sympathetic response from the men.

The old man at the fore wore a robe heavily adorned with magical formulae and all manner of strange symbols, and his face was wrought with terror. The other men's faces were plastered with almost identical expressions, though six of them were also plainly in physical pain. Not surprising in light of the abominable burden digging down into their shoulders.

An oak coffin.

However, more disquieting by far was the heavy chain wrapped around it. It almost seemed like a concerted effort had been made to keep whatever rested within the coffin from getting back out, and the way the chain rattled dully in the wintry light testified to the desperate fear of those who bore the oak box.

The party came to a halt at the center of the bridge. That was where the structure jutted out an extra yard on either side, forming a small gathering place over the river.

The old man who led them pointed to one side.

With much shuffling of their feet, the men bearing the coffin hustled over to the railing.

Giving a shudder, the sturdy man by the elder's side reached for the weapons girding his waist. Steel stakes a good foot and a half long, to be precise. The man had at least half a dozen of them in a pouch on his belt. His other hand pulled out the hammer he wore through the opposite side of his belt. The old-fashioned gunpowder revolver he had holstered there didn't even merit a glance.

Loosing an anguished scream, one of the women scrambled toward the coffin, but her neighbor and the rest of the men managed to restrain her.

"You simmer down," the old man shouted at her reproachfully.

The woman hid her face in her hands. If not for those supporting her, she undoubtedly would have collapsed on the spot.

Casting an emotionless glance at the slender coffin, the elder raised his right hand shoulder-high and began to intone the words befitting such a ceremony.

"I am here today, my heart like unto a mournful abyss beyond description. Gina Bolan, beloved daughter of Seka Bolan and resident #8009 of the village of Tsepesh, Western Frontier Sector Seven, fell victim to the despised Nobility and passed away last night … "

At this, the faces of the pallbearers grew visibly paler, but the elder may not have noticed.

Six pairs of eyes restlessly shifted about, their collected gaze turning imploringly to the calm surface of the river.

There was nothing to see there. Nothing whatsoever out of the ordinary.

Within the coffin, something stirred. Not someone. Something.

The men's faces inched closer to the coffin, as if caught in its gravity.

Clank, clank went the chains.

The men's faces grew white as a sheet.

The mayor shouted the name of the man with the stakes.

"Down! Put it down now!" the armed man said in a terror-cramped tone as he stepped closer. The other men didn't comply with his command. Brains and nerves and even muscles stiffened as fear stampeded through their bodies. This was by no means the first such ceremony they'd been involved in. However, the phenomenon now taking place in that box on their shoulders was patently impossible. For pity's sake, it was daytime!

Seeing the condition of the others, the man with the hammer and stake clanged them together and shouted tersely, "Set 'er down on the railing!" The results were evident enough.

Whatever spell had held the men waned and the coffin, which was a heartbeat shy of being thrown over the side, came to rest on the thick handrail. Three of the men still supported the other side of it.

It was a weird frenzy of activity on the bridge that fine, pre-vernal day.

The well-armed man dashed over and set the sharpened steel tip of a stake against the lid of the coffin.

His granite-tough face was deeply streaked by fear and impatience. The timing of this flew in the face of his vast personal experience and undermined the confidence he drew from long years on the job.

Sounds continued to issue from the coffin. From the way it shook and the sounds it made, it seemed that whatever it contained had awakened and was fumbling around without any idea of its present predicament.

The man raised his hammer high.

Suddenly, the sounds coming from the coffin changed. Powerful blows struck the lid from the inside, shaking not only the casket but also the men carrying it with their thunderous pummeling.

The elder cried something.

With a low growl the hammer tore through the air. Shouting and the sounds of destruction melded into one.

The stake pierced the coffin at almost exactly the same second a pale hand smashed through the heavy planks and clawed at the air. The hand of a mere child!

Wildly twitching, it clutched at the air again and again. Then, in a split second, it flew to the throat of the man who stood there, hammer still in hand and utterly dumbfounded.

"—coffin … Drop the damn coffin!"

Blood gushed from the man's throat along with those words.

This ghastly tableau did more than his orders to rouse the men's consciousness. Shoulder muscles bulging, they tilted the coffin high on the railing. It fell with the other man still pinned to the lid, sending up a splash that flowered in countless droplets across the surface of the river.

Surely the coffin must've been weighted, for it rapidly sank and merged with the ash-gray bottom. Amid the remaining ripples, crimson liquid bubbled up from one of those who'd sank with it, but in the world above the tranquil light of winter blanketed all creation and only a woman's sobs remained to testify to the gruesome tragedy that had just played out.

B lades of grass that had long borne the weight of the snow took advantage of the reverberations from the heavy footfalls and threw off their burden. After all, their day would be here soon enough.

The footsteps came from a number of people. Each and every one of them looked as tough as a boulder and as beefy as a Martian steer. Their well-developed muscles bulged through their heavy fur coats. All of them were in their twenties. Not even their apparent leader, a man a bit taller than the rest, had hit thirty yet. They belonged to the village's Youth Brigade.

The reason they were all breathing so heavily was because they'd already been climbing this slope for nearly nine hours. But it was clear from their expressions and the look in the eyes of all that they weren't here for a picnic. Their faces were so hardened by brooding, they might as well have been on the verge of tears from sheer frustration and rage. From the look of it, they were trying in vain to hold back the pitch-black terror welling up inside them with the ferocity only the young possessed. The pair bringing up the rear was especially short of breath. Although that was partly due to the fact each had a wooden crate full of weapons strapped to his back, the real reason was the gently rolling hill they were climbing.

It was a rather odd piece of geography.

A mile and a quarter in diameter at the base and roughly sixty or so feet high, it looked like any ordinary hill from both the ground and the air. Those who set foot on its slopes with an aim to reach the summit would find that it took several hours to do so no matter how great they were at hiking.

Black ruins rose from the summit of the hill.

That was where the men were headed. However, that simple goal, glowering down at the surrounding landscape from a scant altitude of sixty feet, was not unlike the mirages that were said to occur in the Frontier's desert regions—it taunted these men as they tried to reach it, and would do the same to anyone else who accepted the challenge.

The distance never decreased.

Their feet clearly trod the slope, and their bodies told them they were indeed steadily gaining elevation. And yet, the further reaches of the incline and the ruins they sought never got any closer.

Taking the accounts of all who'd experienced the phenomenon into consideration, it was estimated to take a man in prime condition thirty minutes to climb three feet. Ten hours to the top—even on level ground that much walking would leave anyone exhausted. Climbing the hill, it only got worse, as the slope grew steeper and the trek became ever more fatiguing. It came as little surprise that no one had even tried to climb it in the last three years.

The man at the forefront of the group—Haig, their leader—seemed to take no notice of his compatriots as he scanned the western horizon. Beyond the forest and the silvery chain of peaks far behind them the sun would be going down in two hours. That made it roughly three o'clock Afternoon, Frontier Standard Time.

If they didn't reach the top, accomplish their aims, and take their leave in the one hundred and twenty minutes remaining, Haig knew as well as anyone what fate awaited them when darkness fell.

To make matters worse, once they eventually made it to the summit, the fact of the matter was they didn't have the faintest idea where in the ruins the thing they sought would be slumbering. Although a roughly sketched map was stuffed in the leader's breast pocket, it'd been drawn decades earlier by someone who'd since passed away, so they weren't entirely sure whether they could rely on it or not.

And then there was their exhausted state to consider. Though this group had been selected from the proudest and strongest of the Youth Brigade, the physically taxing climb was actually far more fatiguing mentally. When no amount of struggling would bring you any closer to a goal that was right before your eyes, sheer impatience could physically destroy you. This was said to be a particularly effective defense against intruders from the world below. Once they set foot in the ruins, there was some question as to whether or not they'd even have sufficient strength remaining to search out its resting place.

The only thing they had working in their favor was the fact that on the way down, at least, the hill lost its mystic hold over climbers. If they ran all the way, they could be down to the foot of the hill in less than two minutes.

Suddenly, Haig's sweat-stained countenance was suffused with joy.

He knew the distance between the summit ahead and him was "real" now. Less than thirty feet remained. Ignoring the panting of his air-starved lungs, he shouted, "We're there!" From behind him, satisfied grunts rose in response.

A few minutes later, the whole group was resting in the courtyard of the ruins. The shadow of fatigue fell heavily on each and every face, rendering them almost laughable.

"Just about time to get down to it. Break out the weapons," ordered Haig. He alone had remained standing, surveying their surroundings.

The lot of them huddled around the two wooden crates.

Off came the lids. Inside were five hammers, ten wooden stakes honed to trenchant points, and twenty Molotov cocktails fashioned from wine bottles filled with tractor fuel and corked with rags. In addition, they had five bundles of powerful mining explosives with individual timers. Each of the men also had a bowie knife, sword, or machete stuck through the belt around his waist.

Everyone took a weapon.

"You all know the plan, right?" Haig said, just to be sure. "I don't know if we can put a whole lot of stock in this copy of the map, but right about now we ain't got any other options. If you think you're in trouble, give a whistle. You find out where it is, give two."

Bloodshot eyes bobbed up and down as the men nodded and got to their feet. Their grand scheme was going into action.

An unexpected voice stopped them in their tracks.

"Just a second. Where the blazes are you boys off to all charged up like that?"

Every one of them moved like they'd been jerked back on a leash, turning to where they heard the voice even as they went for their weapons.

From a shadowy entrance in the sole remaining wall of the stony ruins—a cavernous opening that faced the courtyard—a lone girl stepped casually into the afternoon light. Raven hair hung down to the shoulders of her winter coat, and what showed of her thighs looked cold but inviting.

"Well if it ain't Lina! What brings you up—" one of the men started to ask before swallowing the rest of the question. The eyes of all took a tinge of terror, as well as the scornful hue of someone whose suspicions have proved correct. They'd known the answer to that question for quite some time.

"What the hell do you boys think you're doing? You'd better not go and do anything stupid," said Lina as she looked Haig square in the eye. Although her visage was still so innocent it couldn't look stern if she tried, it shone with sagacity and all the allure of a mature woman. She was at that awkward stage, a neat little bud waiting for spring and a heartbeat away from bursting open into a glorious blossom.

"Suppose you tell me what the hell brings you up here?" said Haig, his words dripping like molasses. His gaze had fallen to Lina's bare feet. "It ain't like you don't know the shit that's going on in town. The whole place's been turned inside out and we still didn't find it. Meaning this is the only place left for it to hide, wouldn't you say?"

"Well, that doesn't mean you have to haul a load of bombs up here, does it? Stakes and Molotov cocktails should do the job."

"That's nothing that concerns you," Haig said scornfully. "Now answer the damn question. Why the hell are you here? We sure as shit didn't see you on our way up here. Just how long you been here, anyway?"

"I just got here. And for your information, I came up the other side. So of course you didn't see me."

As the men looked at each other they had a strange glint in their eyes.

"Well in that case, I guess the hill can't fool you none— looks like we had it figured right all along. Unless I miss my guess, you're the one responsible for what's happening in town."

"Spare me your conjecture. You know I've been at home every time anything happened."

"You don't say. Hell, the whole bunch of you have been screwy since that happened. We got no way of knowing what kind of powers you been using behind our backs."

Haig suddenly had nothing more to say. He gave a toss of his chin to his cohorts. All of them smiled lasciviously as they started to close in on Lina.

"We're gonna have to check you out now. Gonna peel you down buck-ass naked."

"You stop this foolishness right now. Do you have any idea how much trouble you'll get in if you even try it?"

"Ha! That supposed to be a threat?" one of them jeered. "Everybody in town knows full well what's going on between you and the mayor, missy. If we can prove you're a plain ol' woman now, the old geezer'll be happier than a pig in shit."

"And that ain't the half of it," another added. "After all of us have had a turn with you, you'll be feeling so damn good you'll lose your tongue for ratting us out."

Haig licked his lips. These young men were known to be rough customers—that was precisely the reason they were perfect for protecting the village from brutal groups of roving bandits or vicious beasts spawned by the Nobility's technology. But now, their exhaustion and the fear of the work to come churned together in a slimy mess that suffocated what little sense they'd been born with.

Lina made no attempt to escape as Haig grabbed her by the arms and pulled her close. His greasy lips savagely latched onto her fine mouth. Pulling her coat up with one hand, he groped at her thighs while his tongue tried to force its way between her perfect teeth.

Suddenly, there was a dull smack and his massive frame doubled over at the waist. With lightning speed Lina had slammed her knee into Haig's privates, leaving him speechless and on his knees. She didn't even spare him a backward glance as she disappeared into the same entrance from which she'd first appeared.

"You little bitch!" shouted one of the three men who went after her.

While it was still daytime, it was only anger and lust that managed to beat back their fear of entering the ruins.

Weird machinery and furniture seemed to float in the chill darkness, but the men were intent on ignoring these objects as they ran. Twisting and turning down one sculpture- and painting-adorned corridor after another, it was in a vast room, a hall of some sort, that they eventually caught up to Lina.

Stripping off her coat when they caught her by the shoulder, she stumbled and fell face first, but the three of them tackled her and rolled her onto her back.

Lina cried, "Quit it!"

"Stop your squirming. We're gonna do you real good. All three of us at once!"

Just as the men were pinning her pallid and desperately thrashing hands and feet and closing on her sweet lips, the creepiest sensation struck them all. Even Lina forgot her struggles as terror overcame her. Four pairs of eyes focused on the same spot in the darkness.

A single shadowy figure emerged out of the blackness. A figure that seemed to them darker by far than the blackness shrouding this whole universe.

"One civilization met its end here," said a soft voice flecked with rust, the words drifting through the darkness. "While it's impossible to halt the progress of time, you would do well to show some respect for what's been lost."

Lina scrambled up and took cover behind the figure, but the men didn't so much as twitch. They couldn't even speak. Animal instincts honed by more than two decades of doing battle with the forces of nature told them just what this person was. It was something far surpassing what they'd expected to find here.

Footsteps rang out at the entrance to the hall, but soon halted. Haig and the rest of the men had burst into the room with enraged expressions, but then froze in their tracks.

"Wha—What the hell are you?"

Not surprisingly, it was the leader of the suicide squad who finally managed to speak, but just barely, his voice tremulous through the chattering of his teeth. His tone spoke volumes about how he, too, had been laid low by this ghastly aura beyond human

ken. The only thoughts running through the minds of Haig's
men at that moment concerned getting down off the hill as fast as
humanly possible.

"Leave. This is no place for you."

As if at the stranger's bidding, the men got to their feet and
started to back away. The reason they remained facing forward was
not so much due to the old adage about never letting your foe see
your back as it was to their terror at not knowing what might
happen to them if they turned around. The adage "Some things are
worse than dying" passed through the heart of hearts of all the men.

The men regained some of their spirit once they'd fallen
back to the hall's entrance. Sunlight poured in through the
cracked roof of the windowless corridor.

Haig pulled out a Molotov cocktail and another man
produced some matches. Striking the match on his pants, the
Brigade member put the flame to the rags and Haig heaved the
firebomb with such an exaggerated throw he seemed to be trying
to blast his own fears away. No consideration at all was given to
Lina's safety.

The blazing bottle limned a smooth arc across the room
and landed at the pair's feet. But no lake of flames spread
from it. The bottle simply stood upright on the intricately
mosaicked floor. There was a tinkling clink as the neck of the
bottle and the flaming rag it contained dropped to the floor.

The men probably hadn't even seen the silvery flash that
had split the air.

Panic ensued.

Screaming, the men scrambled over each other in their
effort to flee back down the hallway. And they didn't look back.
Reason left them, and the fear of the supernatural world bubbled
forth. The men drove their legs with all their desperate might to
avoid having to see what shape their fear would take.

Once she was sure their footsteps had died away, Lina
stepped from behind the stranger. Sticking out her cute little

tongue, she turned to the exit and made the rudest gesture she knew. She must've been amazingly sedate by nature, because she no longer seemed the least bit troubled as her eyes gazed first at the truncated bottle and the guttering flame, then up at the muscular stranger with admiration.

"You're really incredible, you—" she began to say, but her voice gave out on her.

As her eyes became accustomed to the darkness they took in the face of her savior. An exquisite face, like a silent winter night preserved for all time.

"What is it?" he said.

Shaken back to her senses by the sound of his voice, Lina said the first thing that popped into her mind. She was a rather straight-forward girl.

"You sure are handsome. Took my breath away, you did."

"You'd best go home. This is no place for you," the owner of that gorgeous countenance said once more, his words not so much cold as emotionless.

Lina had already reclaimed enough of her senses to shamelessly eye the man from head to toe.

He couldn't have been a day over twenty. His wide-brimmed traveler's hat and the elegant longsword he wore across the back of his black long-coat made it clear he was no mere tourist. A blue pendant dangled before his chest. The deep, soul-swallowing shade of blue seemed to fit the youth perfectly.

Like hell I'm leaving. I'll go wherever I damn well please, Lina wanted to say, but the words she hastily uttered were the exact opposite of what she actually felt.

"If you insist, the very least you could do is walk me out."

At this unexpected request, the youth headed toward the exit without making a sound.

"Hey, wait just a second, you. Aren't we the hasty one!" Flustered, Lina hurried after him. She thought about latching onto the hem of his coat or maybe his arm, but didn't actually go through with it. This young man had an intensity about him that completely locked him off from the rest of the world.

Mutely trailing after him, the girl stepped out into the courtyard.

To Lina's utter amazement, the youth quickly turned around and headed back toward the entrance. She jumped up again.

"For goodness sake, would you just wait a minute? You didn't even give me a chance to say thank you, you big dolt!"

"Go home before the sun sets. The way down is normal enough."

The shadowy figure didn't even turn to face her as he spoke, but his words made Lina's eyes go wide.

"And just how would you know that? Come to think of it, when did you get here, anyway? It couldn't be you can walk up here like normal, could it?!"

Just shy of the entrance, the young man halted. Without facing her, he said, "So, you can climb the hill normally, too, I take it?"

"That's right. My circumstances are kind of special," Lina said, sounding strangely resolved for once. "Wanna hear about it? Of course you do. After all, you came all the way up here to see these ruins—the remnants of a Noble's castle."

The youth started to walk away again.

"Oh, curse you," Lina cried, stomping her feet in anger. "At least give me your name. If you don't, I'm not heading home—come sunset or not. If I get attacked and maimed by monsters, it'll be on your conscience for the rest of your days. I'm Lina Sween, by the way."

Apparently her badgering had paid off, for a low voice drifted from the silhouette as it melded with the darkness filling the doorway. He said but a single word:

"D."

†

L ate that night, a Vampire Hunter paid a call on the home of the village's mayor.

"Well I'll be—"

Having pulled on a dressing gown over his pajamas and come downstairs, the sleepy-eyed mayor forgot what he was about to say when he saw the beauty of the Hunter standing there at the other end of the living room with his back to the wall.

"I see now why our maid's walking around like something sucked the soul out of her. Well, I can't very well put you up here in my house. I've got a daughter for one thing, and the women's groups are always coming and going through here."

"I've already put my horse and my gear in the barn," D said softly. "I'd like to hear your proposition."

"Before we start, why don't you set yourself down. You must be coming off a long ride, I'd wager."

D didn't move in the slightest. Nonchalantly drawing back the hand he'd used to indicate a seat, the mayor gave a nod. The valet, who was awaiting further instruction after having thrown a load of kindling and condensed fuel into the fireplace was ordered out.

"Never show the enemy your back, eh? Indeed, I suppose you've got no proof I'm on your side."

"I was under the impression you hired Geslin before me," D suggested. It almost appeared he hadn't been listening to a word the mayor had to say.

By the look of him, the mayor was a pushy man, but he didn't let the slightest hint of displeasure show on his face. In part this was because he'd heard rumors about the skill of the Grade A Hunter he was dealing with, but more than that because just having him standing there made the mayor feel in his flesh and bones that here was a being from a whole other world. Though he had exquisite features far more beautiful than any human's, the ghastly aura emanating from him brought to the fore something mankind usually kept buried in the deepest depths of its psyche. The fear of the unknown darkness.

"Geslin's dead," the mayor spat. "He was a top-notch Grade A Hunter, but he couldn't find us our vampire and got himself killed by an eight-year-old girl to boot. Throat ripped clean open, so we don't have to worry about him coming back, but we paid him a hundred thousand dalas in advance—what a fiasco!"

"I understand the circumstances were somewhat unusual."

The mayor pursed his lips in surprise. "You know about that, do you? Well, that's a dhampir for you! Seems there might be something after all to them rumors you can hear the winds blowing out of Hell."

D said nothing.

The mayor gave a brief account of the disaster that had occurred on the bridge roughly two weeks earlier. "And all of this happened in broad daylight. By the look of you, I'd wager you've seen more than I have in my seventy years on this earth. But I don't suppose that'd happen to include victims of vampires who can walk in the light of day, now, would it?"

D remained silent. That in and of itself was his answer.

It just wasn't possible. The Nobility and those whose lives they'd claimed were permitted their travesty of life by night alone, while the world of daylight had been ceded to humanity.

"I think you have a pretty good notion why I've called you here. Think about it. If those damnable Nobles and their retinue were free to move not just by night but by light of day as well, do you have any idea what would become of the world?"

The room seemed to grow darker, chillier. To save wear on their generators, it was commonplace to use lamps fueled with animal fat for lighting at night on the Frontier. The old man's eyes seemed to smolder as he stared at the hands he held out to warm, and D didn't move a muscle, as if he'd become a statue.

Really set my hooks into him that time, the mayor snickered to himself. His words had been chosen for maximum effect on the psyche of his guest, and surely they would've dealt a severe blow to the beautiful half-breed Hunter. Oh, yes—come tomorrow, things are bound to be a bit more manageable around here.

However, all did not go quite as expected.

"Could you elaborate on what's happened in this case so far?"

D's voice carried no fear or uneasiness, and for a moment the mayor was left dumbstruck. So, the horrifying thought of bloodthirsty vampires running amuck in the world by day had no personal impact on this dhampir? Wrestling down his surprise a split second before it could rise to his face, the mayor began to speak in a tone more subdued than necessary.

It all started with the ruins and four children.

Even now, no one knew for sure just how long the ruins had stood on that hill. When the village founders had first set foot in this territory nearly two centuries earlier, it was said the ruins were already choked with vines. Several times the hill had been scaled by suicide squads who produced roughly sketched maps and studied its ancient history, but while they were doing so a number of strange phenomena had occurred. Fifty years ago a group of investigators had come from the Capital to see it, and they were the last—after that, there were very few with any interest in surmounting the hill.

It was about ten years earlier that four children from the village had gone missing.

One winter's day, four children vanished without warning from the village—farmer Zarkoff Belan's daughter (eight at the time), fellow farmer Hans Jorshtern's son (aged eight also), teacher Nicholas Meyer's son (aged ten), and general-store proprietor Hariyamada Schmika's son (aged eight). There was some furor over the possibility that it might be the work of a dimension-ripping nueby beast that'd been terrorizing the area, but then there were villagers who'd seen the four of them playing partway up the hill, forcing the community to eye the ruins with suspicion.

For the first time in fifty years a suicide squad was formed, but despite a rather extensive search of the ruins no clue to the children's whereabouts could be found. Rather, toward the end of a week of searching members of the squad started disappearing in rapid succession, and the search had to be called off before all the passageways and benighted subterranean chambers that comprised the vast complex of ruins could be investigated.

The grief-stricken parents were told their children had probably been taken by slave-traders passing by the village by some strange twist of fate, or had been lost to the dimension-ripping beast. Whatever fate awaited them in either of those scenarios, it was a far more comforting hypothesis than the thought of the children disappearing in the remains of a vampire's mansion.

One evening, about two weeks after the whole incident had started, the tragedy came to its grand—if somewhat tentative—finale. The miller's wife was out in the nearby woods picking lunar mushrooms when she noticed a couple of people trudging down the hill, and she let out a shout fit to knock half the town off its feet.

The children had returned.

That was to be both a cause for rejoicing and source of new fears.

"For starters, only three of the kids came back." The elderly mayor's voice was so thin, it was fairly lost to the popping of the logs in the fireplace. "You see, Tajeel—that would be Schmika from the general store's boy—never did come back. To this day we still don't know whatever became of him. Can't say it came as any great surprise when his father and mother both passed away from all their grieving. I'm not saying we weren't glad to get the rest of them back, but maybe if he hadn't been the only one that didn't make it—"

"Did you examine the children?" D asked as he turned his gaze toward the door.

On guard, no doubt, against any foe who might burst into the room, the mayor assumed. It was said that even among Hunters, there was an incredible amount of animosity, with hostility often aimed at the more famous and capable. D's eyes were half closed. The mayor was suddenly struck with the thought that the gorgeous young man was conversing with the night winds through the wall.

"Of course we did," the mayor said. "Hypnosis, mind-probing drugs, the psycho-witness method—we tried everything we could think of. Unfortunately, we used some of the old ways, too. I tell you, even now the screams of those kids plague my dreams. But it was just no use. Their minds were a blank, completely bare of memories for the exact span of time they'd been missing. Maybe they'd been left that way by external forces, or then again maybe it was something the kids' own subconscious minds had pulled to keep them all from going insane. Though if it was the latter, I suppose you'd have to say that as far as Jorshtern's boy went, the results weren't quite what you'd hope for. To this day, Cuore's still crazy as a bedbug.

"The upshot of this is, exactly what happened in the ruined castle and what they might've seen there remains shrouded in mystery. I suppose the only saving grace was that none of them came away with the kiss of the Nobility. Cuore's case was unfortunate, but the other two grew up quite nicely, becoming one of our school teachers and the village's brightest pupil, respectively."

Having progressed this far in his story, the mayor seemed to finally be at ease, and he walked over to a sideboard against the wall, got a bottle of the local vintage and a pair of goblets, and returned.

"Care for a drink?"

As he proffered a goblet, his hand stopped halfway. He'd just remembered what dhampirs usually consumed.

As if to confirm this, D replied softly, "I never touch the stuff." The Hunter's gaze then flew to the pristine darkness beyond the window panes. "How many victims have there been, and under what conditions did the attacks occur?"

"Four so far. All close to town. Time-wise, it's always at night. The victims have all been disposed of."

Just then the mayor's voice left him. Surely the ghastly task of their disposal had come back to haunt his memory, for his hand and the drink it held trembled. After all, not every victim had been given a chance to turn into a vampire before they met their end.

"Finding missing kids and putting 'em down—this is a nasty bit of business to go through with spring so close and all."

With a strident clang, the mayor slammed the steel goblet down on his desk. The contents splashed up, soaking his palm and the sleeve of his gown.

"It's by no means certain that Schmika's boy Tajeel had a hand in this. There's a very good chance one of the remaining Nobility has slipped in here, or a vampire victim run out of another village is prowling the area. I'd like you to explore those possibilities."

"Do you think there are Nobles who can walk with their victims in the light of day?"

At this softly spoken query the mayor clamped his lips shut. It was the very question he'd posed to D earlier. Suddenly the mayor donned a perplexed expression and turned his eyes toward D's waist. However faintly, he could've sworn he'd heard a strange voice laughing.

"Sometime tomorrow, I need all the information you have on how the victims were attacked, their condition following it, and how they were handled," D said without particular concern. His voice was callous, completely devoid of any emotion concerning the work he was about to undertake. Apparently this Vampire Hunter knew no fear, even when confronted with a foe the likes of which the world had never known: demons who could walk in the light of day. With an entirely different kind of terror than he felt toward the Nobility the mayor focused his gaze on the young man's stunningly beautiful visage. "Also, I'd like to pay a visit to the three surviving abductees. If it's any great distance, I'll need a map to their homes."

"You won't need a map," a feminine voice cooed.

Suddenly the door swung open and a smiling face like a veritable blossom drew the eyes of both men.

Eyes that shone with curiosity returned D's gaze as she said, "Not the least bit surprised, are you? You knew I was standing out there listening in the whole time, I'm sure. I'll tell you all you need to know. Lukas Meyer will be at the school. After classes I can take you to where Cuore lives. And you needn't look far for the third. So, we meet again, D."

Farmer Belan's daughter, now the mayor's adopted child, made a slight curtsy to D.

"Say, are you sure this is okay?" Lina asked the next morning, gripping the reins to the two-horse buggy she drove toward the school.

"Sure what's okay?"

"Going out like this first thing in the morning and all. Dhampirs don't like the daytime, right, on account of having part Noble blood in them."

"Just full of weird tidbits, aren't you?" D muttered as he looked over the backs of the six-legged mutant equines. If a telepath had been there, they might've caught a whisper of a grin deep in the recesses of his coldly shuttered but human consciousness.

Inheriting characteristics of both their human and vampire parents, dhampirs were also physiologically influenced by both sides in different respects.

Humans slept by night and were awake by day, while the opposite was true for the Nobility. When the genes of the respective races came into conflict, it was generally the physiological traits of the Noble half—the vampire parent—

that proved dominant. A dhampir's body craved sleep by day, and wanted to be awake at night.

However, just as a left-handed person could learn to use either hand equally well through practice, it was entirely possible for dhampirs to follow the tendencies of their human genes and live just as mortals did. And while they might have nearly half the strength, sight, hearing, and other physical advantages of a true vampire, it was that adaptability that was their greatest asset. With that fifty percent, they had a measure of power within them no human being could hope to attain, allowing them to cross swords with the Nobility by day or night.

Still, while it was true they could resist their fundamental biological urges, it was also undeniable that operating in daylight severely degraded a dhampir's condition. Their biorhythms fell off sharply after midnight, reaching their nadir at noon. Direct sunlight could burn their skin to the point where even the gentlest breeze was pure agony, like needles being driven into each and every cell in their body. In some cases, their skin might even blister like a third-degree burn.

Ebbing biorhythms brought with them fatigue, nausea, thirst, and numbing exhaustion from the slightest activity. The proportion of dhampirs that could withstand the onslaught of midday without experiencing those tortures was said to be less than one in ten.

"Still, it looks like you don't have any problems at all. That's no fun." Lina pursed her lips, then quickly hauled back on the reins. The horses whinnied, and the braking board hanging from the bottom of the buggy gouged into the earth.

"What's wrong?" D asked, not sounding the least bit surprised.

Lina pointed straight ahead. "It's those jerks again. And Cuore's with them. Yesterday was bad enough, but now what the hell are they up to?"

Some thirty feet ahead of them, a group of men walked past a crumbling stone wall and was just turning the corner. There were seven of them. Three of them, most notably Haig, they'd met in the ruins the day before.

Walking ahead of the group as the others pushed and shoved him was a young man of seventeen or eighteen dressed in tattered rags. He was huge. He must've been six-foot-four and weighed over two hundred pounds. His gaze completely vacant, he continued down the little path pushed along by a man who barely came up to his shoulder.

"Perfect timing. We were just going to see him anyway. What's down that way?"

"The remains of a pixie-breeding facility. It hasn't been used in ages, but rumor has it there's still some dangerous things in there," Lina said. "You don't think those bastards would bring Cuore in there?"

"Get to school."

By the time the last word reached Lina's ears, D was headed for the narrow path, the hem of his coat fluttering out around him.

As soon as he rounded the corner of the stone wall, the breeding facility buildings came into view. Although "buildings" wasn't really the word for them. It appeared the owner had removed all the usable lumber and plastic joists, leaving nothing more than a few desperately listing, hole-riddled wooden shacks on the edge of collapse. The winter sun glinted whitely on this barren lot and on the naked trees frosted with the last crusts of snow.

The men slipped into one of the straighter structures. They seemed fairly confident that few people passed this way, as they never even looked back the way they'd come.

Perhaps thirty seconds passed.

Shouting exploded from within the building. There were screams. Lots of screams. And not simply the kinds of sounds someone makes when they run into something that scares them. Startled, perhaps, by the ghastly cries, the branches of a tree that grew beside the building threw down their snowy covering. Inside, a cacophony of something enormous shattering to pieces could be heard.

Just seconds after the reverberations died away, D entered the building.

The screaming had ceased.

D's eyes got the faintest tinge of red to them. The thick smell of blood had found its way to his nostrils.

Every last man was laid out on the stone floor. Aside from a few steel cages along one wall that evoked the pixie breeding facility's past, the rest of the vast interior was filled with the stink of blood and cries of agony. For something that had been accomplished in the half minute the men had been inside with Cuore, the job was entirely too thorough. There could be no doubt that some sort of otherworldly force had completely run amuck.

Two things caught D's eye as the thugs convulsed in their own puddled blood.

One was Cuore's massive frame, sprawled now in front of the cages. The other was a gaping hole in the stone wall. Six feet or more in diameter, the jagged opening let the morning sunlight fall on the dark floor. Whatever had left the eight strapping men soaking in a sea of blood had gone out that way.

Without sparing a glance to the other young men, D walked over to Cuore. Crouching gracefully, the Hunter said, "They call me D. What happened?"

Muddy blue eyes were painfully slow to focus on D. The boy's madness was no act; his right hand rose slowly and pointed to the fresh hole in the wall. His parched lips disgorged a tiny knot of words.

"The blood ... "

"What?"

"The blood ... Not me ... "

Perhaps he was trying to lay the blame for this massive bloodshed.

D's left hand touched the young man's sweaty brow.

Cuore's eyelids drooped closed.

"What did you see in the castle?" D's voice sounded totally unaffected by the carnage surrounding them. He didn't even ask who was responsible for this bloodbath.

However, could even his left hand pull the truth from the mind of a madman?

A certain amount of "will" seemed to sprout up in Cuore's disjointed expression.

The boy's Adam's apple bobbed up and down, preparing to spill a few words.

"What did you see?" D asked once again. As he posed the question, his reached over his shoulder with his right hand and turned.

The half-dead men were just getting up.

"Possessed, eh?" D's gaze skimmed along the men's feet. The gangly shadows stretching from their boots weren't those of any human. The silhouette of the body was oddly reminiscent of a caterpillar, while the wiry, thin arms and legs were a grotesque mismatch for the torso. Those were pixie shadows!

A single evil pixie who'd been kept here must've escaped and remained hidden somewhere in the factory all this time. Unlike the vast majority of the artificially created beasts the Nobility had sown across the earth, most varieties of pixies were exceptionally amiable. But other varieties, based on goblins, pookas, and imps from ancient pre-holocaust Ireland kept the people of the Frontier terrified with their sheer savagery. The redcap variety of pookas lopped off travelers' heads with the ax they were born holding, then used their victims' blood to dye the headgear that gave them their name. Few types possessed the ability to manipulate half-dead humans, but with proper handling they could help make otherwise untamable unicorns

clear vast tracts of land or boost the uranium pellet
production of Grimm hens from one lump every three days to
three lumps a day. In light of this, some of the more
impoverished Frontier villages were willing to assume the risks
of breeding these sorts of creatures. The blood-spattered and
still unconscious men were being animated by an individual of
the most atrocious species.

The shadow held an ax in its hands.

Smoothly the weapon rose.

The men each raised a pair of empty hands over their heads.

As the non-existent axes whirred through the space D's
head had occupied, the Hunter was leaping to the side of the
room with Cuore cradled in his arms.

With mechanical steps the shadow's marionettes went
after him.

Unseen blades sank into the wall and dented the roof of
an iron cage. Cutting only thin air, one of the men fell face-first
and set off a shower of sparks a yard ahead of him.

This was a battle for control of the shadows.

A stream of silvery light splashed up from D's back, then
mowed straight ahead at the invisible ax one of the unconscious
men raised against him.

There was no jarring contact, but a breeze skimmed by D's
cheek and something got imbedded in the wall.

These weapons weren't invisible, they were nonexistent.

Three howling swings closed on the Hunter, all from
different directions. The blades clashed together, but D and
Cuore flew above the shower of sparks that resulted.

Twin streaks of white light coursed toward the floor.

The men went rigid and clutched their wrists. Thud after
thud rang out in what sounded like one great weight after another
hitting the floor. Actually, it was the men dropping their weapons.

Having already sheathed his longsword, D headed over to
one of the men who'd collapsed in a spray of blood.

Going down on one knee by the man's side, he asked, "Can you hear me?"

As the man's feeble gaze filled with the sight of D, his eyes snapped wide open. The fallen man was none other than Haig.

"Dirty bastard ... " Haig said. "How the hell did you—?"

His pitiful voice, which hardly matched his rough face, ground to a halt when he noticed something on the floor.

Now pinned to the stone floor by two stark needles, the unearthly shadow stretching from Haig's feet was rapidly fading from view. Stranger still, it wasn't just the twice-pierced shadow that was affected. The shadows of the other men contorted and writhed in the throes of intense pain. And yet the movements of all remained perfectly synchronized!

It must've taken incredible skill to hurl those needles from midair and nail the shadow precisely through the wrist and heart, but it seemed doubtful someone like Haig could manage the amount of focus needed to perfect such a technique.

Because, amazingly enough, the needles stuck in the stone were made of wood.

Soon enough the disquieting shadows vanished and those of the men returned.

"I'm hurting ... Damn, it hurts! Hurry up, call the doctor ... please ... "

"When you've answered my question." D's tone conjured images of ice. Not surprising, when he was dealing with the same guys who'd already tried to gang-rape an innocent girl. "What happened after you got Cuore in here?"

"I don't know ... We was thinking one of them's to blame ... So we planned on taking 'em one by one, smacking 'em around a little to see if we was right ... And then ... "

The light in Haig's eyes rapidly dimmed.

"And then what?"

"How the hell should I know ... Get me a doctor ... Quick ... As soon as we got in here and had him surrounded ... all I could see was blood red ... like something was hiding in there ... "

The last word out of Haig's mouth became a leaden rasp of breath that rolled across the ground. He wasn't dead. Just unconscious. As the rest of them undoubtedly were. Though thin trails of fresh blood leaked from their ears, noses, and mouths, their condition was quite bizarre given they showed no signs of external injuries.

D turned around.

Cuore stood groggily in the doorway, but much further outside there was the sound of numerous footsteps getting closer. Either Lina or one of the villagers who'd seen the Youth Brigade with Cuore must've summoned the law. Apparently the bullying these young men did was far from appreciated in these parts.

D glanced at Cuore, then quickly spun to face the hole blown through the wall.

"What's wrong? Aren't you gonna keep grilling him? You'll never get to the bottom of this mess if you're afraid of stepping on the sheriff's toes," chided a villager.

Naturally, this didn't faze D in the least as he and his black coat melted into the morning sun.

To be continued in

VAMPIRE HUNTER D

VOLUME 2
RAISER OF GALES

available August 2005

Hideyuki Kikuchi was born in Chiba, Japan in 1949. He attended the prestigious Aoyama University and wrote his first novel *Demon City Shinjuku* in 1982. Over the past two decades, Kikuchi has authored numerous horror novels, and is one of Japan's leading horror masters, writing novels in the tradition of occidental horror authors like Fritz Leiber, Robert Bloch, H. P. Lovecraft, and Stephen King. As of 2004, there are seventeen novels in his hugely popular ongoing Vampire Hunter D series. Many live action and anime movies of the 1980s and 1990s have been based on Kikuchi's novels.

ABOUT THE ILLUSTRATOR

Yoshitaka Amano was born in Shizuoka, Japan. He is well known as a manga and anime artist and is the famed designer for the Final Fantasy game series. Amano took part in designing characters for many of Tatsunoko Productions' greatest cartoons, including *Gatchaman* (released in the U.S. as *G-Force* and *Battle of the Planets*). Amano became a freelancer at the age of thirty and has collaborated with numerous writers, creating nearly twenty illustrated books that have sold millions of copies. Since the late 1990s Amano has worked with several American comics publishers, including DC Comics on the illustrated Sandman novel *Sandman: The Dream Hunters* with Neil Gaiman and *Elektra and Wolverine: The Redeemer* with bestselling author Greg Rucka for Marvel Comics.